THREE ESSENTIAL PLAYS

Car Door Shave
Gambling Fever
Neither God Nor Master

Lance Tait

with introductory remarks by Yvonne Shafer

Theatre Metropole Books
Los Angeles, California

By the same author

Synesthesia

The Black Cat and Other Plays Adapted From Stories by Edgar Allan Poe

Little Black Book of Comedy Sketches

The Fall of the House of Usher and Other Plays Inspired by Edgar Allan Poe

Mad Cow Disease In America, Something Special and Other Plays

Edwin Booth a Play in Two Acts

Miss Julie, David Mamet Fan Club and Other Plays

www.lancetait.com

THREE ESSENTIAL PLAYS

Car Door Shave
Gambling Fever
Neither God Nor Master

Lance Tait

Copyright © 2013 by Lance Tait
Published by Theatre Metropole Books, Los Angeles.
All Rights Reserved.
No part of this book may be reproduced without the permission of the publisher. These plays are protected under Copyright Law. For permission to produce these works (worldwide), contact: theatremetropole@yahoo.com

Publisher's Cataloging-In-Publication Data
(Prepared by The Donohue Group, Inc.)

Tait, Lance.
  [Plays. Selections]
  Three essential plays / Lance Tait ; with introductory remarks by Yvonne Shafer.

  p. ; cm.

  Contents: Car door shave -- Gambling fever -- Neither God nor master.
  Issued also as an ebook.
  ISBN-13: 978-0-615-82575-5
  ISBN-10: 0-615-82575-3

  1. Comedies. 2. American drama. I. Shafer, Yvonne, 1936- II. Title. III. Title: Plays. IV. Title: Car door shave.
V. Title: Gambling fever. VI. Title: Neither God nor master.

PS3570.A333 A6 2013
812/.54   2013941431

ebook ISBN: 978-1-62840-610-8

Publication Coordinator: Scott J. Tait
Book design by Lise G. Neer

TABLE OF CONTENTS

Overview
1

Car Door Shave
7

Gambling Fever
95

Neither God Nor Master
199

Afterword
286

Acknowledgements
289

Appendix (Songs)
291

OVERVIEW

Three essential plays: it is an apt description of the theatrical work by Lance Tait published here in this distinctive volume. These plays embody his fundamental beliefs and concerns, as well as his approach to character and structure. His anxiety over the environment, a belief in true democracy, his passion for learning, his observations of patterns seen in the past and recurring in the present, his vivid handling of human emotion, his musical instincts and his comic spirit can be seen in each of these plays.

Many plays written today focus on very small, very particular aspects of contemporary life. Many seem like expositions of some stories on a reality show or a tell-all magazine. Tait's large and long view propels him into three different periods of American life in three different areas of the country. The world we see in *Neither God Nor Master* is that of Chicago in 1923. Known here and abroad as a violence-infested city with almost no qualities to recommend it, a city with almost no qualities to recommend it, Chicago was totally dominated by the figure of Al Capone. This man was known as a kingpin criminal, responsible for the almost monthly assassinations in front of hotels, at bus stops, and restaurants. The man who gave out presents of diamond belt buckles was responsible for the deaths of rival mobsters and innocent bystanders, and for the corruption of policemen and judges making it almost impossible to find him guilty of his crimes and bring him to justice. In such an atmosphere it is inevitable that minor figures would be involved in criminal activities. An important element in the same time was the increasing demands by women for equality. They had been given the vote, but many circumstances which made their lives difficult were unchanged.

In *Neither God Nor Master*, Tait sees his Chicagoan "minor figures" through an expansive sequence of dramatic scenes that explores an exploitative, racist and morally and physically polluted city. But this city also has its idealists – characters who insist on respect, change and hope. Though people living in that time had little or no awareness of ecological matters, Tait's characters show us that they had to have felt something was wrong in this regard. Certainly 1923 was more like today than many of us imagine it was. As one character says, "You know where my sister reads all this crap? In *Mother Earth*. A rag you'd swear was published a hundred years from now." Towards the end of play, near a rail yard, two boys hunt rats with a rifle. The biggest rat in *Neither God Nor Master*, the character who was just quoted above, dies. In the play's epilogue, the irony, dark comedy and despair voiced often and sometimes loudly are countered by a defiant call for resistance against undemocratic forces at work in America. Is the way songs (and there are many) are used here reminiscent of *Threepenny Opera*? Not exactly.

With *Car Door Shave*, Tait brings us to a period in which crime, corruption, and greed are less obvious to the average American. This is a time in which many of the phenomena predicted in George Orwell's prescient "1984" are coming true. People are vaguely aware of social injustice but largely hope to ignore it. Orwell's phrase, "Spending is better than mending" defines the society which ignores damage to the environment, which delights in excess consumption, and which revels in the sort of imperial presidency of movie star Ronald Reagan: a president who removes the solar panels President Jimmy Carter had installed on the roof of the White House, a president who falls asleep at cabinet meetings, a president whose wife and her astrologer influence his decisions about national and international affairs. Save the redwoods? "When you've seen one redwood, you've seen them all."

In this time the political division of the country over the war in Vietnam was not over and the play's main character, the one-armed veteran Cappy, does not let us forget it. Nor does he let us forget the devastating fallout from the war, which he personally experiences, while he keeps order, with restraint and subtlety, in a comedic, idealized homeless encampment in sunny Southern California. The contrasts of the play are dramatic, exciting and funny. We hear, for example, of the esoteric sexual thought of Dr. Wilhelm Reich; moments later, ridiculous, common extreme-right platitudes bombard us. Two other great contrasts permeate the play: the Hobo Jungle of *Car Door Shave* seems at times to be idyllic and a magic-hour of nostalgia wants to take shape around it – but there is also a harsh feeling that "something went wrong back there."

Cappy seeks escape from the contemporary world and finds peace in reading and thinking. The conflicts forming the action of the play temporarily disturb the community he has set up. Nevertheless, he remains convinced of the rightness of the path he has chosen although he recognizes how hard it is. The Ghost of Jimmy Carter appears in the play as a reminder of the path America could have chosen. The Ghost says, "Experience tells me that is harder to be a peace monger than a war monger." In retrospect, especially after reading this play, one can only wonder why more average citizens were not at that time concerned about the future of the country – except in relation to the money that they might be able to make.

Gambling Fever is set in 1992, five hundred years after Christopher Columbus arrived to find a continent with clean water, clean air, and open spaces. In the play's first scene we see a skeleton of a dinosaur, a reminder of a far distant past. As Eugene O'Neill wrote, "The past is the present, it's the future, too." As the skeleton lies half-buried in a small crater in the ground we hear the sound of a helicopter presenting a central theme in the play: the intrusion of modern technology into a place where the mountains reign, where there are sounds of birds, there is quiet, and there are echoes: "The sounds here tell of eternity," remarks the assistant to the paleontologist who leads the excavation. In these mile high mountains there is an exhilaration in simply breathing, but the machines are coming and a casino will be built with an enormous parking garage, and will have as a central attraction the dinosaur bones excavated in this "nursery where the dinosaur lies in its cradle." The paleontologist comments to his assistant, "The more we're dependent on machinery, the more our minds are told what to do according to what the machines say." How often have we heard that we can't do something because the computer won't let us?

Present in the play, and the primary force for the casino, is the evil in today's society. This is not evil in the sense presented by some writers who provide excuses for unacceptable behavior, but evil which grows, feeding on itself, and for which there is no repentance. In *Gambling Fever* we see the struggle for commercial advantage (increased tourism, more casinos, growth, "more jobs") in stark conflict with the desire to maintain natural beauty, calm and quiet places as retreats from the exhausting aspects of living in increasingly close quarters with our fellow human beings. Tait composes a multitude of situations in which people compete and conflict with one another furiously; he gives us not only a picture of Colorado, where the play is set, but a dynamic microcosm of the world. Unfortunately, the world we are shown is taking a wild, senseless gamble; it is a world up for grabs, a world in danger. Can we bring about a change? Fortunately, this play has many sublime and comedic moments.

These plays contain so many elements of the theatre of the past and the modern theatre revealing the playwright's wide appreciation of earlier playwrights ranging from Ben Jonson to Bertolt Brecht. His original use of theatrical devices makes each of the plays notable. He presents a kaleidoscope of the world inviting us to imagine the cumulative onstage effect of combinations of music, poetry, metaphor, sound, visual elements, and vivid characterization. Brecht criticized the "culinary theatre" in which the audience is simply to sit back and enjoy. Tait welcomes the audience to participate intellectually and emotionally. These three plays are an invitation to respond imaginatively as you read or see them. He is, like all playwrights, holding the mirror up to nature. But what sort of a mirror? A straightforward reflection? A fun house grotesquery? No, rather a reflection that alters and enhances and introduces unexpected revelations.

– Yvonne Shafer

CAR DOOR SHAVE

a play in two acts

Car Door Shave is mostly set in the woods where there are sweet smelling eucalyptus trees. The place could be, as one character says, a paradise. The play reveals the Tait's wide reading and the numerous influences which form the background of his work. One of the books which contributed to his writing and thinking is *The Comedy of Survival* by Joseph M. Meeker. A significant portion of the book deals with Dante's *Inferno*. Meeker writes, "Paradise is where human awareness expands to comprehend the complexity of things rather than reducing complexity to simple principles easily grasped." But intruders create problems and destroy the peace and satisfaction. Cappy, the organizer of the so-called Hobo Jungle, says, "We have to be constantly on guard against those who could harm the community." Indeed, two intruders representing an extreme conservative outlook and who work for social services come with the intent of destroying the place which serves as a refuge from a world increasingly polluted and self-destructive. Again, Meeker's description is useful: "Dante's Hell is a sink of noxious gasses, polluted water and denuded forests. The people there have caused their own misery and have created the miserable environment in which they are trapped." Unhappily, Meeker's 1974 predictions of the results of what people were doing to the world have come to pass. As Meeker then wrote, "The nature of human pain and joy has not changed in the half-dozen centuries since Dante, but the world has come to resemble Hell more than ever."

In contrast to the outside world, the home of Cappy and the others is ecological. The basic desire expressed by Cappy is "to live at the level of technology that is sustainable for the planet." People are encouraged to learn, to engage is satisfying sensual desires, and to live simply. So different is the atmosphere and are the goals in such a place that the two intruders find it intolerable; they actually do not want this place to exist. Citing the unoriginal phrase "Better dead than red," they think of those who live in the Hobo Jungle as parasites and they complain with predictable phrases such as "If they can walk to the bank to deposit their checks, they can walk to work" or use put-downs like "You're human garbage." Their plans to destroy the encampment include such possibilities as running a highway through it, flooding the nearby creek, and introducing destructive insects. Very nice indeed. While these intruders can be hilarious they are also scary.

In addition to these two, there is another intruder who represents evil; there is nothing funny about her. Tait has written that he was influenced by the playwright Ben Jonson who presents characters who do not change or learn, but represent a kind of behavior which is permanent. I read once that people don't change, they just become more what they are. That is a good description of the character Christine, a strong female character whom the reader will see is not only incorrigible, but a master at introducing chaos and pain. The subject of female characters in this play is a lengthy one. The reader will see that this play abounds with many wonderful opportunities for actresses.

– Y. S.

Car Door Shave

Actors and directors are going to exercise their skills to effectively portray the characters and communicate the ideas contained in the play. A note on the dialogue is important: I have only written the dialogue out as it appears on the page for the sake of ease when reading. (For example, I have written "going to go" instead of "gonna go.") Actors – depending on the character they play and the dramatic circumstances – might drop final consonants and make other phonetic adjustments to their words. As we all know, spoken English hasn't sounded exactly the way it's been written for a long time.

What I say above concerning phonetic adjustment also goes for other plays in this book. However, one should not be too extreme with this practice and one can even elect to opt out of it. What should not be done by the actor is to add, "you know," and "oh, um..." in their speeches. They should learn to manage the rhythms without adding such things.

Car Door Shave appears first in this book because, judging by audience reception in readings, this is the most popular of the three plays.

– Lance Tait

CAR DOOR SHAVE

Characters

CAPPY	*Male, 40.*
HUEY	*Female, Asian, 30s.*
SHELLY	*Female, 40-50s.*
ANGELA	*Female, mid 30s.*
PUNK JIM	*Male, early 20s.*
MEG	*Female, early 20s.*
BRIDGET	*Female, 18.*
KEVIN	*Male, 28 to 38.*
GEORGE	*Male, 50 to 55.*
CHRISTINE	*Female, 40.*
THE GHOST OF JIMMY CARTER	*Male, over 60.*

Place: Ventura, California.

Time: The end of May, 1984.

CAR DOOR SHAVE

ACT I

Scene 1

It is a sunny day in the "Hobo Jungle" in Ventura, California. It is the end of May. To one side of the stage, towards the back, there is a wooden structure that looks like an outhouse. Towards the other side of the stage at mid-stage is a junked front door of a car that is propped up in the position that it would be in if it were still attached to a car – the rest of the car is nowhere to be found. The area is shaded by a large eucalyptus tree.

Near the car door is an overturned metal barrel which functions as a seat. CAPPY *sits on it. His face is lathered with shaving cream. In his right hand he holds a razor. He is missing his left arm. Nearby is a small old wooden table. On the table is a water basin filled with water. The mirror is still attached to the car door. It is turned in such a way that* CAPPY *can see himself in it as he shaves.* HUEY *stands by as* CAPPY *shaves.*

CAPPY: Punk Jim visited England. *(Pause.)* Well, if I had the money, I'd go to Florence.
HUEY: Where's Florence?
CAPPY: In Italy.
HUEY: What do they got there?

Cappy: Art museums. *(Pause. Expansively.)* To see it in person! Botticelli's Venus on a half shell. Michelangelo's sculpture of David. I hear they have a Galileo museum there.
Huey: Oh.
Cappy: And they've got the house that Dante lived in.
Huey: Who's that?
Cappy: Ever heard of Shakespeare?
Huey: Yeah.
Cappy: Well, he's like Shakespeare. He's important. *(Pause.)* Other things can be chancy. When you get as old as me, you want the Pure and the Bona Fide. And you don't want to see it like it is here where some corporate sponsor's name's plastered all over the place. *(Pause.)* Give me the classics. They won't waste your time.
Huey: *(Pause.)* You're not that old.
Cappy: Forty is plenty old.
Huey: I don't think so.
Cappy: I'm old. I've seen war. That'll age you. *(Pause.)* You cooking today?
Huey: Yeah.
Cappy: Ah, cooking over an open fire! Just like in the old country, huh?
Huey: Sometimes.
Cappy: The simple life. That's what I like. *(Pause.)* Well, we got enough money to eat good, but not enough money to go places – except in our minds. *(Pause.)* So what do you have for me today, Huey?

Cappy *is half done shaving.*

HUEY: *(Reciting by heart.)* "For many ages, the human race has felt the existence of Universal Energy. This feeling was categorized as a *belief.* With Reich's scientific work, the energy's parameters are identified and measured. Its output can be collected and stored."

CAPPY: *(In heaven.)* Ah, yes. From the "Archives of the Orgone Institute". *(Pause.)* Memorizing things is a gift that keeps on giving. Underappreciated these days. *(Pause.)* Here's one: "Universal Energy regulates itself naturally without resorting to compulsive duty or compulsive morality – both of which are sure signs of antisocial impulses."

HUEY: Oh. I don't understand that so well.

CAPPY: You're doing all right, kiddo. *(Pause.)* We lost a great man when we lost Wilhelm Reich. But he lives on in his writings.

HUEY: Is Dante as great as Wilhelm Reich?

CAPPY: There's no comparing two geniuses – though the bourgeoisie does. They do it 'cause they hate it that some people become gods.

HUEY: Cappy, I believe in God.

CAPPY: Well, *women* are more likely to believe in God, I'm told.

HUEY: You think you ever will?

All the lather is off CAPPY's *face now. He sets the razor down on the table.*

CAPPY: Never. Universal Energy moves me the same way it moves all geese. Those big birds don't call the energy, "God" – and they're certainly not *afraid* of it. Nor are they looking to it for comfort. *(Pause.)* Geese're only capable of seeing towards the horizon – but not *over* it. That's our capability, too – though science extends the horizon some.

CAPPY: *(Continued.)* Now humans, they speculate foolishly on what is *beyond*. Geese just live the Universal Energy. If geese get uneasy they don't act like feeble humans and go cry to an imaginary god. No, they just open up their butts and out goes the bad stuff. *(Pause.)* Can you do me a favor?

HUEY: Yeah.

CAPPY: Can you bring that basin a little closer, please? (HUEY *picks the basin up and moves it closer to* CAPPY.) Thank you. *(He splashes some of the water on his face with his right hand.)*

HUEY: You want me to get you a towel?

CAPPY: Sure, that'd be great. *(Pleasantly.)* You're a good gook, Huey, good gook.

Scene 2

SHELLY *works for Ventura County Social Services. She is in her office at her desk. Among the usual office items, there is a cassette recorder.* SHELLY *dictates into it.*

SHELLY: May 28, 1984. Angela will take over while I'm gone. I made sure everyone knows that I'm all packed for Ensenada – and I have my camera and tripod… and rolls and rolls of film. *(Pause.)* So we shall see. Hm. Haven't been camping in a *long* time. *(Pause. In response to other people's criticism of the Hobo Jungle:)* They can't be right. I'll be safe enough. The Vietnam vet in the Hobo Jungle doesn't stand for any nonsense. *(Pause.)* If they were moved out of there, where would they go? The city's streets. *(Pause. Sarcastically.)* Yeah, that's an outcome we can all love. *(Chuckling.)* Well, if I don't come back, at least this tape shows that I'm me. And *I* need to know.

That is the end of her memo. SHELLY *turns off the cassette machine. She picks up her telephone, pushes a button and speaks loudly.*

SHELLY: Angela, can you come in here now, please?

Pause. ANGELA *enters.*

SHELLY: My calls will be routed to you. But that doesn't mean you have the authority to make any decisions on my behalf. You understand?

ANGELA: *(Dismissively.)* No problem. *(Wanting to go.)* Is that all, Shelly?

SHELLY: *(Does not like her attitude.)* We're clear on that point, right?

ANGELA: *(With a sour look on her face. Pause.)* Yeah.

SHELLY: Okay then. *(Pause.)* Uh... and just be sure nobody goes down to the Hobo Jungle. *(Firmly.)* There's no approval for that. Is that clear?

ANGELA: *(Not happy.)* What?

SHELLY: You heard me.

ANGELA: They're drug addicts and thieves. They live in filth.

SHELLY: Then of course nobody would want to go down there unless they were from the police department.

ANGELA: They're squatting. They should be working and renting somewhere.

SHELLY's *position of authority is very much in evidence.*

SHELLY: May I remind you that as an employee of Ventura County Social Services you are to leave your political views outside this building? *(Pause.)* May I also remind you that there

SHELLY: *(Continued.)* are those with legitimate disabilities who live in our state? *(Pause.)* There is such a thing as *misfortune* – a concept which I don't have time to get into with you right now – nor should I. *(Longer pause.)* Have you ever thought about taking another kind of county job? One where you might not have to interact with people? *(Pause. Obviously contradicting her first comment.)* Reaganites supposedly want the government to leave everybody alone. Why is it then that you're so concerned about the Hobo Jungle people?
ANGELA: Government money goes down there. Down the drain.
SHELLY: You think you see some larger, better picture, don't you?

ANGELA *does not answer. Pause.*

SHELLY: The Hobo Jungle's neither your property nor mine. If you stop to think, the people there are saving our agency money. We don't have to put them up in a hotel, for example.
ANGELA: There shouldn't be hotels available to them.
SHELLY: *(Pause.)* Maybe I shouldn't leave you in charge while I'm gone.
ANGELA: No, do. *(Pause. Apologizing.)* I'm sorry.
SHELLY: Well. *(Pause.)* That's it, then.
ANGELA: *(Fake pleasantly.)* Have a nice vacation. I hope you get plenty of good pictures in Ensenada of the eclipse. (ANGELA *leaves.*)
SHELLY: *(Shaking her head negatively.)* If I had any other alternative, Angela, *you* would not be the one.

Scene 3

The Hobo Jungle, as in Scene 1: the car door and barrel under the eucalyptus tree, as well as the wooden structure that looks like an outhouse. PUNK JIM *has a Mohawk haircut. He wears punk clothes, but instead of the de rigueur Doc Martens boots, he wears dark green suede pointy shoes. His girlfriend,* MEG, *is a "goth". She is dressed in black and wears black Doc Martens boots. She wears simple silver and stone jewelry and her fingernails have black nail polish on them.* PUNK JIM *and* MEG *sit under the tree that shades them a little from the sun. They share a joint of marijuana.*

PUNK JIM: *(After exhaling.)* The U. S. is really weird.
MEG: Jim, life here is like... they're on a planet they don't know.
PUNK JIM: They think 'cause they have good weather, there's a chance. They think 'cause they have money, they might have life.
MEG: *(Pondering that.)* Yeah.
PUNK JIM: You call life shopping malls? And wine coolers? *(Pause.)* What about slums? And heroine from the C.I.A....
MEG: People don't see the bomb that exploded. There's a kind of damage that's related to the kind of bomb that fell, man.
PUNK JIM: London has shopping malls, Meg. What a mistake. *(Pause.)* American "success". American excess. American Express.
MEG: Yeah, a big bomb. Or lots of medium-size ones.

PUNK JIM: I hate malls. *(Pause. They are stoned.)* Everything's in patterns, you know? *(Pause.)* You can't get a shirt in only one color. Everybody has to be some ... goofy pattern advertisement for a clothing designer.

MEG: It's totally the wrong energy.

PUNK JIM: Yeah, that's what Jimmy Carter was warning about. Patterns at the gas pumps and with the international banks.

MEG: *(Pause. Continues to be spacey.)* God, I really like your shoes, man. So pointy, wow!

PUNK JIM: Yeah, you can only buy them in London. *(He looks down at the Doc Martens' that* MEG *is wearing.)* Doc Martens don't fit me.

MEG: *(Pause.* PUNK JIM *and* MEG *are spaced out.)* What's going to happen to The Clash? So many groups don't stay together for very long.

PUNK JIM: *(Pause.)* The eclipse, man. *(Pause.)* Yeah, it's too bad they split up. They were a great band. *(Pause.)* This dope is strong but like... it wears off faster than you think.

Pause. The joint is finished. They gaze off into the space in front of them. After a few seconds BRIDGET *wanders in, handbag on her shoulder. She enters near where the "outhouse" is. She looks around. Finally, she notices* PUNK JIM *and* MEG.

BRIDGET: Sorry. I hope I'm not bothering you.

MEG: *(To* PUNK JIM.) Do you see that?

PUNK JIM: I think there's a chick standing in front of us.

BRIDGET: The day warms up pretty fast here, doesn't it?

MEG *and* PUNK JIM *do not answer – they are high.*

BRIDGET: Um, I don't mean to intrude. *(Pause. Referring to the wooden structure.)* Hey, is this an outhouse?

Again, MEG *and* PUNK JIM *do not answer.*

BRIDGET: I'm not asking 'cause I have to go to the bathroom. *(Pause.)* I'm just wondering.

(She walks over to the wooden structure and opens its door. She is surprised that someone is inside it.) Oh, my god! Oh, I'm sorry. Excuse me. I didn't… *(She closes the door quickly.)* Excuse me!
HUEY: *(From inside the structure.)* You don't need to excuse yourself.
BRIDGET: I didn't know anybody was inside.
HUEY: Don't worry. It's okay. (HUEY *comes out.*) I was just sitting. *(Pause.)* It's not what you think it is. *(Pause. She pronounces "Henway" like it is a brand name.)* It's actually… a… Henway.
BRIDGET: A Henway? *(Pause.)* What's a Henway?
HUEY: *(She is proud of knowing this joke. Cappy taught it to her.)* Oh, between five and seven pounds.
BRIDGET: *(Pause. She finally gets the joke.)* You got me. *(Motioning to the wooden structure out of which* HUEY *just stepped.)* So what is it, anyway?
HUEY: An orgone accumulator.
BRIDGET: What's that?
HUEY: Something Wilhelm Reich invented.
BRIDGET: Oh. *(Pause.)* Does he live here?
HUEY: No.
BRIDGET: *(Pause.)* I'm looking for somebody named Christine McClure. Do you know her?

HUEY: Why do you want to know?
BRIDGET: So you know her?
HUEY: Did I say I did?
BRIDGET: *(To* PUNK JIM *and* MEG.) Do *you* know Christine McClure? *(To* HUEY.) Do they know her?
HUEY: You have to ask them.
BRIDGET: I just did.
HUEY: They're not available.
BRIDGET: *(Pause.)* Look, I'm not out to do anything to Christine.

This does not have any effect on HUEY. *She does not respond.* BRIDGET *does not know what to do next.*

BRIDGET: Well then, I guess I better ask somebody else.
HUEY: Here?
BRIDGET: Yeah. This is where I was told to go.
HUEY: Yeah? Hmp. *(Pause.)* You better watch out. This place can be dangerous.
BRIDGET: It doesn't look like you're in any danger. *(Pause.)* Do you know a guy named "Cappy"?
HUEY: *(Defensively, but proud.)* He's not just some guy.

BRIDGET *perceives something special about Huey's feelings towards* CAPPY.

BRIDGET: Oh, is that so? *(Pause.)* Um. You know, I heard you're all on welfare.
HUEY: *(Pause.)* I think you should go.
BRIDGET: *(Pause. Realizing her mistake, she tries to be as nice as can be.)* My name is Bridget.

CAPPY *walks in. He has not heard what* BRIDGET *has just said.*

CAPPY: Hi, Huey. *(Pause. He looks* BRIDGET *up and down.)* Who's this?
HUEY: Oh. This is Allison.
BRIDGET: I just told you. My name's Bridget.
HUEY: You look like an Allison. *(To* CAPPY.*)* Doesn't she?
BRIDGET: I'm not. That's not my name.
CAPPY: *(Pause. He smiles at* BRIDGET.*)* Well, my name's Cappy.
HUEY: *(She dislikes* BRIDGET.*)* She's trespassing.
CAPPY: *(Pause.)* So... Bridget. What's up?
HUEY: I said, she's trespassing!
CAPPY: *(To* HUEY.*)* We're all trespassing, Huey. *(To* BRIDGET.*)* Though Huey's right – you are trespassing trespassing.
BRIDGET: What's that mean?
CAPPY: You're trespassing above and beyond trespassing. *(Pause.)* It's like... metaphysical. Like you're the *meta* and we're the *physical*.
BRIDGET: Do you know Christine McClure?
CAPPY: You mean Christine Huber?
BRIDGET: No, Christine McClure.
CAPPY: No, I don't know anybody named Christine.
BRIDGET: Then how come you just said *Christine Huber*?
CAPPY: I don't know. Uh... it just... uh... I don't know... came out of nowhere, I guess. *(Pause.)* Hey, you know what? Let me find you a chair.
BRIDGET: Why?
HUEY: There aren't any.
CAPPY: *(Answering* BRIDGET.*)* You could sit on my lap, huh? And we'll talk about the first thing that pops up.

BRIDGET: I don't need to sit down.
HUEY: *(To* BRIDGET.*)* Let me show you the way out of here. There's a shortcut.
CAPPY: Huey, what's the rush?
HUEY: *(Under her breath.)* She's not your type.

SHELLY, *disguised, in worn clothes, and with a different hairstyle, enters.* CAPPY *sees her.*

CAPPY: What is this, Grand Central Station?
SHELLY: Hi.
CAPPY: Hi to you. You looking for somebody, too?
SHELLY: No. I'm uh... I'm looking for a place to crash.
CAPPY: This isn't really that kind of place.
HUEY: People *live* here. They don't crash here.
SHELLY: Well, I'd uh... I'd like to live here, maybe.
CAPPY: *(Mocking her.)* Oh, you would, huh?
SHELLY: Yeah.
CAPPY: Just like that. ...I mean, with no references?
SHELLY: I have my own tent. It doesn't cost anything to live here.
CAPPY: Maybe not money-wise. *(Pause.)* This isn't a free-for-all. I run a tight ship.
SHELLY: Is ... uh... this your place?
CAPPY: Yes and no. It depends on your metaphysics.
SHELLY: What do you mean?
CAPPY: Ask her. *(He points to* BRIDGET. *Pause.)* I have another client to service at the moment.
SHELLY: Client?

CAPPY: Yeah, client. That's what they call them at the V.A. I hear they're starting to use "customer" at Social Services. The Republicans are looking at everything now like it's a business – even welfare. *(Pause. To* SHELLY.*)* Anyway, we got a system here. And um... just like anywhere else, it takes a while for somebody to get processed. It takes time for the wheels to turn.

SHELLY: Well, I'll wait my turn, then.

CAPPY: Sometimes there's not even a chance for turn-waiting. We have to constantly be on guard against those who could harm the community.

SHELLY: I'm not crazy and I can do chores.

CAPPY: Yeah, you look like an intelligent woman. I'm sure you can appreciate the amount of effort that goes into keeping this place running smooth.

BRIDGET: I'm not a "client". I'm not waiting to get in here. I'm in college. I'm just looking for somebody.

CAPPY: *(To* BRIDGET, *nicely.)* I never finished college. War came between me and it and gave me an education I never asked for. *(Sexual innuendo.)* But I'll take some education from you. *(He eyes* BRIDGET.*)*

BRIDGET: *(To* SHELLY.*)* You might want to think twice about staying here.

SHELLY: It's just that I don't want my husband to find me.

CAPPY: Where's he live?

SHELLY: San Diego.

CAPPY: Maybe he'll think you stopped at L.A., right?

SHELLY: Yeah, something like that.

CAPPY: Got any friends in the Big Onion?

HUEY: You could stay with them.

SHELLY: I don't have friends *here*. That's the point. He won't look here. I'm safe here.

CAPPY: You're safe here? How do you know we don't have any flesh-licking lesbians on the premises?

KEVIN *walks in with a slight limp. He uses a cane.*

KEVIN: Hey, what's going on, man?
CAPPY: There's been a spike in the local population. Weatherman says it's going to be clearer tomorrow.

KEVIN *looks at the women, not particularly happy to see them.*

KEVIN: Two females.
CAPPY: Yep, news of my sexual prowess has apparently been broadcast statewide.
BRIDGET: *(To* CAPPY.*)* You know, you're kind of fresh.
CAPPY: "Fresh"? Hm. *(He says "dainty" but means "preppy".)* How very dainty of you to use the word that way. I haven't heard that expression in quite sometime! *(Pause.)* Unbelievable! It's Reagan times and we're back to talking like we're in the fifties.
BRIDGET: It's not the sixties anymore.
CAPPY: *(To* BRIDGET.*)* Maybe you're in training to be an old maid. *(Pause. To* SHELLY.*)* Excuse me, Our Lady of the Husband. But... uh... your future doesn't look good here. Huey, can you show her the way out, please?
BRIDGET: I don't want her to go. She needs a place.
CAPPY: Oh? *(To* SHELLY.*)* You have a mysterious supporter, it seems. *(Pause.)* Listen. This isn't a commune. We don't sprout our own vegetables. We *play* all day long, and I don't mean volleyball.
SHELLY: Play at what?

KEVIN: *(Joking.)* We play with each other's minds.

SHELLY: *(Sarcastically.)* That sounds like a very healthy thing to do.

BRIDGET: *(To* KEVIN.*)* Do you know Christine McClure?

CAPPY: *(To* KEVIN, *referring to* BRIDGET.*)* I want this one to stay. She's a type that's "searching".

BRIDGET: I'm *not* staying. I was just told that I could find people here who know Christine McClure. If nobody does, then I'll go. Gladly.

KEVIN: But what if somebody does know?

BRIDGET: Are you playing with my mind?

CAPPY: Kevin's not that type. He used to be an engineer, not a psychologist. But he will cheer on the jester in me sometimes. He does assist nicely when there's a point needs to be scored. It's all in keeping with his kind, giving, good nature. (CAPPY *sighs. He makes motions to leave.*) Kev', if you don't mind, maybe you can take over? This is all beginning to feel like too much work to me.

HUEY *is glad that* CAPPY *is going to leave.*

BRIDGET: Hey, wait a second! Just let me be sure. You don't know anything about Christine McClure?

CAPPY: Later, my peach.

CAPPY *exits and* HUEY *follows him. Pause.* BRIDGET *almost follows, but stays.*

BRIDGET: *(Frustrated, but still being nice to* KEVIN.*)* He blew me off! *Pause.* KEVIN *looks at* PUNK JIM *and* MEG.

KEVIN: *(To* BRIDGET, *motioning in the direction of* PUNK JIM *and* MEG.) Look at those guys. Getting stoned when accelerated access to Universal Energy is standing right next to them.

KEVIN *walks over to where* PUNK JIM *and* MEG *are open-eyed and staring into space. He moves his hand vertically first in front of* PUNK JIM's *eyes, and then* MEG's, *to see if he can get them to blink. They do not blink.*

BRIDGET: *(Proudly.)* I don't smoke marijuana.
KEVIN: Have you experienced the benefits of an orgone accumulator?
BRIDGET: No. It's the first time I've ever seen one.
KEVIN: *(Explaining.)* Universal Energy surrounds us. *(He points to the orgone accumulator.) That* will help you tap into it, *(Pause.)* ...get it in a more concentrated form. *(Pause. To* SHELLY, *inferring that she cannot stay.)* Look, um, ...I'm sorry but the elevator here can only carry a certain number of people.
SHELLY: *(To* KEVIN.) You're not even giving me a chance!
KEVIN: Usually there's a fair amount of quiet here. In fact, ...your voices – that's why I came out of my house.
BRIDGET: You live in a house?
KEVIN: I call it my house.
SHELLY: You live here in the Jungle in a house?
KEVIN: *(He motions far upstage.)* Yeah, my "mansion".
SHELLY: *(Suspiciously, but subtle about it.)* It's a big place?
KEVIN: It's not bad. It has all the modern conveniences.
SHELLY: I'd like to see that! *(Guarded.)* How can you afford it?
KEVIN: I use my noggin. It's not always money you need.
SHELLY: Will you show it to me?

KEVIN: *(Appraising her, he looks her up and down.)* I don't know. *(Pause. He thinks.)* Um… There's an admission price.
SHELLY: What?
KEVIN: *(Pointing to* BRIDGET.) Her.
SHELLY: *(Indignant.)* What do you mean?
BRIDGET: I'm only here looking for somebody – my birthmother. I'm adopted.
KEVIN: *(To* SHELLY.) I have an idea. If you let me do something with this idea, I'll let you stay in the Jungle. *(Pause. To* BRIDGET.) What's your name?
BRIDGET: Bridget.
KEVIN: Well, Bridget. Have patience and don't be afraid. This lady will watch out for you while you wait for an answer.
BRIDGET: Answer? To what?
KEVIN: Anything you ever wanted to know about a certain person that you *seem* to be interested in.
BRIDGET: Why do I have to wait? Tell me now.
KEVIN: *(Pause.)* There was once a woman named Christine. She was consumed into orgone energy and now lives on another planet where sex is free – but you have to pay for the love part.
BRIDGET: You know Christine McClure?
KEVIN: Just, just… just wait. I'm trying to get you acclimated as fast as I can.
BRIDGET: What does *that* mean?
KEVIN: I'd like to go through your handbags now.
SHELLY: What?
KEVIN: The only way you ever get to know a woman is to go through her handbag.

SHELLY *and* BRIDGET *are appalled.*

SHELLY: That's an invasion of privacy.

KEVIN: Nothing compared to the invasion of privacy that I need to discuss with you.

SHELLY: I don't know if I want to go to your house.

KEVIN: Something tells me Bridget would want us to go to my house. *(Pause. Dangling the prize.)* I do have pertinent information.

BRIDGET: What do you have?

KEVIN: Just what you want. *(To* SHELLY.*)* And I probably have some information that *you're* after, too.

SHELLY: *(To herself.)* God, does he know?

BRIDGET: I'm not going to let you go through my handbag!

KEVIN: *(Pause.)* Well, anyway, it was fun asking. *(Pause.)* But before we go home, I should familiarize you a little more with Wilhelm Reich.

SHELLY: What?

KEVIN: *(To* SHELLY.*)* You need to be familiarized. 'Cause it's about who we are. *(Pause.)* You know anything about him?

SHELLY: … I once saw a movie called, …um, "W.R.: Mysteries of the Orgasm." It was like… an underground film. That was about him, right?

KEVIN: Yep, that's our man. The philosopher of Universal Energy, … of Orgone. *(Pause.)* Energy, the orgasm, life, love, freedom, sex… all the things dear to life. We're an island of rationality in the sea of the insane, you know.

SHELLY: *(Sarcastically.)* I can tell that.

PUNK JIM *and* MEG *are still stoned.*

PUNK JIM: *(To* MEG.*)* You feel it? Starting to wear off, huh?
MEG: Yeah. Wow. That was like, *boom*, and then... Now.
PUNK JIM: *(Pause.)* You know, the squat I was living in in London didn't get too much sun.
MEG: I like the sun.
PUNK JIM: Me, too.
KEVIN: Oh, the babies are awake now.
BRIDGET: *(Going over to* PUNK JIM *and* MEG.*)* I'm looking for somebody named Christine McClure. Do you know her?
PUNK JIM: No. You have a cigarette?
BRIDGET: I don't smoke. *(To* MEG.*)* Have *you* ever heard of her?
MEG: No. Do you have five bucks?
BRIDGET: *(Trying to hold her frustration in check.)* I don't think so. *(Pause.)* So neither one of you knows Christine McClure?
PUNK JIM: *(He thinks Bridget's questioning is too "intense".)* Whoa. Chill out.
BRIDGET: *(Still frustrated but trying to be nice.)* Look, I'm . . . well... *(Pause. A bit calmer now to* PUNK JIM *and* MEG:*)* Should I believe what that man Cappy says? Or Kevin?

PUNK JIM *thinks for a moment then smiles. He is still stoned even though he thinks he is not. He shakes his head positively. Pause.*

PUNK JIM: Do you have a nuclear reactor?

Scene 4

KEVIN's *ramshackle place in the Hobo Jungle. It is an "indoor-outdoor" type of improvised shelter that takes advantage of a warm climate. The "house" is constructed with cast-off lumber, used tires, and used just-about-anything. Three folded up lawn chairs lean against a wall.* KEVIN *shows* SHELLY *and* BRIDGET *around.*

KEVIN: So. This is it. My humble abode.
BRIDGET: Impressive. You must've put some money into this.
SHELLY: *(Under her breath.)* Yeah, where did the money come from? *(To* KEVIN.*)* Some things fell off the back of a truck, huh?

KEVIN *does not reply.*

SHELLY: You're resourceful.
KEVIN: Yeah, I'm quite the collector.
SHELLY: *(Looking things over.)* This house says a lot about you.
KEVIN: I even have a burglar alarm system.
SHELLY: Things are worth that much, huh?
KEVIN: Sentimental value.
SHELLY: *(To* KEVIN.*)* Do you feel guilty at all?
BRIDGET: *(To* SHELLY.*)* Why do you say that?
SHELLY: Well, there must be some things here that are bought with taxpayer money. Welfare money.
KEVIN: I'm not on welfare, lady. *(Pause.)* I had a real job. But there weren't any real people there. That's one of the reasons I came here.

BRIDGET *touches an object.*

KEVIN: Hey, please. Don't touch that. I'm holding it for somebody. Who's in jail.
SHELLY: How many people live like you do in the Hobo Jungle?
KEVIN: You mean, in such uh... "luxury"?
SHELLY: Yeah.
KEVIN: Nobody. Just me. *(Pause.)* Has anyone ever told you you're nosy?
SHELLY: Yeah.
KEVIN: It's not a good trait. *(Pause.)* By the way, you can pitch your tent out next to me for the night. Tomorrow at noon we review your case.
SHELLY: So maybe I'll be able to stay for a while?
KEVIN: We go through things the way we're supposed to. That's all I can say for now.
SHELLY: Tough terms. Does Cappy lay down rules here?
KEVIN: Nosy, nosy, nosy. Stop it!
SHELLY: Why is it that Cappy has so much sway over what goes on here?
KEVIN: Women! *(Pause.)* He's bigger and stronger than any other one of us.
SHELLY: That can't be the only reason why you let him be the leader.
KEVIN: (KEVIN *does not like* SHELLY.) No. We *like* him. *(Pause. Changing the subject.)* So. You see where I live.

KEVIN *takes the three folded lawn chairs that are against the wall and gives one to* SHELLY *and one to* BRIDGET. *He keeps one for himself. He unfolds it and sits down.*

KEVIN: Have a seat.

SHELLY *and* BRIDGET *remain standing with the folded chairs in their hands.*

KEVIN: Let's get down to business.
SHELLY: Business?
KEVIN: Excuse me for sitting down before you. I have days when I'm tired.
SHELLY: What kind of business are we getting down to?
KEVIN: Well, please sit down, I said. Then we can talk. *(Pause.)* Might do you good to get off your feet. You won't find too many chairs in this neck of the woods.
SHELLY: *(Apprehensively.)* Okay. Thank you.

SHELLY *glances at* BRIDGET *and the expression on her face says*, "*Let's hear him out*". *They unfold their chairs and sit down. Pause.*

KEVIN: You know you've answered a girl's prayers?
SHELLY: Who has?
KEVIN: *(He points straight at* BRIDGET.*)* She has.
BRIDGET: I have?
KEVIN: Yeah. We have to move as fast as we can. Tonight, in fact.
SHELLY: Move – where?
KEVIN: We're not moving anywhere. *(Pause.)* Um, *finally* Huey's going to get laid.
SHELLY: Excuse me?
KEVIN: You heard what I said.

Pause. SHELLY *and* BRIDGET *have no idea what* KEVIN *is talking about. He explains.*

Kevin: Huey's from the old country. She's never been married. She came to the U.S. – and um... nobody's ever really gone for her. ... She's not the most gorgeous woman that's ever walked the planet... And she's shy. She feels ... quite rightly ... that she's ... missing something. *(Pause.)* I mean, come on. She's here in the Jungle – that almost makes it worse. 'Cause as many people know, Reich – well, ... let's put it this way: energy and actually, *sexual* energy, is central to his philosophy.

Shelly: Huey's heard all about sex but she hasn't had it.

Kevin: Yeah, you're catching on. *(Pause.)* Now it so happens that Huey has taken a shine to Cappy. But he's not physically attracted to her. He fought in Vietnam, and he's got his complexes. I don't think she's his "physical type" either, but nevertheless, there *will be* a sexual union between Cappy and Huey. Tonight.

Shelly: And you're going to make that happen somehow.

Kevin: *(Points at* Bridget.*)* She's the decoy.

Bridget: I beg your pardon.

Kevin: Cappy's going to think he's having sex with you.

Bridget: I don't want anything to do with that man.

Kevin: Well, you'll just have to get over that.

Shelly: What if she can't?

Kevin: Then she goes back empty-handed in regards to Christine McClure. *(Pause. Smiles to* Bridget.*)* Don't you?

Bridget: How do I know you really have any information?

Kevin: *(Shrugging.)* Okay, okay, go through your life not trusting anybody. See how far that gets you. *(Pause.)* What if I told you the stuff that I'm holding here for that person in jail, ...that that "person in jail" is Christine McClure?

Bridget: You could be lying.

KEVIN: All right, go ahead, kick me in the teeth – I'm just giving you a free sample.
BRIDGET: Why can't you tell me everything now?
KEVIN: 'Cause I can't have you skip town. We need you.
BRIDGET: *(Pause. She reconsiders. Not looking forward to hearing his plan.)* Tell me how your plan is supposed to work.
KEVIN: Well, in conjunction with you and some of Cappy's favorite whiskey, Huey's wish is going to come true. *(Happily.)* At last!
SHELLY: *(Not hearing any details from him.)* Whatever. You're confident. *(Pause.)* If you're successful, what if Huey finds out the real truth?
KEVIN: What, that she's had sex with Cappy? That's what she wants!
SHELLY: What if she finds out that Cappy didn't think that she was *her*?
BRIDGET: You could hurt her feelings.
KEVIN: *(Mocking* BRIDGET.*)* Oh, goodness, me! *(Pause.)* Well, then, she'll just have to get over it. It isn't always easy. It doesn't always *flow*. For God's sake, especially the *first* time! How many of us have been *there*? *(Pause. To* BRIDGET.*)* You still a virgin?
SHELLY: *(For* BRIDGET, *who refuses to answer.)* That's none of your business!
KEVIN: *(To* BRIDGET.*)* I bet you're not. *(Pause.)* You don't want Huey to remain a sexually frustrated human being. That's just not nice.
BRIDGET: She wasn't nice to me.
KEVIN: Well, that's probably 'cause Cappy's attentions were on you.

BRIDGET: *(Confirming* KEVIN's *observation.)* They were. *(Pause.)* Um, why did you say Christine got consumed into orgone energy and now lives on another planet?
KEVIN: You need to have a sense of humor around here.
BRIDGET: To me, this is a serious matter.
KEVIN: *(Heatedly.)* Well, if you want, we could stay right here and I could tell you about another serious matter. Probably much more serious than what you have on *your* plate! *(Pause. Calming down a little.)* I'm simply asking you to be a decoy!
BRIDGET: All right, all right. *(Pause.)* All right. *(Pause. She is still thinking.)*
KEVIN: Look, my plan is to make someone happy. There's nothing wrong with that.
BRIDGET: *(More or less resigned.)* Okay.
KEVIN: *(To* BRIDGET.*)* So, we're good to go? *(Pause.)* The deal is that you act as a decoy and afterwards I'll tell you everything I know about Christine McClure – including exactly where you can find her.
BRIDGET: Yes.
SHELLY: *(Pause. To* KEVIN.*)* Hey, wait a second. Um, can you, like, describe to us a little bit about the mechanics of your plan and how you know it'll work?
KEVIN: It'll work. *(Pause.)* It'll be dark. He'll be drunk.

Long pause.

SHELLY: That's it? You were an engineer once. Don't engineers usually have it worked out to the finest detail?
KEVIN: Well, there's going to be a curtain.
SHELLY: Okay – *(Pause.* SHELLY *expects more information from him but gets none.)*

BRIDGET: I don't look anything like Huey!

KEVIN: That doesn't matter. *(Pause.)* There's a little light that comes from the glow of the city but that's it. And I have other ideas too about how to make this work.

SHELLY: *(Not yet convinced.)* Oh.

KEVIN: *(Pause. Then, to* BRIDGET.*)* Cappy's going to be pleasantly surprised when I tell him that suddenly you're lusting after him.

BRIDGET: Ugh. He'll believe you after how I acted towards him?

KEVIN: You don't know Cappy like I do. *(Pause.)* Huh! Sweet young you? *(Pause.)* He's vain enough to fall for it.

BRIDGET: This better not be a trick to get *me* into bed with Cappy.

KEVIN: No. Huey's the one that's in need.

BRIDGET: Cappy's going to be drunk. Other people might be drunk. I could get raped!

KEVIN: *(Assuring her.)* I'll be there, sober. *(Referring to* SHELLY.*)* And so will she, *(He turns to* SHELLY.*)* won't you?

SHELLY: *(Shrugging, thinking the plan is crazy.)* Yeah, I'll be there.

KEVIN: Very good. So now all I have to do is inform the parties concerned.

Scene 5

At an edge of the Hobo Jungle. GEORGE, *from the Public Works Department, and* ANGELA survey the area.

ANGELA: George, this place is an eyesore.
GEORGE: I know. But a lot of it's hidden by the trees. Most people can't see it unless they're looking for it.
ANGELA: It's an embarrassment. I don't understand why we can't raze this dump by having the landowners step in.
GEORGE: Because it's private property *and* a combination of state, county and city land.
ANGELA: Can't we get the private owners to throw their weight around?
GEORGE: No, there's original owners that are dead and their heirs are fighting among themselves.
ANGELA: If the property owners can't do something, my agency can.
GEORGE: You can?
ANGELA: Yeah. Welfare fraud is rampant here. People are faking mental disability. The current crackdown is well overdue. *(Pause.)* I don't get it with these people. There are plenty of jobs for everybody – even people with "mental problems". If they can walk to the bank to deposit their checks, they can walk to work. They're stealing from the taxpayers – it's as plain and simple as that!
GEORGE: I know.
ANGELA: *(Pauses, visualizes.)* If we say a road needs to be built through here, that's one way to get this place condemned.
GEORGE: I don't think the environmentalists will stand for that.

Angela: All they want to do is wreck our economy so we can become socialists. *(Pause.)* I did some more homework on the Hobo Jungle. You know there's that new disease called AIDS... *(Pause.)* Well, somebody has it here.

George: *(Shook up.)* They do?

Angela: You're not going to catch it from standing at this distance. *(Pointing into the Jungle, with concern.)* There's a guy who's been in the hospital with Kaposi's sarcoma.

George: What's that?

Angela: It's what a lot of people with AIDS get before they die. Just think what would happen if AIDS spread from the Hobo Jungle.

George: *(He forms an idea.)* Well... maybe somehow... we in Public Works can raise the water level of the creek nearby. Flood them out.

Angela: Yeah, but the water wouldn't last *(With disgust.)* and they'd come back. We have to think of some better way.

Punk Jim *approaches.* Angela *takes one look at his Mohawk haircut.*

Angela: What planet are you from?

Punk Jim: The same one as you, unfortunately.

Angela: Do you live here?

Punk Jim: Who are you to ask me?

Angela: I work with the county. *(She refers to* George.*)* So does he.

Punk Jim: Oh. Me, too.

Angela: Oh, yeah? Which department?

Punk Jim: The Department of Collections.

Angela: There's isn't a department of collections. *(Pause.)* Oh, I get it. *(Pause.)* Why don't you find a *job?*

PUNK JIM: I don't see the point of it.

ANGELA: The point is to earn money. You have to eat.

PUNK JIM: That's what food stamps are for.

ANGELA: *(To* GEORGE, *gritting her teeth.)* The fraud and decadence in this country is shocking!

PUNK JIM: I agree with you on that.

ANGELA: Yeah, sure!

PUNK JIM: Reagan, Bush and the rest of them. Hang them for treason! The evidence is there for everybody to see.

ANGELA: Well, there are millions of us that *don't* see it that way.

PUNK JIM: Yeah, that's the scary part.

ANGELA: *(Proudly.)* I voted for Ronald Reagan.

PUNK JIM: *(To* GEORGE.*)* Did you vote for Ronald McDonald, too?

GEORGE: Yes!

PUNK JIM: I'm so glad I left this country. My only regret is that I came back.

ANGELA: *(Smiling.)* We're sorry you came back, too.

PUNK JIM: It's nice that we're all so sorry. It says a lot about how pathetic things have become.

ANGELA: You know, you might not have a home here for long.

PUNK JIM: What, are you going to deport me?

ANGELA: Not exactly.

PUNK JIM: Yeah, just remember, bitch: *I'm* an American, too.

GEORGE: *(Shocked.)* Did you just call her a bitch?

PUNK JIM: I think I did, um... yeah! So what are you going to do about it? Make me *your* bitch? *(Pause.)* I don't work for minimum wage, man. It's not a *living* wage.

GEORGE: It's types like you who are better off dead.

PUNK JIM: Watch out. Last I knew, lynching was murder and murder was like… not only unbrotherly, but also against the law.

GEORGE: Better Dead than Red!

PUNK JIM: *(Sarcastically.)* That's what I like about you right-wingers – you have that gift Like …you know how to *rhyme*. *(Pause.)* No, I think it's better to be Red than dead. The dead don't get no free handouts like the Reds do.

GEORGE: You're human garbage.

PUNK JIM: At least I'm human. You're slime.

GEORGE: You bastard! Put 'em up! Come on!

GEORGE *positions his hands like those of a boxer in a ring.* PUNK JIM *puts up his hands. They "dance" around in a circle like boxers, sparring.* GEORGE *throws a few punches.* PUNK JIM *manages to avoid each one of them.*

ANGELA: *(Yelling.)* Get him, George! If you kill him, I'll swear you hit him in self-defense.

PUNK JIM: *(To* ANGELA.*)* Yeah, pipe right up – now that your *pimp* is here to defend you.

ANGELA: He's not my pimp!

PUNK JIM: There aren't many whores who can afford to be without them these days!

ANGELA: George, did you hear what he just called you? And me?

GEORGE *and* PUNK JIM *continue to revolve around an imaginary center point as* GEORGE *throws most of the punches but never lands one.*

GEORGE: *(Trying to concentrate.)* I can't talk when I'm fighting.
PUNK JIM: Yeah, focus, or something might happen to your eye.

PUNK JIM *almost manages to hit* GEORGE *in the eye.*

ANGELA: *(Yelling.)* I'll pull out your hair, piece by piece!
PUNK JIM: You're never going to lay your hands on my head, bitch. And my hair would *cut* you, anyway.
ANGELA: *(Outraged.)* George, he called me a "bitch" again.

GEORGE *manages to hit* PUNK JIM *lightly on the shoulder. They continue fighting.*

GEORGE: *(Happy that he landed a punch.)* There!
ANGELA: *(To* PUNK JIM.*)* How do you like that!?
PUNK JIM: Sorry. Wind has hit me harder.
ANGELA: Yeah, sure. *(Pause. Yelling.)* George, knock him out cold!

GEORGE *and* PUNK JIM *continue to circle like sparring boxers.* PUNK JIM *is able to dodge any punch that* GEORGE *throws at him and vice versa. After a while,* CAPPY *enters.*

CAPPY: Well, what do we have here! Hey, go team, go! Ha! *(Pause.)* Jimbo, you know what? You have real warrior spirit in you! Add orgone to that and you're unbeatable. *(He goes over towards* GEORGE.*)* I myself would run away from him 'cause his intimidating face scares the hell out of me. *(Pause. To* GEORGE.*)* I don't know who you are, but you are one tough guy! It takes a lot to stand up to frisky young Jim. Aim for his jaw! Everybody thinks it's the eyes that'll get you further, but if you take out the jaw, you take out the man! *(Pause.)* I haven't seen a fight like this since we were fighting hand-to-hand in *("-nam" almost rhymes with "man".)* Vietnam.
GEORGE: You fought in Vietnam?

Caught up in speaking, GEORGE *barely manages to dodge a punch by* PUNK JIM *that would have hit him in the head.*

CAPPY: I did.

GEORGE *distances himself from* PUNK JIM *and lowers his hands.*

GEORGE: I don't want to fight in front of a vet. I have too much respect.
CAPPY: That's very ceremonious of you, but I was just starting to enjoy a good fight.
PUNK JIM: *(Sorry that the fight is ending.)* I could've knocked him out.
ANGELA: No, that would have been too much *work* for you. *(Pause. To* PUNK JIM.*)* That's what you get for calling us names!

By this time PUNK JIM *and* GEORGE *are well away from each other.* GEORGE *has stopped challenging* PUNK JIM, *so the fight has been abandoned.*

CAPPY: Names? Oh, that's the only thing you were fighting over?! *(Fake disappointment.)* Aw. *(Pause.)* At least in 'Nam we murdered women and children for a good reason.

GEORGE: I thought you said you were a vet. *(Pause.)* You don't talk like one!

CAPPY: Maybe not like the ones that *you* know.

CAPPY *clears his throat and throws some spit that hits* ANGELA.

ANGELA: *(Horrified and angry.)* You rude, disgusting pig!

CAPPY: Whoops, I'm sorry! – A habit I picked up in Asia. *(Pause. To* GEORGE.*)* You know, it's a different culture, *not ours*, and we were *there*. *(Pause.)* They often spit. It *is* a little too much – from *our* point of view.

ANGELA: Don't try and philosophize your way out of it!

CAPPY: You're right, Angela. I shouldn't beat around the bush. *(Pause.)* You and your kind are a disgrace.

GEORGE: I can't let him get away with it, Angela. Spitting is foul and revolting!

CAPPY: Some of us call this place Camp *Resistance*, but at this juncture, I'm all for revolt.

GEORGE *would fight* CAPPY, *but he does not want to hit a one-armed vet.*

ANGELA: Don't get worked up, George. He's not worth it. This is Nick Bocaro – otherwise known as *(With loathing.)* "Cappy".

GEORGE: So?

ANGELA: So, he runs the Hobo Jungle. You just don't want to mess with him.

GEORGE: How can anybody "run" the Hobo Jungle?

ANGELA: I don't know, but he does.

GEORGE: You should put him in jail for it.

ANGELA: If only we could.

CAPPY: Wait a second – before you condemn me without a trial. We do *good* here. Most of us try to live at the only level of technology that's sustainable for the planet: the Stone Age. How do *you* stack up against that?

GEORGE: Angela, how does he know you?

PUNK JIM: *(To* CAPPY, *still frustrated that the fight ended.)* Man, man! I was winning!

CAPPY: *(To* PUNK JIM.*)* Winning against these people is an illusion. They have the military-industrial complex on their side – you don't.

ANGELA: That's right. We're strong. We're the law. And you know, Mr. Bocaro? I think it's time to schedule that periodic psychologist's evaluation that people like you are supposed to be getting on a regular basis.

CAPPY: That sounds fine. I'm a dedicated student of psychology if there's ever been one.

ANGELA: Are you still trying to sexify everybody that lands up in the Hobo Jungle?

CAPPY: I like that word, "sexify". It's new for me. Thank you for expanding my vocabulary, Angela.

GEORGE: *(To* ANGELA, *finding it hard to believe.)* The two of you actually know each other –

ANGELA: *(To* CAPPY, *ignoring* GEORGE.*)* Disseminating propaganda written by a foreign doctor – Wilhelm Reich – who, need I remind you, was a convicted felon that died in federal prison!

CAPPY: We all have our bad days. Reich was no exception.

ANGELA: Bad days? Your hero had a few bad years!

CAPPY: It's tough for those who agitate for a revolution in sex. And he wanted a political one, too, so... *(Pause. To* ANGELA.*)* It's good of you *(He makes an obscene gesture to accompany the word.)* to *bone* up on him.

ANGELA: I'm onto your scam. When you come up for review, you start raving about Reich – that's how you confirm to them that you're "insane". How many years has this worked for you?

CAPPY: Wait. Sorry. Wrong! You're making some of it up as you go along. *(Pause.)* And George, you were so impressed by her. *(Pause.)* The thing is, um, my file's with the Veteran's Administration, and I'm not on mental, but *physical* disability.

ANGELA: *(To* GEORGE, *angry that she has been proved wrong.)* George, they're swine here. They don't work. They just take handouts and fornicate!

CAPPY: And we've never been happier in our lives.

ANGELA: *That* I'm sure is a big lie.

CAPPY: Angela, since you have had some personal experience in the Hobo Jungle, I suppose you have a right to say that.

GEORGE: What's he mean?

CAPPY: She stayed here – for a short time. Years ago. She was a teenage runaway. I guess somebody beat untruth back into her after she was forced to go home.

ANGELA: George, he's completely off his rocker. Don't listen to a word he says!

CAPPY: If I'm off my rocker I should apply for mental disability. *(Pause.)* I'd donate the extra money to the American *Socialist* Party – that's what I'd do. *(To* GEORGE.*)* Cool, huh, George?

PUNK JIM: Who *is* this georgy-porgy guy that I want to pop in the face?

45

ANGELA: You watch your mouth. George is from Public Works. And you know what they have there? *Bulldozers!*
PUNK JIM: *(Sarcastically.)* I'm really afraid now.

MEG *enters.* ANGELA *looks her up and down with displeasure.*

ANGELA: What is this... freak?

MEG *ignores what* ANGELA *has said.*

MEG: *(To* PUNK JIM, *nicely.)* Hey, Jim. I was looking for you.
PUNK JIM: I went for a walk and I ran into *these* guys *(Gestures to* ANGELA *and* GEORGE.) who are like deeply committed to greed and planetary rape.
ANGELA: We don't have to stand here and take this.
CAPPY: That's why I think you should go.
ANGELA: *(To* CAPPY.) You realize your days are numbered.
CAPPY: I do use a calendar like a lot of people.
ANGELA: *(To* GEORGE.) Let's get out of here.

ANGELA *and* GEORGE *turn and exit.*

CAPPY: *(Pause.)* They've made us one of the new enemies.
MEG: What do you mean?

Car Door Shave

CAPPY: They need us to fill the vacuum left by the Vietnamese – or the "Viet Cong" as they called them – an enemy on par with the *Devil*. Those poor villagers were considered dominos in the global game of countries falling to communism. *(Pause.)* Well, we still have communists and they're great to hate. You can get a lot of money for hating. *(Pause.)* Now you can get money for even hating us. There's never enough enemies! Always need *more* – reach right down into the regular folk for them. Eeny meeny miny moe, label someone an enemy and get the dough. *(Pause. To* MEG.*)* You know why they want the Hobo Jungle?

MEG: I don't know... um ... it's like uh, a bomb went off and they can see it in other places but they can't see it here.

CAPPY: Yeah. Well. Something like that. They want to put their war-dependent civilization on top of this land. *(Pause.)* You know what I say to them? I fought for you once. And I will never, ever... stick up... for you... ever again.

Scene 6

The Hobo Jungle, as in Scenes 1 and 3: the car door and barrel under the eucalyptus tree, the orgone accumulator some distance away. CAPPY *sits on the barrel. His face is lathered with shaving cream. He faces the car door mirror and shaves. The basin filled with water is on the table near him.* HUEY *stands by, close. There is a small bottle of men's cologne on the ground near her.*

CAPPY: What a sublime late afternoon. It almost makes me forget the disagreeable encounter I had earlier today. Well. Onward and upward... to ...*tonight!*

HUEY: *(Dreamily.)* Yes, tonight.

CAPPY: The arrangements have been made.
HUEY: *(Dreamily.)* The arrangements have been made.
CAPPY: I feel as strong as a bull.
HUEY: *(Dreamily.)* I feel as strong as a bull.
CAPPY: Best to get rid of this five o'clock shadow.
HUEY: *(Dreamily.)* Best to get rid of this five o'clock shadow.
CAPPY: Thank you, Kevin.
HUEY: *(Dreamily.)* Thank you, Kevin.
CAPPY: Tonight the stars in the sky will shine.
HUEY: *(Dreamily.)* The stars in the sky will shine.
CAPPY: And I will be deeply satisfied.
HUEY: *(Dreamily.)* And I will be deeply satisfied.
CAPPY: Is there an echo here?
HUEY: What?
CAPPY: Did I hear an echo? I never had trouble with my hearing, except when I was in combat.
HUEY: I don't think there's an echo here. There's too many trees and stuff.
CAPPY: *(Pause. Supposes she is right.)* Oh. *(Pause. Very happy.)* I have a python in my pants.
HUEY: I'm a little nervous.
CAPPY: Just bask in the glory of this golden afternoon. Leave your worries far behind.
HUEY: I just can't help being nervous.

CAPPY: Nobody's going to throw us out of the Hobo Jungle, Huey. At least not for a good long while. *(Pause. He means "good in bed".)* Obviously, I'm known to be good. *(Pause. Thinks. Expansively.)* You know, Reich discovered orgone energy through consistent, thorough study of energy functions – in our psyches, in our bodies, in our politics. He was always aware that smaller minds especially want to get their hands on *sex* and hold *it* hostage – making everyone a prisoner, making it impossible for them to break free.

HUEY: *(Not understanding him.)* I guess so…

CAPPY: *(Trying to explain.)* The nature of oppression, Huey. And RE-pression. It's deep stuff. It gives us war. And not only the namby-pamby war-of-the-sexes. But enough of that. *(Looking around him.)* What a fine place we have here.

HUEY: I got some cologne. I'll put a little bit in your hair.

HUEY *puts a few drops of cologne in her palm and then runs her hand through* CAPPY's *hair.*

CAPPY: Thanks. Could you get me some aloe, please?

HUEY: Yeah, sure.

HUEY *exits to get an aloe vera leaf.* CAPPY *rinses the soap off his face with some of the water from the basin.*

CAPPY: *(With a pleasurable sigh, referring to Huey's good-heartedness.)* You're good, Huey. *(Pause.)* I admire Bridget's openness and curiosity. But sometimes you can be too curious and too open. It's a bad idea – I'm sure people tried to warn her off from finding her birthmother – that low-down piece of corruption whose only worthy deed was to put her baby up for adoption!

Huey *returns. She has an outer leaf of aloe vera. She is radiant. She has a smile on her face.*

Cappy: You're in one of the happiest moods I've ever seen you in.
Huey: *(Sighing, happily.)* Yeah, well...
Cappy: Sometimes we *do* live in a wonderful world. Just look at this: you standing there with that plant – a healing force in your hands. *(Pause.)* Yeah, that Bridget – she is coming into her own. You know what she's doing?

Huey's *expression sours at the mention of Bridget's name. She remains silent.*

Cappy: She took that woman Shelly for a walk along the creek. To get her out of our hair so we could get things ready for the party tonight. All Bridget's asking the lot of us is if we can re-collect our thoughts, think back, and remember any stories that might involve Christine McClure in these parts.
Huey: I don't know no Christine McClure.
Cappy: It's a good thing you don't.

Huey *is ready to spread some aloe gel on* Cappy *but he takes the aloe leaf out of her hands, gets some gel from it, and spreads it on his face and neck.*

Cappy: I can't have you touching me, Huey. Otherwise you'll be stalking me in my nightmares with the rest of Charlie on the prowl.

An Unknown Woman *enters. She is loud-mouthed and she talks tough.*

Unknown Woman: Sitting on his ass! What else is new!

Cappy: *(Unhappy.)* Jumping Jesus! I hope I'm seeing a ghost. And on this most glorious day.

Unknown Woman: Glorious day?

Cappy: Yeah, Jimmy Carter was going to be sworn back in as president. The last four and a half years have just been declared a bad dream.

Unknown Woman: *(Dryly.)* Yeah, dream on.

Cappy: Hope you're on your way somewhere else.

Unknown Woman: My stuff's here. I need to get at it.

Cappy: Nobody wants you here.

Unknown Woman: You mean *you* don't want me here.

Cappy: Me and a few others. *(Pause.)* Do what business you need to do and split, huh?

Unknown Woman: I'll leave when I feel like it.

Cappy: Don't push your luck.

Unknown Woman: How's the Reich scam holding up? Getting laid enough? *(Quoting.)* "I hate abstinence. The few bad poems that are occasionally created during abstinence are of no great interest." *(Pause.)* That's what Reich said. Or least that's what *you* say he said. *(Pause.)* Reich is right. Sex *is* where it all begins. Your trouble, Cappy, is you always want to begin… and begin …and begin again.

Cappy: Okay, you're starting to push your luck.

Unknown Woman: What are you going to do about it? *(Pause.)* I have to see Kevin.

Cappy: If I hear that you've "borrowed" any money from him, I will find you and I will kill you.

UNKNOWN WOMAN: You wouldn't do that. You're just too plain lazy. *(Pause. She refers to* HUEY.) So you've got a little oriental now. What a surprise. Asians like to *work*. For most of them, this place with its lack of activity would really get on their nerves. But maybe she does work. As your slave.

The UNKNOWN WOMAN *exits.*

HUEY: *(Turns up her nose.)* She's weird. You know her, huh?
CAPPY: Jail's the only place where she's remotely capable of behaving herself. It appears they let her out early.
HUEY: Who *is* she?
CAPPY: That Huey, is Christine McClure. And we must do everything to not let her ruin this evening.

ACT II

Scene 1

At the edge of the Hobo Jungle, alongside a small creek that borders it. BRIDGET *and* SHELLY *are walking.*

BRIDGET: I wonder if this creek ever has much water in it.

SHELLY *does not answer.*

BRIDGET: I have to say, the Hobo Jungle is one of the seediest places I've ever been in.
SHELLY: Yeah, well... I'm adaptable. *(Pause.)* It's all *I* have at the moment.
BRIDGET: I'm sorry. I didn't mean to criticize it so much.
SHELLY: I just pretend I'm away at camp. *(Pause. Reflecting.)* When you think about it, Mother Nature never intended any one species to be affluent. *(Pause.)* We *think* we should live in big, comfortable houses – but that's just us thinking.

There is a pause in the conversation. They continue to walk. BRIDGET *is struck by Shelly's intelligence. She wonders:*

BRIDGET: You're smart – don't you call the police when your husband is violent towards you?
SHELLY: You can – but then there's the problem that you live together in the same house. Where you going to go? I may be smart but I don't have enough money to rent somewhere else.
BRIDGET: There are shelters for battered women.

SHELLY: Yeah, but you can only live there for so long. And there's hell to pay if you're away from home too long.
BRIDGET: What do you mean? Do you have kids?
SHELLY: *(Making it up as she goes along.)* Yeah.
BRIDGET: How many?
SHELLY: One.
BRIDGET: How old is she?
SHELLY: About your age.
BRIDGET: How does she deal with the situation?
SHELLY: She... um... moved out. Just. *(Pause.)* She's a freshman in college.
BRIDGET: Good for her.
SHELLY: Can we change the subject? The whole thing upsets me.
BRIDGET: Sure.

There is a pause in the conversation. They walk some more.

BRIDGET: Kevin is certain. I'm not. Kevin told me I'm not to say anything once I show Cappy into the room. Cappy's not just going to start taking off his clothes – drunk, in the dark – and *not* want to talk to me. I mean, he's not going to want to just... stick it in right away.
SHELLY: *(Agreeing.)* You're going to have to talk to him.
BRIDGET: But Kevin doesn't want Huey to know what's really going on. So, say I'm standing near Huey, so I can do a little talking, while Huey's lying down. Huey will know I'm there. There's no way around it. It's not going to work.
SHELLY: Maybe he thinks that Huey will be drunk. Or that she'll be in such a state that she's blocking you out. *(Pause.)* No, I don't see how it's going to work, either.

BRIDGET: What am I getting myself into!?

SHELLY: *(Pause.)* This is an interesting place. I won't mind getting to know it better.

BRIDGET: *(Surprised.)* Really? Not me! *(Pause.)* So you've heard of Wilhelm Reich?

SHELLY: Vaguely. *(Pause.)* He's in the Sigmund Freud category. Funny that they've adopted an author of psychology books as a mascot. *(Pause.)* I will say this: Cappy's not a stupid guy. Kevin's a clever man. Huey, the rest of them – real characters. A colorful way to begin my new life.

BRIDGET: This is like the last place I would ever think of beginning a new life in.

SHELLY: Oh, well. Life's about learning. *(Pause.)* Learning doesn't stop when you get out of school or college. Or after you turn thirty. It goes on and on – unless you learn *not* to learn, I guess. *(Pause.)* These people can teach me something.

BRIDGET: They're pretty weird.

SHELLY: You can think they're weird. But in general, humans are strange. Or at least they're born strange. They're born strangers to themselves. It takes them a lifetime to get to know themselves. *(Pause.)* Excuse me for asking, but are you sure you um… want to meet your birthmother?

BRIDGET: They said she's been more or less a drifter her whole life. But I'm older. I think I can take it.

SHELLY: And what if she doesn't want to see you?

BRIDGET: Well, that's life.

SHELLY: You're brave to come out here.

BRIDGET: Brave, or it's just something I want to know.

They continue walking for a while. Then:

SHELLY: Bridget, tonight – for Huey – tonight's a real big night for her. Actually, I would like Kevin's plan to work. Don't think it's just about sex.
BRIDGET: What else is it about?
SHELLY: It has to do with fitting in. *(Pause.)* I'm not talking about peer-pressure… conforming mindlessly… *(Pause.)* I'm talking about her sense of wholeness, her sense of dignity. *(Pause.)* I believe that Huey feels that until she's had sex, she hasn't yet joined the human race.
BRIDGET: I think it's pretty sad if she believes that.
SHELLY: I don't want to sound condescending but… you're young and… you're not Huey.

They walk some more.

Scene 2

KEVIN's *ramshackle place in the Hobo Jungle. A couple of chairs are positioned around a small portable table.* KEVIN *sits at the table.* PUNK JIM *stands nearby.* KEVIN *reaches into his pocket and takes out his wallet. He takes some money out and puts it on the table.*

PUNK JIM: Why can't Meg go out and buy the stuff?
KEVIN: She won't be able to carry it all. There's other things to get. *(Pause.)* She had to go somewhere else. For some cloth and thread.
PUNK JIM: Why that?
KEVIN: I don't know how to sew. She says she does, okay? *(Pause.)* It's nothing that concerns you. *(Pause.)* So you'll remember?

PUNK JIM: I don't need to remember. I made a list.
KEVIN: Don't forget your list.
PUNK JIM: I'm cool. I'll get everything you want.
KEVIN: Okay, so it's Johnny Walker *Black* Label, not Red.
PUNK JIM: Yeah, I know.
KEVIN: Seven-Up, not Sprite.
PUNK JIM: I wrote it all down. *(He takes the money off the table and stuffs it into his pocket.)*
KEVIN: I appreciate it.
PUNK JIM: No problem, man. *(Pause.)* You didn't throw a party for me when *I* got here.
KEVIN: Yeah, well, this is different.
PUNK JIM: How is it different?
KEVIN: It's just... there's a difference, okay? *(Pause.)* You know the difference between AM and FM radio?
PUNK JIM: *(Pause. At first puzzled that Kevin would be asking this.)* Yeah. FM broadcasts in stereo. What's that got to do with anything?
KEVIN: FM signals are much higher frequencies. A lot higher than AM ones.
PUNK JIM: Yeah, so?
KEVIN: When you got here you were *FM*, man. *way* high. A party wouldn't have meant anything to you.
PUNK JIM: Oh. *(He starts to leave.)*
KEVIN: Buy whatever kind of beer you like – I don't care.

PUNK JIM *leaves. After thinking to himself for a while,* KEVIN *gets up, gets a book, and sits back down. He finds a favorite passage in the book.*

KEVIN: *(Reading aloud.)* "The unity of nature and culture, of sexuality and morality – longed for from time immemorial – will remain a dream as long as man continues to condemn the biological demand for natural, orgastic sexual gratification. *(Pause. He turns some pages. He finds another passage that he likes. He reads it aloud.)* "Man is basically an animal. Animals, as distinct from man, are *not* machine-like, they're not sadistic. Animal societies – within the same species – are incomparably more peaceful than those of man. The question then, is: what made the animal, man, degenerate into a war machine? *(Pause.)* Sexual *re*-pression and political *op*-pression – both so interdependent upon one other – *(Pause.)* both move in a terrorizing feedback loop that rejects the orgone energy that nurtures all species on the planet."
CHRISTINE: *(Offstage. Loudly.)* Kevin, you in there?

KEVIN *looks in the direction of his front door.*

CHRISTINE: *(Offstage. Yelling.)* Kevin!

KEVIN *puts the book down and gets up from his chair.*

KEVIN: *(Not loudly.)* Yeah. Coming.
CHRISTINE: Kevin! *(She enters.)*
KEVIN: Well, this is a surprise!
CHRISTINE: You didn't hear that I was around?
KEVIN: No.
CHRISTINE: *(Maliciously.)* Stupid bastards! *(Pause.)* I got here an hour ago! I just had to go get something to eat. *(Not nicely.)* I didn't want to sponge off from any sponger here.
KEVIN: So, you're out, huh?

Car Door Shave

CHRISTINE: Yeah, I'm *out*. *(Making fun of the gay usage of the word, "out".)* Do you think I'd be here if I wasn't... "out"?

KEVIN: No.

CHRISTINE: You've been a good boy keeping my stuff for me. I really appreciate it.

KEVIN: You're welcome. *(Pause.)* So I guess you're here to pick it up?

CHRISTINE: I'm not sure. Not sure what my next move is yet.

KEVIN: Well, I can still hang onto it for you.

CHRISTINE: Thanks. *(She stretches both arms up in the air like a cat.)* It's so good to be on the outside.

KEVIN: Listen, Christine. I don't want to rush you or anything but... something's like... happening now. *(Lying.)* The police have been coming around to talk to me. They think some of the things I have is stolen stuff. They actually were supposed to come here like right now – to um... interview me.

CHRISTINE: They think *you're* a thief? Boy, are they wasting their time!

KEVIN: I know. I know, but they're hoping one of these times I'm going to confess. So they keep stopping by. At all sorts of hours. I mean, they're harassing me. *(Pause.)* I'm thinking, it's not good for you to be here – um, I don't want to be seen with you – no offense – but also, I know you don't want to be seen with me – and all the stuff here – especially since you just got out of jail.

CHRISTINE: I served my time.

KEVIN: Christine McClure may have, but has Christine Huber?

CHRISTINE: *(After being silenced momentarily.)* True. *(Pause. Suspiciously.)* There's people here that have things against me. *(Taking the offensive.)* Have they had any influence over you?

KEVIN: No. Look, I'd hate for you to have to deal with the cops. You've seen enough uniforms.

59

CHRISTINE: So you want me to leave, basically, now?

KEVIN: It'd be a good idea. *(Pause.)* Come back tomorrow.

CHRISTINE: How will I know the coast is clear?

KEVIN: I don't know. But… any minute now they could show up. Can you find a place to stay away from here, for like… the next twenty-four hours?

CHRISTINE: Why does it have to be twenty-four hours?

KEVIN: Well, okay – let's say twenty hours or maybe twelve. It's just better if you're not seen here now …or tonight.

CHRISTINE: So what's going on tonight?

KEVIN: Nothing. Listen, there's a few violent people that live here now. One of them might think you're here to steal something or to hurt somebody.

CHRISTINE: So the Hobo Jungle's been going downhill since I've been gone?

KEVIN: There's been more crime since the Republicans got in.

CHRISTINE: I don't know if what you're saying is true. Are you trying to hide something from me?

KEVIN: No. I'm telling you, please. The cops are bugging me and I'm thinking of *you*, too.

CHRISTINE: *(Not happy with him.)* Okay, okay. You're telling me a couple of stories… *(Pause. Determined.)* But I'm coming back. I'm going to live here if I want to. Nobody can throw me out. Not even Cappy!

KEVIN: Don't worry about that. *(Pause.)* Well… look… I'll see you tomorrow morning?

CHRISTINE: All right, then. *(She looks at the title of the book that he was reading.)* Unbelievable. Even you on the Wilhelm Reich kick! Where will it end!

Kevin: Um... you still have a minute, if you're fast... maybe there's something in your stuff that you need right away. Go ahead, take it. It'll be one less suspicious thing for the cops to see. But get it quick, and go, please. *(Pause.)* I'm sure you must have some business as Christine Huber to attend to.

Christine: *(When she says "pleasure", she does not mean sexual pleasure.)* Oh, yeah. And business for her is much more a pleasure.

Scene 3

Angela's *office at Ventura County Social Services. It is the end of the day. Angela stands and looks out her office window.*

Angela: I'm so tired. *I* could use a vacation in Ensenada! Eclipse – yeah, sure. Whatever floats Shelly's boat. *(Pause.)* I hope she's having a terrible time! I hope she gets mugged down there. *(Pause.)* That's where they should send the Hobo Jungle people: Mexico.

She sits down behind her desk. She is tired. She puts her elbows on the top of the desk and her head in her hands. The Ghost of Jimmy Carter *walks in.* Angela *talks to him as if she were speaking from inside a dream.*

Ghost of Jimmy Carter: We're at a turning point in our history. There are two paths to choose. One is a path that leads to fragmentation and self-interest. Down that road lies a mistaken idea of freedom, the right to grasp for ourselves some advantage over others. That path would be one of constant conflict between narrow interests ending in chaos and immobility. It is a certain route to failure.

ANGELA: Jimmy Carter, *you*? Won't you ever go away?

GHOST OF JIMMY CARTER: As long as there are educated citizens with a conscience – and many poor folks too – people will bring me back.

ANGELA: You're not welcome back. We have the economy under control. We're cutting taxes for the rich. They're the ones who create the jobs.

GHOST OF JIMMY CARTER: *(Shaking his head negatively.)* Trickle-down economics means *I* will line my pockets and *you* better hope that there's a hole in one of them.

ANGELA: You lost the election.

GHOST OF JIMMY CARTER: I would not have if there had been a run-off. It was a three-candidate race – John Anderson siphoned off votes that would've been mine. *(Pause.)* Well, now, Ronald Reagan, he postures himself as a law-and-order man. He and your current governor both build a lot of new prisons for those who can't conform. *(He shakes his head negatively.)*

ANGELA: We need to clean up our country.

GHOST OF JIMMY CARTER: Then why not start at the top? One hundred and fifty of Mr. Reagan's appointees will wind up being convicted felons. *(Pause.)* It's sad – the direction this country is taking.

ANGELA: No, it was sad under you. Our embassy in Teheran was attacked and our people were taken hostage. Something which you could do nothing about.

GHOST OF JIMMY CARTER: Worse will happen. I dare say that people like that will come to our shores and will kill a few thousand of us.

ANGELA: That'll never happen. Once again, you're wrong! *(Pause.)* I'm so glad Reagan tore down those ridiculous solar panels you installed on the White House roof!

GHOST OF JIMMY CARTER: Yeah, that sent a clear signal to the oil barons that we're going back to business as usual. Doom, I tell you. Doom. Big Oil will someday sit in the Oval Office. *(Pause.)* Well, there's a choice. A choice between whether our country wants to be an empire or a democracy. We can't be both.

ANGELA: We *are* a democracy. And we will spread democracy throughout the world.

GHOST OF JIMMY CARTER: *(Worried.)* You will spread your type of Americanization throughout the world. *(Pause.)* Well, I'd better go. My work is never finished.

ANGELA: *(Sarcastically.)* I'm sure it isn't.

GHOST OF JIMMY CARTER: *(Pause.)* Experience tells me that you have to work twenty times harder and longer to be a peacemaker rather than a warmonger.

He smiles. The GHOST OF JIMMY CARTER *glides easily out of the room. There is a pause.* GEORGE *walks in.*

GEORGE: I have the answer.

ANGELA: *(Startled from her dream-state.)* What? *(Pause.)* George, how'd you get in here?

GEORGE: I called you. You said come in at the end of the day. You just buzzed me in.

ANGELA: *(Still coming to.)* I did? Oh, okay.

GEORGE: The answer is the white ashfly.

ANGELA: What?

GEORGE: The answer to the problem. It's perfect for the Hobo Jungle. The white ashfly is a parasite. It attacks and destroys shrubs and shade trees. Once I set it loose, the Department of Agriculture will have no choice but to seal off the Jungle and fumigate it. The people down there will be gone.

ANGELA: *(She collects herself. She thinks for a moment and visualizes the situation.)* That's perfect! When can you get these flies into the Jungle?
GEORGE: A couple of weeks.
ANGELA: That long?
GEORGE: It'll take time to keep our tracks covered.

ANGELA *thinks about it. It makes her happy. It* is *a plan that is worth the short wait.*

ANGELA: You know what? We're going to fix their little red wagons!

Scene 4

Somewhere in the Hobo Jungle before nightfall. The pace of SHELLY's *talk with* HUEY *is at first leisurely.*

SHELLY: The smell of eucalyptus trees here is amazing.
HUEY: Just don't get near the laurels. They stink.
SHELLY: It's a kind of paradise here sometimes, isn't it? *(Pause.)* But you still need *some* money. Where do you get it?
HUEY: We sell things.
SHELLY: Where do you get things to sell? Do you steal them?
HUEY: We don't steal. We go for walks. We find lots of things on the street. Empty bottles – we pick them up and take them back. That's good money, actually.
SHELLY: Do you get money from Welfare?

Car Door Shave

HUEY: I don't. Most people here don't. Welfare only pays a few bucks. Why bother?
SHELLY: *(Pause. Baffled.)* I'm just wondering... how did you ever wind up here?
HUEY: *(Chuckles.)* Oh, that's a story! *(Pause. She does not elaborate.)*
SHELLY: Well, can you tell me?
HUEY: I guess. *(Pause.)* I met Cappy outside a hamburger restaurant. He wasn't feeling right. He was acting strange.
SHELLY: Is he on medication?
HUEY: Cappy? *(She turns up her nose.)* No. *(She pauses. She wistfully thinks back in time.)* It was hot. High humidity, too. He shouldn't have eaten there. I didn't eat there and I worked there. I was on one of my breaks and I was going to those newspaper vending machines on the street. Sometimes I like to look at the little ads, you know? So much stuff that people want to get rid of! *(Pause.)* Anyway, Cappy saw me. *(Pause.)* Like he saw something in my face – I'm from Thailand, you know, so that's close enough to Vietnam. And then all of a sudden, he starts freaking out. I spooked him. It wasn't just me. He was scared of everything. He thought he was in Vietnam. In the war.
SHELLY: He was having a flashback.
HUEY: I think so. He said something about gooks. I told him he wasn't in Vietnam anymore. He said he once had two arms. *(Pause.)* I felt sorry for him. Such a strong man. And handsome, too. But not in good shape that day. Finally I figured out he lived in the Hobo Jungle and I helped him get back here. There's a lot more shade here than there was outside that hamburger restaurant.
SHELLY: *(Pause.)* You helped him back and you never left.

Pause. HUEY *makes no comment.*

SHELLY: You like him, don't you?
HUEY: Yeah.

There is a long pause.

SHELLY: I don't consider myself "repressed". But I don't like all this talk here about "the orgasm".
HUEY: *(Pause.)* I'm not sure what an orgasm is.
SHELLY: *(Surprised.)* You don't know?
HUEY: *(Innocently.)* No. Not really.

SHELLY *pauses to "regroup" her thoughts.*

SHELLY: Um, do you know what sexual fantasies are?
HUEY: I'm not sure.
SHELLY: People have them about a person when they desire that person and they can't have them. *(Pause.)* The person *isn't there* for some reason – maybe they don't *want* to be there. Maybe they have no interest in being desired… *(Pause.)* Fantasies, and… sexual fantasies can be healthy to have. They give you an emotional outlet. If a real relationship doesn't develop, well, fantasizing stays as only dreams, and you can either let it calm your nerves or let it drive you crazy.
HUEY: What are you talking about?
SHELLY: I don't want you to be disappointed, Huey.
HUEY: I don't get disappointed.
SHELLY: Well… enjoy your time with Cappy and when tomorrow comes, think of all the good things that have happened between you two. *(Pause.)* If you find out later that something wasn't real the way you thought it was real, I hope you'll take comfort in knowing that it was all done with good intentions in mind.

HUEY: *(Pause.)* I don't get it. What are you saying? *(Pause.)* Have you been smoking some of Punk Jim's stuff?

Scene 5

An open space in the Hobo Jungle. There is a party tonight and its theme is "Harem Night". A long string of small lights stretch from Kevin's roof to a tree. A few balloons are tethered to whatever can be found. Small portable tables and chairs are here and there. Food, beer and other drinks are available. Pop music with pan-Arabian influences plays in the background.

j

HUEY, SHELLY, BRIDGET *and* MEG *wear their normal clothes but they also wear thin veils that drop from the bridges of their noses and down to their chins.* MEG *and* HUEY *have had a little bit to drink.* MEG *has a box of wheat crackers called "Sociables" in her hand.* KEVIN *and* CAPPY *are loud.* KEVIN *has his cane.* CAPPY *is drunk.* PUNK JIM *is stoned.*

CAPPY: Only a genius like Kevin could create a "Harem Night." Isn't it something! *(Pause.)* Life sure can be sweet.
SHELLY: *(To herself.)* It makes you wonder if it's better not to have any money at all.
CAPPY: *(To* SHELLY.*)* What did you say, Bridget? *(Winking.)* Are you ready? *(He has made a mistake and he does not realize it.)*
SHELLY: I'm not Bridget. *(Pointing.)* She's over there.

KEVIN *and* MEG *start singing.* HUEY *joins in on the second line.*

KEVIN and MEG: *(Singing.)* My pillow's soft but it's stone cold.

KEVIN, MEG and HUEY: *(Singing.)*
You could make it warm – I'm nice to hold.
Take me in your arms, let's get to bed.
Don't be so hard – yeah, I know what I said...
CAPPY: Man, how I love old-timey country music. Country music has that Broadway tinge to it now that I can't stand!

MEG and HUEY sing a fragment of another song and now clap hands and stamp their feet. KEVIN sings and thumps his cane on the ground to keep time.

KEVIN, MEG and HUEY: *(Singing.)*
My dog might be dead and my lover did leave me
But I'm still open to getting a cat.

From the same song they sing another fragment. They also clap and stamp as before.

KEVIN, MEG and HUEY: *(Singing.)*
Saltwater taffy and I'm dancing with a tuna!
MEG: *(Letting out a yell.)* Whoo-ooh!
CAPPY: *(Euphoric.)* All the world sings with us tonight!
MEG: *(Pause. She picks up the box of "Sociables" crackers and offers some of them to PUNK JIM.)* Here, have a Sociable.
PUNK JIM: *(With little expression.)* What's that?
MEG: It's one of these. *(She moves the box of crackers even closer to him. He takes a cracker out of the box and eats it. She continues, tenderly.)* Aren't you having fun?
PUNK JIM: *(He is having fun, only he does not show it outwardly because he is high.)* Sure, this is great.
HUEY: I feel like I'm floating on a cloud.

SHELLY: *(Pause.)* I propose a toast to Cappy.

KEVIN: A toast to Cappy!

SHELLY: Will somebody please tell me how he got that name? You were a captain in the army, right?

CAPPY: *(Factually, and with some pride.)* No. Private First Class. My name did cause some tension with my sergeant and the captain. *(Pause.)* Huey, tell this woman how I got my name.

HUEY: When Cappy was born and his eyes were open and he could see… his mother noticed him staring up and trying to grab something. *(Pause.)* In hospital nurseries, the nurses wore white hats. That's how his mother came to call him Cappy. That's the first thing he reached for!

CAPPY: Always happy to relieve a woman of an article of clothing. *(Pause. To* BRIDGET.*)* Bridget… time for bed?

SHELLY *is not happy to hear that last remark. She rushes to speak.*

SHELLY: Like I said, I want to propose a toast to Cappy, who seems to be holding the Jungle together pretty well.

CAPPY: Do you know what the name of this place *really* is?

SHELLY: It's not the Hobo Jungle?

CAPPY: It's "New Orgonon".

SHELLY: That's an interesting name.

CAPPY: Well, Wilhelm Reich, he founded a settlement called "Orgonon" back East. So, we're *New* Orgonon.

SHELLY: Anyway. In addition to a man who creates names for places, add to that that you're a brave man who marches to the beat of his own drum. I admire you. … And that's my toast!

SHELLY, MEG *and* KEVIN: *(Raising their cups or bottles or cans in a toast.)* To Cappy!

BRIDGET and PUNK JIM: *(Less enthusiastically.)* To Cappy!

SHELLY: *(To* KEVIN *only.)* Okay, Kevin. Have I done enough to move things along?
KEVIN: Good job, lady.

Pause. CAPPY *takes center stage.*

CAPPY: *(Feeling no pain. But not slurring his words.)* Well, friends. It's nice to have friends. Thank you. Here we are, living in the real nineteen eighty-four. Despite the mind control and *other* forms of control by the corporations and the military and the government, we're eating, drinking and making merry. So there! *(Pause.)* But I can't end my speech like that. *(In a serious tone.)* No. *(Pause.)* We pause to remember our fallen comrades. *(Pause.)* We pause to remember those who don't live the bejeweled life that we live here. *(Pause.)* We party for those poor slaves who are caught up in the super-expensive nightmare world where there's no chance to kick back like we do. *(Pause. Solemnly.)* Long Live New Orgonon.
MEG: *(Not solemn, with convivial spirit.)* Long Live New Orgonon!
HUEY and KEVIN: New Orgonon, right on!
CAPPY: Ah, just feel it! All that great orgone energy! *(To* BRIDGET.*)* You feel it?
BRIDGET: *(Lying, but going along with him.)* Sort of, I guess.
MEG: *(To* PUNK JIM.*)* What's up, anyway?
PUNK JIM: Orgone's cool, but I'm like... really stoned. *(Pause.)* Potato chips and prezels. Corn chips. Cheese doodles... I mean, where's it stop? Those crackers are called Sociables. I wasn't even hungry before and I ate oranges and dates from ten miles away.
MEG: *(Placing her hand on* PUNK JIM's *hand for a moment to comfort him. Sweetly:)* Ah, Jim.

PUNK JIM: Nice party. It was a stressful day. I could've knocked that guy out, man.

MEG: *(Comforting him.)* I know, I know.

PUNK JIM: It's a good thing you weren't there. *(Pause.)* Terrible people.

KEVIN: *(To* HUEY, *only.)* Okay, now. Pretty soon we're going into the bedroom. You're going to wait there for Cappy. You know he's a little, um… self-conscious… about being seen taking his shirt off. So it's going to be dark. Don't worry. Don't get confused. You might feel that somebody else is there, but that would only be if Cappy needs help getting his clothes off 'cause he's had a little too much to drink. You don't have to help him, huh? You just lie there. Keep your veil on as long as you can.

HUEY: What about my clothes?

KEVIN: You won't be wearing them.

HUEY: *(Nervously.)* Oh.

KEVIN: Just do what I say, all right? *(Pause.)* I think you're going to need another beer. Let me get you one.

KEVIN walks with his cane over to where the cans of beer are. The recording of the pan-Arabian-inflected pop music stops abruptly. CHRISTINE walks in.

CHRISTINE: Hey, folks, having a good time? *(Pause. She looks around.)* Well, lah-dee-dah, look at all those veils!

KEVIN shouts at her, but his voice almost cracks because a sudden weakness comes over him.

KEVIN: What are you doing here? I asked you to stay away.

CHRISTINE: *(Mock pleading with him.)* Oh, come on, gay boy, be *gay*. There's a party here!
CAPPY: *(His heart is sinking.)* No, no, no, no, no. I can't believe this is happening!
PUNK JIM: *(To* CAPPY *and* KEVIN, *referring to* CHRISTINE.*)* What's the deal with her?
CHRISTINE: *(To* PUNK JIM.*)* The deal with me? Who are you?
PUNK JIM: *(Louder than* CHRISTINE.*)* Who are *you*?
CHRISTINE: Oh. *(Pause.)* He's a "punk".
KEVIN: Christine, this is really… you can't imagine what a horrible cow you are to come here tonight!
CHRISTINE: Cow? I've never been called a cow before.
PUNK JIM: They call lots of women "cows" in London. It's slang there.
CHRISTINE: So is it slang here now? Put a lid on it, *punk!*
PUNK JIM: My name is Nancy Boy.
CHRISTINE: What's that supposed to mean?
PUNK JIM: It means I'm as queer as Kevin, so you better watch out what you say to him, or I'll punch you out.
CHRISTINE: You think so? *(To everybody:)* You're having a party without me? How… inconsiderate. After all I've done for this place.
CAPPY: You haven't done anything for this place!
KEVIN: *(Pause.)* Except give it a bad name! *(Pause.)* You said you wouldn't come back until tomorrow!
CHRISTINE: Christine McClure said that. *(Pause.)* But Christine *Huber* didn't!
KEVIN: You just couldn't stay away! You are so… so selfish!
CAPPY: It's true, Christine. It's always about *you*, no matter what.

CHRISTINE: *(Pause.)* Just one minute ago this place was jumping with joy. There's no need to get heavy. Let's be light as veils. *(Pause.)* Man, what a way to welcome me back!

KEVIN: This party wasn't for you.

CHRISTINE: I'm hurt, Kevin. Really hurt.

CAPPY: Christine, there are those who are hostile to us from *without*. And with you, here, we have someone who is hostile to us from *within*. We don't want that. *(Pause.)* But there's no point in explaining to you, huh? You're a child. *(Pause. Speaking clearly and perfectly.)* Now, be a good child and do us all a favor and take yourself out of here at once, so that we might get back to the... *(He loses his temper and shouts.)* good time we were having when you weren't here!

CHRISTINE: I have as much right to be here as you do.

KEVIN: Why would anybody want to be somewhere where they're not welcome?

CHRISTINE: Jail isn't fun. I have good memories of this place. *(Pause.)* You know, when you get out of jail, you go home – that's the thing, it's usual – that's all I'm doing, what's usual. *(Pause.)* I want to do things the regular way, I want to go home.

CAPPY: This isn't a... lair for monsters.

BRIDGET: Why is she a monster? What's she done?

CAPPY *is displeased that* BRIDGET *has spoken up, but he answers her.*

CAPPY: She writes bad checks. And under other names, there's welfare fraud, harassment of abortion clinics, and a whole slew of things you don't want to know.

CHRISTINE: *(To* BRIDGET.*)* Who are you?

BRIDGET: I don't know.

CHRISTINE: *(Snaps at her.)* What do you mean, you don't know?
BRIDGET: I don't know. But like you, I have two names at least... I'm sure.
CHRISTINE: You're too *clean* looking to live here.
BRIDGET: I don't live here.
SHELLY: *(Not angry. Thoughtfully.)* You've blown it, Christine. *(Pause.)* You've blown it – not just for you.
CHRISTINE: *(To* SHELLY.*)* Who the hell are *you* behind that stupid veil? *(She swings angrily around to* CAPPY.*)* Who are these people, Cappy, in those ridiculous veils?
CAPPY: Time passes. Places change. *You*... don't change.
CHRISTINE: I asked you a question! *(Pause.)* You just don't like me 'cause I never signed on with the Wilhelm Reich shit. *(Pause.)* Now you've added veils? *(Pause.)* Anything to feed your sick sexual appetite for young girls... *(She looks over to* HUEY.*)* and *exotic* ones. Pity the female that strays here.
KEVIN: *(Nervously strained, shaking, not feeling well.)* That's enough, Christine. We need you to go. Now.
BRIDGET: She can't go.
CHRISTINE: *(Haughty. To* BRIDGET.*)* What? *(Pause. Egotistically.)* I can go if I want to!
BRIDGET: You can't go because I don't want you to go.
CAPPY: *(Half-whispering at first.)* Oh, come on, Bridget – let her go. She'll go and things'll get back to normal. We'll all get in the mood again. Remember, there's so much ... *(Searches for the word.)* ...enjoyment ... to be had.
CHRISTINE: *(To* BRIDGET.*)* I don't know who you are. But that doesn't matter 'cause I don't know who half of the people here are.
BRIDGET: *(To* CHRISTINE.*)* There's something I'd like to discuss.
CAPPY: *(Loudly, to* BRIDGET.*)* No, no, no, don't do that, please!

KEVIN: *(To* BRIDGET, *trying to warn her off* CHRISTINE.) There's no time for discussions now. *(Pause.) Huey* has a real big problem – with all this...

CHRISTINE: *(Interrupting.)* You mean with *me?*

KEVIN: *(Continuing. Pressing his point.)* People think that if Cappy's happy, then the Jungle is. That's not actually the case. It's when *Huey's* happy that the whole Jungle is happy.

CHRISTINE: Wow. I just heard an amazing fairy tale. You even wrapped it up with a Princess-of-the-Jungle bow. *(Shoots a glance at* HUEY. Pause.) Am I in Disneyland? Let's all ride zebras... and look at tigers and shake hands with Asian Snow White! *(Pause.)* What is your point, Kevin?

KEVIN *feels ill. He does not answer.*

PUNK JIM: *(To* CHRISTINE.) Man, it really sucks that you're not in jail anymore.

CHRISTINE: I got out for good behavior.

CAPPY: You'd never know.

SHELLY: You got out because they haven't finished building some of the new jails yet. Only last week a judge ruled that Verde Segundo had to release some of its prisoners due to overcrowding.

CHRISTINE: *(To* SHELLY.) Oh, there's somebody here who follows the news? That's new. *(Outraged.)* What is it with these mysterious, veiled voices in the Hobo Jungle!

MEG: *(Correcting her, softly.)* New Orgonon.

CHRISTINE: *(She goes over to* SHELLY.) What are you? A spy? A reporter? *(Pause.)* You're not for this place. I can *smell* it.

KEVIN: Ah! *(He groans and faints, falling to the ground.)*

Everyone is caught off guard. In a split second SHELLY *is over at* KEVIN's *side.*

SHELLY: Kevin! Are you all right? What's the matter?

KEVIN *has a seizure. It does not last long. Soon he is silent and motionless.*

SHELLY: Has this happened to him before? *(She moves to make him more comfortable.* KEVIN *has lost consciousness.)*

HUEY *sees what is happening. The night she had hoped for is ruined – the certainty of this hits her like lightening. Her reaction: she rips off her veil and runs, taking a flying leap at* CHRISTINE *and tackles her to the ground.*

CAPPY: *(Seeing* CHRISTINE *being tackled.)* Wow. That's orgone energy unleashed!
HUEY: *(Beating* CHRISTINE *with her fists.* CHRISTINE *defends herself easily.)* I hate you, I hate you. (HUEY *breaks out in tears.)*

SHELLY *tears off her veil.* MEG *and* BRIDGET *do the same. They are in no hurry to pull* HUEY *away from* CHRISTINE. BRIDGET *goes over towards* HUEY *and* CHRISTINE. MEG *goes over to* SHELLY *and* KEVIN.

HUEY: *(Crying and beating* CHRISTINE.) It was my chance! My chance. Now see what happened to Kevin!
CHRISTINE: *(Struggling, not harmed.)* Get off me! I can kill you if I want!

HUEY: *(Crying and continuing to beat her.)* Kevin helps us all. We need him. You wrecked it. It's all over now. You *lied* to Kevin. Kevin's a *nice man!*

CAPPY *and* PUNK JIM *go over to* KEVIN, *who lies motionless on the ground.*

CAPPY: Hey, Kev? Are you all right?
SHELLY: He's not.
HUEY: *(Crying and pummeling* CHRISTINE.*)* You... you... you *evil person!*
CHRISTINE: You stop now, or I'll knock you all the way back to Asia!

HUEY *pulls herself off* CHRISTINE. *In tears, she runs over to* CAPPY *to take refuge.* CAPPY *lets her bury herself between his arm and his chest. He comforts her.*

CAPPY: You're a good girl. *(Pause.)* Kevin's going to be all right.
HUEY: But we didn't... *(She sobs, heaving with emotion.)*
CAPPY: This was supposed to be such a night! *(Pause.)* We never got to it. *(Pause.)* Kevin'll be okay. *(He shoots a piercing look* at CHRISTINE.*)* Christine, you ought to rot in prison! *(Pause. Continuing to comfort* HUEY:*)* It'll be all right. Calm down, sweety, calm down.
HUEY: *(Still crying.)* Kevin had it all planned...
CAPPY: Yeah. He knows how to plan a fun party.
PUNK JIM: *(Looking at* KEVIN.*)* He doesn't look good.
CAPPY: *(Looking down at* KEVIN.*)* He needs medical attention.
SHELLY: *(To everyone.)* We need an ambulance. Right away.

Scene 6

It is night. A path leads to a campfire on the edge of the Hobo Jungle. In the darkness, BRIDGET *and* MEG *walk, flashlights in hand.*

BRIDGET: I knew she might turn out to be bad – but not as bad as that.
MEG: I don't think you should have anything to do with her.
BRIDGET: I can't do that. *(Pause.)* This'll be the first and last time I ever talk to her. *(Pause.)* Kevin was going to tell me some things – but for all I know I'll never be able to talk to him again.
MEG: He looked pretty sick.

There is a pause in the conversation. They walk some more.

BRIDGET: I hope I've only inherited my mother's good genes – if she has any. *(Pause.)* I wonder what made her turn out the way she did.
MEG: I don't think you want to know. *(Pause.)* If you don't mind me saying, I think you should... set a limit on how far you go... with this. I mean, give yourself five minutes or so – and that's it.

BRIDGET *and* MEG *approach the campfire.* CHRISTINE *is not far away from the fire. She has stacked some small logs on tree stump. She chops more firewood with a hatchet. There is a bottle of beer next to her on the ground. She sees the young women.*

CHRISTINE: Visitors from Arabia. Haven't you gone to bed yet?
BRIDGET: My day isn't over.

CHRISTINE: *(She stops chopping and puts the hatchet down.)* Mine is.
BRIDGET: I hope you got what you want.
CHRISTINE: You've got a lot of nerve talking to me like that when I have a hatchet right next to me.
BRIDGET: You wouldn't use it on me.
CHRISTINE: No? *(Now she thinks of a reason.)* No, 'cause then I'd have to kill her, too. *(She means* MEG.*)* You don't want anybody talking.
BRIDGET: Have you always been this rotten?
CHRISTINE: If you think I'm rotten you should have met my mother.
MEG: *(To* BRIDGET.*)* Don't go there with her.
CHRISTINE: *(To* MEG.*)* So, where's your stoned boyfriend?
MEG: *(Pause.)* He went to bed.
CHRISTINE: Passed out on you, huh? *(Pause.)* I wish the world would just pass out.
BRIDGET: Why?
CHRISTINE: Nothing good comes from this world.
BRIDGET: There isn't anything good?
CHRISTINE: Sure, there's good – afterwards – in heaven.
MEG: What if you get sent to hell?
CHRISTINE: I'm a Christian. My confessions are up to date. I'm forgiven.
MEG: I think you have some confessing to do for what happened tonight.
CHRISTINE: What on earth are you talking about? I still have a few sins to go before it's time for me to see a priest again.
BRIDGET: *(She is disheartened by what she is hearing.)* Great.
CHRISTINE: Yep.
BRIDGET: *(Pause.)* You live like a hunted animal.

CHRISTINE *lets out a roaring laugh. The campfire crackles.*

BRIDGET: Does it really have to be like that?
CHRISTINE: Kid, you have no idea.
MEG: The best thing you did was to give her up for adoption.
CHRISTINE: What are you saying?
MEG: She's the daughter you gave up for adoption.
CHRISTINE: *(Emotionless.)* Oh, is that so.
MEG: Yeah.
CHRISTINE: I didn't give her up. *(To* BRIDGET.) You were taken from me.
BRIDGET: Taken? *(Long pause.)* That doesn't... really... paint a ...very good picture.
CHRISTINE: You can only do so much when there's a judge involved.
BRIDGET: *(Pause.)* What's my biological father like?
CHRISTINE: I don't know.
BRIDGET: You don't know?
CHRISTINE: There were two or three men in my life. For all I know, your father could be Cappy.
BRIDGET: You had sex with Cappy?
CHRISTINE: Cap and I go way back. Like when he had *two* arms.
BRIDGET: Wasn't he away in Vietnam?
CHRISTINE: The guys would visit home now and again.
BRIDGET: Does Cappy know I could be his daughter?
CHRISTINE: Not unless he's some kind of psychic. *(Pause.)* When those boys were back from 'Nam they were so out of it that they didn't know if they were taking a shower or it was raining outside.
BRIDGET: Oh.

CHRISTINE: I wouldn't want to be Cappy's daughter – he's a total con man.
MEG: You're wrong about that.
CHRISTINE: Am I?
MEG: I don't trust what a convict like you says.
CHRISTINE: *(To* MEG.*)* Back off, Kewpie doll. *(Jealous, to* BRIDGET.*)* It looks like you've had a nice upbringing.
BRIDGET: It wasn't bad.
CHRISTINE: Well, congratulations. *(Pause.)* You must be a little smart – I'm not that easy to find.
BRIDGET: I don't give up when I want something.
CHRISTINE: You getting what you want?
BRIDGET: No.
CHRISTINE: So, what do you want, kid?
BRIDGET: *(Pause.)* Two things: peace of mind... and for you to leave the Hobo Jungle.
CHRISTINE: Why should you care about the Hobo Jungle?
BRIDGET: I don't know. I just do.
CHRISTINE: Well, go to the Lord, He'll give you what little *peace of mind* there is to be found in this world.
BRIDGET: You think so? I think it's more psychologically complex than that.
CHRISTINE: You would think that way. You're middle class.
BRIDGET: You could've gotten an education.
CHRISTINE: Not in my circumstances. The American Dream isn't there for everybody.
BRIDGET: No. You chose to be ignorant.
CHRISTINE: *(Pause.)* Well, you've found me, you've seen me, we've had our little chat. It's getting chilly. *(Pause.)* I'm surprised you lasted more than sixty seconds in the Hobo Jungle. Maybe there's a little bit of me in you.

BRIDGET *is too afraid to respond.*

MEG: *(To* CHRISTINE.*)* You're really messed up.
CHRISTINE: *(Taking issue with that.)* On one level I'm a saint.
BRIDGET: You, a saint?
CHRISTINE: You'll have to ask God.
MEG: *(Challenging the notion that* CHRISTINE *is a saint.)* Kevin's in the hospital. He might be dead – and you helped.
CHRISTINE: He got what's coming to him. Homosexuality's a deadly sin according to the Bible.
BRIDGET: Okay, I've had enough! *(She cannot stop herself from bursting into tears. To* MEG.*)* I want to go home.

BRIDGET *cries.* MEG *comforts her.* MEG *takes her by the hand and leads her out. Once the two have exited,* CHRISTINE *picks up the hatchet beside her and chops a piece of kindling.*

CHRISTINE: Girl Scouts! *(Pause.)* We all want to go home.

Scene 7

The Hobo Jungle, as in Act I, Scene 1. The car door and overturned barrel are under the eucalyptus tree. The orgone accumulator is some distance away. CAPPY *sits on the barrel. His face is partly lathered with shaving cream. He looks in the car door mirror. He is half finished with shaving. The water basin and a towel are on the nearby table.* HUEY *stands by, close to him.*

CAPPY: Huey, we cope. We're strong. There are people against us and above all we want them to embrace orgone energy so it can change their lives. *(Pause.)* We let another gorgeous day inspire us. We soldier on. We have land – so what's there to worry about?

HUEY: It's not ours.

CAPPY: I'm so used to it not being technically my land or your land that the concept of mine and yours has undergone a transformation. We live like the Indians of old.

HUEY: I don't want to leave here. They treat us like whiskers that they want to shave off the face of the Jungle.

CAPPY: Well, times have been worse for me – it's not like in 'Nam where we were staring down barrels of guns and who knew what would happen. Here the battle goes on in slow motion. And instead of guns we have a crank. The rich turn the crank ever-so-slowly, like an old organ grinder grinding out a dirge.

HUEY: What's a dirge?

CAPPY: It's music for the dead.

HUEY: *(Shudders.)* Don't say that word!

CAPPY: What word?

HUEY: You know what word. Don't say it as long as Kevin's in the hospital.
CAPPY: *(He puts his razor down. He is finished shaving.)* Now, Huey, superstition's a relic of the past. If Wilhelm Reich didn't put it exactly like that, I know that's what he thought. *(Points to the towel.)* Could you hand me that, please? *(She hands him the towel. He dries his face.)* Thank you.

MEG *has been in the orgone accumulator. Its door opens and she emerges from it.*

CAPPY: *(To* MEG.*)* Well?
MEG: It didn't happen all at once. At first I was just sitting there. There was a little light seeping in. I thought about Jim still being asleep. I thought about all that went on last night.
CAPPY: The stars were against us. *(He sets the towel to one side.)*
MEG: I started thinking about Kevin. But then I stopped thinking about him because I started to feel my breasts getting heavy.
CAPPY: Now that… that's orgone energy!
MEG: It was almost like maybe milk was going to be in them.
CAPPY: Wow!
MEG: Yeah, I thought, "Wow!" *(Pause.)* "I'm charged up like a battery!"
CAPPY: You need to wake Jim up and spend that sexual energy right now!
MEG: *(With a wide smile on her face.)* You're right!

MEG *leaves, possessed. She heads in a bullet-straight trajectory to where* PUNK JIM *is. There is a pause.* CAPPY *gets up from his seat.*

Huey: So what are you going to do today?
Cappy: Well, after I stride through one interesting part of the universe or another in my mind, I think I'll just read myself a book.
Huey: I hope you'll be able to do that. There were a lot of people here yesterday.
Cappy: May it be a lot less busy today.

Shelly *enters. She is tired.*

Cappy: Oops. I spoke too soon.
Shelly: Hi.
Cappy: Well, don't look so chipper.
Shelly: The only sleep I got was in the waiting room at the hospital.
Cappy: So, uh... how's Kev'?
Shelly: That's what I came to tell you. Kevin passed away. Just over an hour ago.
Huey: Oh, no.
Shelly: I'm sorry. *(Pause.)* I know how much he meant to you. *(Pause.)* You know he had a lot of health issues. His body just gave out.
Cappy: Another courageous soldier enters the night.
Huey: *(Angry.)* Christine killed him!
Shelly: No, the disease called AIDS did. Though Christine's antics didn't help.
Huey: *(It appears that she might cry.)* And he helped Christine so much – he kept her stuff while she was away!

CAPPY: Kevin, may you rest in peace. *(Pause. Reflecting.)* Kevin never lived to see the day when we all drive electric cars. That was an advance that he as an engineer looked forward to.

HUEY: I didn't know that.

CAPPY: Men talk about cars among *men*. No other subject is of so little interest to women.

HUEY: *(In tears now.)* Kevin was so *good! (She goes over to* SHELLY *for comfort.* SHELLY *holds her, hugs her.)*

SHELLY: Yes, I know. *(A long pause. Then, to* CAPPY.) You don't listen to the radio, do you?

CAPPY: Not much. *(Pause. He thinks more about* KEVIN.) Poor Kev'.

HUEY: What are we going to do without him?

CAPPY: Life is transitory. I don't want to sound religious when I say we have to count the blessings that come to us: friendship, nature, sex, what-have-you. *(Pause. Softly.)* I guess I'll never see that Bridget again...

HUEY *stops crying when she hears the name "Bridget"*.

CAPPY: ...'Cause she's vanished into the lesser night. The cool clammy night of Coastal California. June Gloom.

HUEY: Christine should be arrested.

CAPPY: Yeah. We'll find a way to do that.

SHELLY: Yeah, how?

CAPPY: Huey and I will arrange that when you're out of earshot, my lady.

SHELLY: *(Pause. To* CAPPY.) Look, maybe you don't know... the radio mentioned the exact time the eclipse is going to happen here today – and it's pretty soon.

CAPPY: Oh, yeah. I heard something about that the other day. *(He does not care.)* Whatever... I still get a bigger kick out of seeing a yucca plant bloom.
HUEY: *(Asking herself, mispronouncing.)* Do I know what an eclibs is?
SHELLY: It's a solar one.
HUEY: What's that mean?
SHELLY: It'll make the sky go dark for a minute or so.
CAPPY: A fitting memorial to Kevin.
HUEY: How does that work?
SHELLY: The moon will block the sun, Huey.
CAPPY: Would be great if it takes Christine by surprise! *(Pause.)* Maybe she'll believe it's the End Time and the Final Judgment's upon us. She'll be quaking in her boots. *(To SHELLY.)* Thank you for bringing this to my attention, Eclipse Woman.
SHELLY: *(To herself.)* Christine's the Eclipse Woman.

ANGELA *enters.*

CAPPY: *(Upon seeing her.)* Okay, Grand Central Station all over again. I might turn into a dissatisfied passenger.
ANGELA: (Taken off guard, seeing SHELLY.) I thought you were in Mexico!
SHELLY: I never went to Ensenada. What are you doing here?
ANGELA: I was going to take a walk on the beach but it was crowded with people setting up cameras.
SHELLY: I told you specifically not to come down here. Why are you here, then?
ANGELA: Why are you here?
SHELLY: It's not for you to ask.

CAPPY: Oh, you know each other.

ANGELA: Yeah, from *work*. *(Pause.)* Most people have to do that sort of thing. *(Pointing to* CAPPY *and* HUEY.) You and you should be no different.

CAPPY: Angela, you're such a broken record. *(Pause.)* If you insist on being a recording, you really should change your tune – to something more upbeat. Don't dwell on missed opportunities. Accentuate the positive, everyday, like I do. Give thanks to your lucky breaks. For example, I'm thankful how fortunate I am not to live around people like you.

SHELLY: *(Stating flatly to* ANGELA:) Your job is in jeopardy.

HUEY: Are you her boss?

ANGELA: *(Paying no attention to* HUEY *but answering* SHELLY.) No, it's not.

SHELLY: What were you hoping to accomplish here on this visit of yours?

CAPPY: She was here yesterday, scoping things out. I guess you didn't see her. She wants to tear this place apart. She had a companion with her who got a little out of hand – just ask Punk Jim.

SHELLY: Somebody else was with her? Angela, you haven't wasted any time, have you?

CAPPY: *(To* ANGELA.) The Hobo Jungle hasn't changed all that much from the way it used to be, has it? You didn't need to case out the joint. *(Pause. To* SHELLY.) So let me take a wild guess. You're with Social Services, actually.

SHELLY: Yeah.

The sky begins to darken.

HUEY: Hey, it's starting to happen – look!
SHELLY: *(Pause.)* Don't look into the sun, Huey.

It gets darker. The faint sound of tree frogs is heard.

Huey: Why not?
Shelly: It can hurt your eyes.
Cappy: *(Taking advantage of the increasing darkness.)* Hm, this is cozy. *(Pause. Joking.)* Angela, even though you're a bit too old for me now, I always thought you were hot. The fact that you were a runaway – kind of gets me warm and fuzzy inside. Add to that the hard-nosed, uptight woman-in-authority exterior that you have now and wow! – it really makes me want to share some orgasms with you!
Angela: You pervert!

Cappy laughs. Huey has been busy looking up at the sky. She did not hear what Cappy said to Angela.

Huey: Wow, it's getting dark.

The lights are dim, but a spotlight slowly comes up on the orgone accumulator. Pause. The door to the orgone box opens. The Ghost of Jimmy Carter *steps out and takes a few steps forward – with the spotlight following him.*

Ghost of Jimmy Carter: As I say, we're at a turning point. Another day has passed and another half billion dollars has been transferred from the middle class to the ultra rich. We have the philosophy of "It's Morning in America" to thank for that.
Huey: Do strange voices come with an eclibs?
Cappy: I would say sometimes they do.

Ghost of Jimmy Carter: I guess I do have a strange voice. And a very recognizable one, at that. *(He chuckles and flashes his trademark "chipmunk" smile.)* Oh, well. *(To* Angela.*)*

Angela, that's naughty of you and your friend George to want to spread the white ashfly around here so you can clear out the Hobo Jungle.

Angela: How do you know about that? *(Pause.)* They have no right to be here!

Ghost of Jimmy Carter: Oh, Human Rights – that's not part of your program, is it? *(Pause.)* You don't want to know about people who are at the mercy of others who have gained power over them. You've never heard of somebody who inadvertently looked the "wrong way" at someone in a position of authority – and was taken out and shot for it. *(Pause.)* The people here do have a right. The right to life, liberty and the pursuit of happiness.

Angela: Spare me your country preaching! We need to grow this country economically or we'll be run by Moscow.

Ghost of Jimmy Carter: A life based solely on supply and demand is no life at all.

Angela: You're no longer president. You're not in demand. You don't have a voice. You can't be talking.

Ghost of Jimmy Carter: But I am.

Angela: *(Frustrated.)* What are you? *Who* do you think you are, anyway?

GHOST OF JIMMY CARTER: Well, I'm... I'm... *(Spoken as if "Anyway" were his actual name.)* ...Anyway. *(Pause. He slowly makes its way over to* HUEY. *Once nearer her, he says:)* Huey, everybody knows from my famous magazine interview *(He smiles.)* that I *have* looked at women with lust in my heart. And uh... I know you have passion in yours, and you want to do something about it. *(Pause.)* Hm. There's a nice young Democrat from Arkansas by the name of Bill that I'd like to introduce you to – if you'll just accompany me.
HUEY: *(Surprised, but delighted.)* Um... sure.

The GHOST OF JIMMY CARTER *extends his hand to* HUEY *and she takes it. They slowly walk offstage together as the eclipse comes to an end. The sound of the tree frogs fades away as daylight is restored.*

CAPPY: There's something in that eclipse that I haven't appreciated in other ones before.
SHELLY: *(Pause.)* Where did Huey go?
CAPPY: Probably went to the bathroom. She's always a little squeamish about that during daylight hours.
SHELLY: *(Pause. To* ANGELA.*)* Leave, Angela. Go back to the office.
ANGELA: You better not try anything against me. I have friends. *(She exits.)*
SHELLY: She makes working in my office a nightmare sometimes!
CAPPY: You'll have to join us.
SHELLY: *(Chuckling.)* Yeah.
CAPPY: *(Pause. He sees somebody in the distance.)* Well, look who's coming!
SHELLY: Who? *(Pause. Nervous.)* Christine?
CAPPY: No. *(Pause. Relieved.)* Thankfully.

Pause. It is BRIDGET. *She enters.*

CAPPY: *(To* BRIDGET.*)* The sun's come back and so have you, my radiant one. You look even more luminous than yesterday.

BRIDGET: Your remarks on my appearance have absolutely no effect on my thinking better of you. *(Pause.)* I just came by to thank Shelly. *(To* SHELLY.*)* Thanks for watching out for me.

SHELLY: You don't have to thank me.

BRIDGET: I do. *(Pause. She glances at* CAPPY.*)* Because I have manners.

CAPPY: Are they just manners or do you actually feel the warmth of gratitude?

SHELLY: *(To* BRIDGET.*)* I hope this has answered some of your questions.

BRIDGET: *(Unhappily.)* For better or worse, yeah.

SHELLY: I'm sorry.

BRIDGET: No, it's okay.

CAPPY: We're going to miss you. We're running a fine social experiment – retesting ideals of freedom.

BRIDGET: *(She chuckles. Then, courteously.)* Excuse me for missing the high-mindedness here.

CAPPY: People miss it because we're so low key.

SHELLY: *(Pause.)* Well, my business is done here, too.

BRIDGET: Business?

SHELLY: Yeah.

BRIDGET: I don't understand.

SHELLY: I work for the County. Social Services. There's been a lot of talk about the Hobo Jungle and what to do about it – if anything can be done about it.

CAPPY: She found out we're not murderers and thieves. Nope, that's reserved for the Republicans.

BRIDGET: Gee, Republicans… I guess I just haven't heard enough about them yet.
CAPPY: Actually, you're right. I should focus more on Wilhelm Reich. That's where the life-affirming energy is. It'll purify you. It will.
SHELLY: *(Bringing the conversation back to where it was.)* Anyway, I wanted to see the human face of the problem. Now I've seen it and it'll help with finding a solution.
CAPPY: *(The idea of a "solution" seems absurd to him.)* There is no solution here because there's no problem.
SHELLY: *(Pause. To* BRIDGET.*)* Well. *(Pause.)* I'll go with you, so… *(To* CAPPY.*)* Goodbye.
CAPPY: *(To* BRIDGET, *bidding her farewell.)* You're young. Enjoy it. *(He winks at her.)*
BRIDGET: Thanks for the advice.
CAPPY: Pretty feathers don't last forever.

SHELLY *and* BRIDGET *leave. There is a pause.*

CAPPY: They go back to the land of the *real* moochers. *(He looks over to the barrel that he was sitting on. He looks up at the beautiful sky, then looks down and around and finds a book to read. He thinks heavenly thoughts.)* Ah, yes. To read. A book. *(He looks at the book and reads its title.)* "The Mass Psychosis of Fascism" – by Wilhelm *(Pause.)* Reich. *(Pause. Blissfully.)* Light reading for a mid-morning that's coming into heavenly Being.

With book in hand, CAPPY *goes over to the barrel, slides it with his foot to reposition it, and very slowly sits himself down.*

GAMBLING FEVER

a play in two acts

The theme of a dinosaur fossil is ironically very present-day. There are lawsuits that attempt to stop the private auction and sale of some dinosaur specimens, including, for example, ones taken illegally from Mongolia and brought into our country. Instead of being in museums, these skeletons are purchased by wealthy persons who have buildings constructed to house them. These are lovely settings for cocktail parties, no doubt.

Casino gambling is as well a very up to date topic. Victoria is the moving force behind the founding of a new casino in *Gambling Fever.* Her continual chain smoking despite the knowledge that it will lead to her death is a symbol of her irrational, self-destructive nature. Like her equally immoral acquaintance Boots, she has masses of money and she has power. But for both of them there is never enough. So to gain more of both they buy a candidate for office who will oppose anything aimed at protecting the environment. How much a part of present day life is the candidate who is elected because of major funding by rich, profit-seeking, selfish persons who care nothing for the future as long as they come out ahead. Some years ago, a governor in Delaware, for example, opposed drilling for oil and a creation of a major area for shipping oil on the grounds that it would be a dangerous prospect for the beaches. He succeeded but was later thrown out of office because he had opposed progress and kept people from getting jobs.

Tait's Colorado play – for it is set entirely in and around the Denver and the nearby Rockies – is full of poetry and spectacle. In addition to the dinosaur skeleton, we see a chorus of aboriginal characters representing those to whom the land once belonged. The Indian Ed appears in a feathered cape causing him to appear like a giant magpie. He should be standing up for the rights of the people who are descended from the natives of 1492, but all he wants is a cut of the casino – or so it seems. As the play progresses it moves further from reality. A waiter in a restaurant is dressed like the Grim Reaper. In a snow scene figures appear magically on a toboggan. There is a mysterious figure of a man in the politician's bedroom. All of these elements heighten the dramatic qualities of the play. In the course of the action a man is tragically killed, but his body is replaced in the next scene by the magical appearance of a pine sapling—a sign of hope for the future. But the final scene shows the success of the money grabbers and is punctuated near its end with the Cassandra-like cries of young Melanie.

– Y. S.

The action in the first act of *Gambling Fever* seems to take place within a twenty-four hour period. "Time" loosens in the second act. In Act II the drama begins to "zoom out" purposefully. It shows us highly selective, unpredictable scenes. The consequences of earlier actions are dramatized in an epilogue-like last scene where new "minor" characters help take the play (with Ed's help?) where it needs to go. The fact that the air is thin in the high country has undoubtedly influenced the aesthetic of this work.

– L. T.

GAMBLING FEVER

Characters

IRENE	*female, 40s to early 50s.*
DOROTHY	*female, 30s.*
MALCOLM	*male, 40s to mid 50s.*
"T"	*male, late 50s to early 70s.*
MELANIE	*female, 18 years old.*
VICTORIA	*female, 40s to early 50s.*
ED	*male, American Indian, 20s.*
MS. PAROLE	*female, late 20s to early 40s.*
SCOTT	*male, mid 20s.*
RANDY BRUCE	*male, late 30s to early 50s.*
MARIE	*female, brawny, 19 years old.*
BOOTS	*male, 60s-70s.*

Minor Characters (to be doubled)

GEOLOGIST	*can be doubled by the DOROTHY actor.*
ABORIGINAL CHORUS	*comprised of available actors from the cast; they wear masks.*
FAT WAITER	*heavily costumed; played by an available actor from the cast.*

MYSTERIOUS MAN	*played by the actor who plays* ED.
TERRY	*played by an available actor from the cast – but not the* ED *actor.*
CHORUS OF TOWNSPEOPLE	*can be played by the actors who play* DOROTHY, MS. PAROLE, SCOTT, RANDY BRUCE *and* MARIE. *They wear masks.*
MIDDLEBURG	*can be doubled by the* RANDY BRUCE *actor.*
OUTERMAN	*can be doubled by the* "T" *actor.*
GRUMBLER	*can be doubled by the* MALCOM *actor.*
BITTERMARCH	*can be doubled by the* SCOTT *actor.*

Doublings are suggestions. A total of twelve actors can manage the cast requirements.

Place: Colorado.

Time: 1992-1993.

GAMBLING FEVER

ACT I

Scene 1

It is night at an excavation site in the Rocky Mountains in Colorado. IRENE *and* DOROTHY *walk across the ridge of a ravine and up a mountain trail. They have backpacks on. They have become separated from each other.*

DOROTHY: Irene?

IRENE: Gritty sand. Steep plunges of rock and ravine. *(Pause. She wonders where* DOROTHY *is.)* Dorothy, where'd you go? *(Pause. To herself.)* It's so quiet. *(Pause.)* When you think, your thinking echoes. *(Pause. Thinking to herself.)* You can't minimize the importance of a shard of stone. It's still something. With energy inside.

DOROTHY: *(Pause.)* Irene? Irene? Don't go so fast. What's the hurry? Slow down! *(She does not find* IRENE.*)*

IRENE: *(Continues thinking to herself.)* Stones *are* and wild beings just *are*. *(Pause.)* And night-creeping deer respond to smells and light. Like my sister they only respond when the danger is immediately upon them. Like my sister they have no gratitude. If it weren't for me, she wouldn't be alive now. Victoria would never admit that in a million years!

DOROTHY: *(Still not close to* IRENE.*)* Irene? Can you stop for a minute?

IRENE: *You* say I should try to get along with her? She should try to get along with me. I saw those signs in her eight years ago and *I* was the one who forced her to go see a doctor.

IRENE: *(Continued.) (Aside.)* Thereby saving her life. There'd be no way she could hack this trail. This is no smoker's paradise. *(Pause.)* I'm not making light of her and her hysterectomy. But it doesn't make her a martyr.

DOROTHY: *(She has almost caught up to* IRENE.) You doing all right?

IRENE: I'm feeling sorry for myself, Dorothy. I shouldn't, but I do. And I should never think Victoria's going to be anybody other than who she really is. But, hand on my crystal necklace, I will survive.

DOROTHY: I hope you're not wrong about this trail.

IRENE: *(Confirming that it is the correct trail.)* This is it. *(She stops and rests for a moment. She feels the gemstone pendant around her neck.)* The vibrations calm me.

DOROTHY: What happened a minute ago?

IRENE: Nothing. Echoes.

DOROTHY: It sounded like somebody.

IRENE: No. Echoes love this canyon.

DOROTHY: I didn't hear you say anything.

IRENE: I was thinking.

DOROTHY: I heard a voice.

IRENE: I was talking to myself.

DOROTHY: I heard a loud voice.

IRENE: I don't like your line of questioning. *(Sighing.)* The wicked city below and its sounds. I'm through with it. Let's press on.

DOROTHY: The voice didn't sound like you.

IRENE: It was Nature. *(Nonchalantly.)* The eaters or those to be eaten.

A long pause. IRENE *and* DOROTHY *continue to walk up the mountain trail.*

DOROTHY: Maybe it's all for the best.

IRENE: What?

DOROTHY: That you're not going to work for her anymore.

IRENE: Oh, so that's your *(As in, "your reality".)* perspective.

DOROTHY: But you don't need to run away.

IRENE: I'm not. I was sent away.

DOROTHY: Don't exaggerate.

IRENE: If I wasn't sent away, why did you agree to come with me?

DOROTHY: 'Cause I didn't want you coming up here alone.

IRENE: You don't have to worry about me.

DOROTHY: But I do.

IRENE: *(Pause.)* Dark works well. It's harder for people to follow you.

DOROTHY: I can go most of the way up. But then I have to turn around and go back.

IRENE: It's kind of late to do that.

DOROTHY: I've got stuff to do tomorrow. We get to Malcolm, and then I'll go.

IRENE: *(She is afraid of being left alone but she hides it.)* Yep. *(Taking in a deep breath.)* We're almost there.

DOROTHY: Should we start yelling?

IRENE: Why?

DOROTHY: So they'll know it's us.

IRENE: *(Meaning, "It's a bad idea".)* No. *(Pause.)* Malcolm doesn't like strangers around.

DOROTHY: We're not strangers. That's the whole point. He needs to know it's you.

MALCOLM *appears out of the darkness. He has light in his hand but he does not turn it on. The women do not see him as he walks slowly, getting ever closer to them.*

IRENE: *(Anxious about that she'll be crossing paths with* MALCOLM.*)* Well, there's no way around it. We're going to have to say hello. There's no other trail that avoids the excavation site.
DOROTHY: Irene, you said you needed to come up here.
IRENE: I said the cabin was protected from the wind on two sides.
MALCOLM: *(Even-toned.)* Wind?, you say?

The women are startled.

DOROTHY: *(Whispering to* IRENE.*)* Ah! What's that?
IRENE: Nothing.
MALCOLM: It's a rather verbal nothing.
DOROTHY: There's somebody here.
MALCOLM: You bet there is.
IRENE: M... M... Malcolm? Where are you? I can't see a thing.

MALCOLM:
Sounds of humans at night can mean to me
Poachers creeping across the sandstone,
Hoping to rob bones.
Bones of the Cretaceous, the Jurassic –
Even the Oligocene.
You saber-tooth cats!

MALCOLM *switches on his flashlight.*

IRENE: I guess you've had your drinks and you're ready to go to bed. Sorry, we don't mean to disturb you.
MALCOLM: I don't drink, Irene.
IRENE: Why are you talking weird? *(Pause. Composing herself.)* We're just on our way up to the cabin.
MALCOLM: You're with someone?
IRENE: My cousin, Dorothy.
MALCOLM: *(He cannot see* DOROTHY *very well.)* I'd shake your hand, but in this dark my hand is likely to touch something else less decent.

"T": *(Entering, with his flashlight on.)* Oh, boy. I should've known. *(He lectures the two women.)*
This is a place of scientific research.
We're serious about trespassers, ladies.
Beware the bones that come up here.
I once had a grip that could bust three arms.
Don't disturb this nursery
Where the dinosaur lies in its stone cradle.

IRENE: We're not. We're going up to the cabin.
"T": Say what? And I'm on my way to a drive-in movie! You're intruding on private property. Of course, it's your own property. But we can't have nobody but experts at the excavation. *(Pause.)* All people have it hard seeing in the dark. *(After this remark, he looks* IRENE *over, examining her quickly.)* In this terrain – I will not enumerate the dangers. And if you happen to fall into the site, you'll get hurt *and* you'll set our work back. *(Pause.)* It's painstaking work. It comes to fruit slowly. Respect what Doctor Malcolm needs and give him his sway.

IRENE: *(She digs into her pocket and finds a piece of a bone which she shows to* MALCOLM.) Look here.
MALCOLM: What is it?
IRENE: I brought you this.
MALCOLM: *(Looking at it.)* A piece of bone.
IRENE: I know this isn't a convenient time. I can show you another day.
"T": Okay, what are you doing here? You know he has better things to do. You could have asked them at the rock and mineral shop where you got it!
IRENE: You're right. I'm just nervous.
MALCOLM: *(Caring.)* Oh, Irene. You shouldn't be on the trail at this hour.
IRENE: I know. But...
"T": But what?
MALCOLM: *(To* "T".) That's enough, "T".

IRENE *is touched by* MALCOLM's *insight. She has to rein in her emotions – one feels she could almost burst into tears.* IRENE *calms herself but blurts out:*

IRENE: I had to come up. Victoria said I was banished.
DOROTHY: Irene had a fight with her.
"T": *(Muttering under his breath.)* So what else is new!
MALCOLM: No one can banish you.
"T": Banish? What's that all about?
MALCOLM: "T", let her be.

IRENE *is silent. Then she speaks. Her voice wavers. She is upset.*

IRENE: She said I would never have a job with the company again. *(Pause.)* I'll be gone from your camp soon. *(Pause.)* You're right. It's dangerous. I've already been accosted on the trail.

The others don't know what to make of this last statement.

DOROTHY: What?
IRENE: There are predatory animals. For those, you carry a piece of striped agate.

Offstage, MELANIE *moans.*

"T": *(Hearing the moan.)* Hey, what's that?
DOROTHY: *(Looking accusingly at* IRENE.*)* Oh, no. *(Looking accusingly at* IRENE.*)* Irene!

Again, offstage, MELANIE *moans.*

"T": In the ravine. *(Getting excited.)* We got one, Malcolm! A poacher! Hope he's not carrying a gun. *(Pause.)* If he knows what's good for him he should run away fast.
DOROTHY: I don't think it's a "he".

IRENE *fidgets and takes a step away from* MALCOLM *and the rest.*

DOROTHY: *(Explaining.)* I heard a sound before. When Irene was ahead of me on the trail. *(To* IRENE.*)* Irene, you said it was just an echo.
IRENE: Some thing was trying to kill me.

MELANIE *struggles up the ravine to approach the others.*

MALCOLM: Irene, was there someone else on the trail?
IRENE: A *thing*, really bad.

MALCOLM *shines his flashlight across the stage.* MELANIE *is faintly seen in the distance. She rests against a makeshift alpenstock as she struggles up the steep grade.*

"T": *(Relieved.)* Oh, it's Melanie. *(Concerned.)* She needs help.
MALCOLM: No, stay, "T". You could slip. She'll make it on her own.
"T": *(Loud.)* We're coming. Don't move.
MELANIE: No, don't come. I've got my footing. *(She is now fully visible and walks towards* MALCOLM *and* "T".) Keep her *(She means* IRENE.) away from me. *(Pause.)* I didn't do anything to her.
MALCOLM: We know. Irene, Melanie could have been killed.
"T": You should have used that staff to defend yourself.
MALCOLM: *(He gives* "T" *a scolding look. Then, to* MELANIE.) Are you hurt?
MELANIE: Bruised, maybe. *(Concerned that he'll send her home and wanting to stay.)* I'll still be able to work.
IRENE: She's part of the banishing forces. Trying to push me down.
MELANIE: I didn't even get near you! You came to me. I was just out looking at the stars.
DOROTHY: We're sorry.
IRENE: Banished! *(Pause. Although is referring to* MELANIE, *the person, she also means "this situation" when she says "this".)* And she sends this. *(Pause.)* To stop me from getting to land that's also rightfully mine.

MALCOLM: No, you're wrong, Irene.

IRENE: *(Matter-of-factly.)* I'm entitled to be here.

MALCOLM: No, what I'm saying is you're wrong about Melanie. She's one of my assistants.

"T": And she was out looking to see the mountains match their peaks against Draco and Hercules!

MALCOLM: Irene, I don't know what to say. Luckily it looks like Melanie hasn't been hurt too badly. *(Pause.)* You've got to be less suspicious of things here. Your cousin's trying to help you.

"T": Melanie, let me help *you*.

"T" offers his shoulder to MELANIE, *she rests on him and they start for her tent - there are two tents at the site, one for* MELANIE *and the other for* MALCOLM *and "T". But as everyone starts to go their way they are stopped in their tracks by the distant sound of a helicopter getting ever more closer.*

Each person looks up to the sky. A powerful searchlight from the helicopter shines on an open area in the canyon. The excavation site near them is illuminated: a large dinosaur skeleton still embedded in rock sits in the earth. A makeshift lifting-machine stands nearby. The machine is a tripod - three strong poles joined together near each of their tops. At the juncture of the poles a chain runs down on two sides. One end of the chain is hitched to the skeleton. The other end of the chain passes through a block and tackle system (in technical terms, this type of system is a "luff block and tackle") which is itself attached to another chain anchored to an outcrop of rocks. A shallow circular pit, like a small moat, has formed around the skeleton.

Malcolm's tent is close by. It is shaken by the "wind" stirred up by the helicopter. The loud sound of the helicopter's engine and propellers steadily diminishes, finally ending with a whining sound. Though the "helicopter" has landed offstage, part of its searchlight remains shining. VICTORIA *enters, smoking a cigarette. She quickly finds her way to the others. She first takes special note of* IRENE.

VICTORIA: There you are... "What's that in the mountain brush?" you say. "Shh. Who's that?" *(Pause.)* I told you before, Irene. You crossed me. For that, you will never be forgiven. *(Nicely, to* MALCOLM.*)* Malcolm, my apologies. My sister's bothering you. She needs help. You're not *that* kind of doctor. Your hands are full with urgent matters that require your full attention. *(To* IRENE.*)* Just as mine are. *(To all.)* There's no excuse for it. No way she gets off this time. *(To* IRENE.*)* You think you're being smart, don't you?

IRENE: *(Matter-of-factly.)* It was April Fool's Day.

VICTORIA: On the first of September?

IRENE: My pen was controlled - not by me.

VICTORIA: By a *force* of some kind? The company doesn't have "forces" on staff. It has employees. Even the quote-unquote creative ones that work in graphic design are still employees. *(To* DOROTHY.*)* I'm glad our poorer country relations reach out to us from time to time. You're a good sport. She's a lot to put up with. There's not much left to your or my family. Thanks, Dorothy. *(She takes a drag on her cigarette.)*

DOROTHY: No problem, Victoria. You know how much I respect you and how much I love Irene.

IRENE: *(To* VICTORIA.*)* You don't control the world. You and business only think you do. Your punishing me means nothing in this canyon.

VICTORIA: Grow up, Irene! *(To the others.)* Sisters! How lovely. *(To* IRENE.*)* How dare you draw strange faces in the vegetables pictured in our supermarket circular! I was kind to give you a job in the advertising department. But no, you couldn't stop being yourself and screw it up! *(Pause.)* You needed to spit at me – no, needed to spite me. Oh, it's because I don't have a sense of humor? *(Pause.)* Sketch or cartoon? "Funny" or just "interesting"? Eight hundred thousand people saw your ink on my pages. Liver-brown ink peeking from behind the lettuce, the tomatoes, the grapes and the newsprint. *(Sarcastically.)* You're a recognized *force* now! I hope that makes you happy. Your prank will be remembered as one of the most bizarre manifestations of our once-great family's brilliance. *(To* MALCOLM.*)* I'm sorry, excuse me. I shouldn't bring my business concerns up in front of you. There are other, more important, matters. *(Glancing at* IRENE.*)* What she did was grotesque. *(To* MALCOLM.*)* What you do is serious, grand. Though I do wish you could finish things up quickly. Yet, I know it's a monumental task. But there's only so much time.

"T": Well, you've got your own urgent matters. You want things done in a hurry. But pardon me for asking: why are you here?

VICTORIA: *(She ignores the question. To* MALCOLM.*)* Before long, the skeleton you're excavating will be on view for all to see. No one's to gain personal profit from it. I only ask that some mention of me be made on a plaque next to it.

IRENE: It's my land, too.

VICTORIA: Malcolm, you can breathe a sigh of relief. Randy Bruce has triumphed at the polls today. He's won the Republican primary. He's all but sewn up the general election. This means the Democrats won't come in with that horrible legislation that they're drafting that will mess things up. We'll get your skeleton, keep it in private hands, and you'll move on to other great conquests. Thank you for your excellent work. This is a very happy time.

"T": We're happy to the sound of chopper blades.

VICTORIA: Mr. Bruce supports the rights of ranchers and people like you and me. And he'll help us make this economy grow.

"T": If I understand correctly, Mr. Bruce has won a primary – not an election.

VICTORIA: I don't like the way you address me.

"T": I don't like how you treat your sister.

VICTORIA: *(Irked, to* MALCOLM.) Malcolm, your man here doesn't measure up to you by a mile.

"T": *(To* VICTORIA.) You are many miles from the city. All indications are that you have plenty to do there.

VICTORIA: Apparently you don't know what side your bread is buttered on. *(She is caught off guard by "T"'s impertinence. But she quickly collects herself and is a model of one who is in control and puts out her cigarette. To* MALCOLM.) Malcolm, you're a painstaking person. You might also take pains with holding your team more in check. (Pause. Starting to go.) Well, there's nothing more exhilarating than progress! *(Pause.)* So, make progress!

MALCOLM: We'll do our best.

"T": But we have to go to sleep now.

VICTORIA: *(She does not hear the remark. She shouts in the direction of the helicopter pilot.)* We're leaving!

"T": I guess you're not going to take your sister with you.

VICTORIA: *(Not revealing any hostility in her face, to* "T".*)* Back down, Bub, if you know what's good for you.

The sound of the helicopter motor starting up is heard.

VICTORIA: *(To all, with a false smile.)* Well, good-bye. And Good Night! Have dreams of... Completion! *(To herself.)* God, these people are taking forever with their damn dinosaur! *(She exits to get in the helicopter.)*
"T": What was that all about? Whirling blades, a crazy bat swooping down on us! *(Pause. He thinks.)* Human beings strive to kings and queens. If we really want to survive we have to study lizards, who were once kings of the hill, but who are now quiet creatures who've lived longer than we'll ever live. *(To* IRENE *and* DOROTHY.*)* And you two, showing up like a pair of starved wolves. We got science going. We number everything. Later we think about what it might mean. Your unmeasured steps are out of place here.
MALCOLM: "T", settle down.
IRENE: We'll be going, too.
MALCOLM: "T", we could lend them another flashlight.
"T": I guess we're a full-service oasis here. *("T" gives his flashlight to the women.)* Now, you be especially careful.
DOROTHY: We will.

DOROTHY *and* IRENE *exit.*

MALCOLM: Thanks, "T". *(Satisfied that matters are coming to a close for the evening.)* All may not be right but all seems *(Positively.)* well.

"T": *(Protesting slightly.)* Huh. I would not say "well". Up here we can be too positive sometimes. It's called having a "Rocky Mountain High". *(Pause. But he is, after all, content to be here. He lets go.)* But it *is* nice up here. *(He deeply breathes in some mountain air. Then:)* It's the *life* of it – don't you know!

Scene 2

It is late morning at the excavation site in the canyon. MALCOLM *is in the pit surrounding the dinosaur skeleton.* MELANIE *and* "T" *help him with his work, they have dry paintbrushes in their hands; they brush and sweep away little by little at the rock. When they move, they move carefully.*

MELANIE: *Calavera.* La *calavera.*

"T": *La calavera.*

MELANIE: That means "skull". *(Pause.) Quijada. La quijada.*

"T": *La quijada.*

MELANIE: Jaw. Malcolm, say, *quijada.*

MALCOLM: *Quijada.*

MELANIE: Now say, *hueso. Hueso de la cadera.*

"T": *Hueso.*

MALCOLM: *Hueso de la cadera.*

MELANIE: That means hipbone. Now you know the four most important dinosaur bones – in Spanish. *(Pause.)* If you ever go to Mexico or any Hispanic place you'll know what to ask for. But be sure to tell people you're a scientist. Otherwise, if you say you're looking for a *calavera*, people might think you're looking for a party. Because *calavera* means skull but it also means someone who likes to party.

"T": We speak languages. Books are written in languages. We have ourselves a library here. A library of stone and soil. Pages of fossils and bones. Colorado sat down on the globe where Florida is now. These mountains have risen three times.

MALCOLM *takes hold of the hook at the end of the chain that hangs down and is attached to a series of steel cables that encircle the rock/skeleton. He rearranges and refastens some of the cables.*

"T": Moses had stone tablets – they were scratch pads compared to what we find here. Isn't that right, Malcolm?

MALCOLM: "T", make sure the chain doesn't slip.

"T": *(He puts down his brush and checks to see if the chain is secure. It is.)* I don't know, Malcolm. I appreciate you wanting to do this with a chain and stuff. But it's easier if the chain was hooked to a backhoe.

MALCOLM: Yeah, well, how would we get that up here?

"T": I don't know.

MALCOLM: That's the challenge of our work. *(Pause. Looking at the rock/skeleton.)* It would be to our advantage if we could nudge this up just a little bit.

"T": *(Doubtful.)* I wouldn't use the word, "nudge". *(Pause.)* I guess the contraption will hold.

MALCOLM: It will hold and it does help us.

"T": But do we have enough muscle?

MALCOLM: We only have to raise it a couple inches.

"T": I wouldn't use the word "raise". Not with no machine at our disposal.

MALCOLM: "T", the more we're dependent on machinery, the more our minds are told what to do according to what the machines say.

"T": I don't fully understand the workings of an internal combustion engine but I still use it.

MALCOLM: Yeah, and see what problems that causes for the world. *(Looking at the apparatus, pointing with his finger.)* This'll bear the weight. We bring it up. *(Slightly defensively.)* We can try, can't we? *(He motions.)* Then we chisel and brush. *(Pause.)* We just need to get *at* it. At it, *better.*

"T": *(Not convinced.)* You're only thinking this because the sledgehammer hasn't arrived.

MALCOLM: I'd rather this not be in two pieces.

"T": We have to. *(Eyeing the rock/skeleton.)* It's the only way we'll get at it. It won't move, otherwise. Look, there's a crack already started for us. Don't be impatient. That's what you're telling me all the time.

MELANIE: The *marro.*

"T": What's that?

MELANIE: I'm saying the same thing you said. Just in Spanish. *Marro* is a sledgehammer.

"T": ...Which was supposed to here yesterday. There's only so many other things we can find to do until we get it. *(Turning to, and eyeing,* MELANIE.*)* What is your sister doing? Where is she?

MELANIE: Marie's bringing it today. At this moment.

"T": Oh, "at this moment". *(He is the first to spot* DOROTHY *approaching. He stares at her as she approaches. Finally, to* DOROTHY.*)* It's you again.

MELANIE: Where's Irene?

DOROTHY: She's staying up in the cabin. I was supposed to go back down last night but it got too late.

MELANIE: Is she all right?

DOROTHY: Well, we had an argument this morning. I stuck around longer than I intended. I was worried. But, what can you do?

MELANIE: It's good you stayed with her.

"T": (*He takes one look at* DOROTHY *and* MELANIE. *Peeved at the interruption, he says to* MALCOLM.) Malcolm, a man my age is going to need at least five minutes before he embarks an impatient push to roll a stone away from where it wants to be. Or even thinks about trying to do so.

MALCOLM: (*Looks at the apparatus.*) The chain's secure. (*Agrees.*) All right.

"T": (*To* MALCOLM.) And I want you to take the break with *me*. So we can *talk*.

MALCOLM: Fine.

"T": (*To* MELANIE.) Break time for five minutes.

MALCOLM *and* "T" *get out of the pit and walk over to where some supplies are. They are out of earshot of* DOROTHY *and* MELANIE.

DOROTHY: I don't know how much effect I can have on her. I'm sorry Irene pushed you. She got away from me.

MELANIE: What did you argue about this morning?

DOROTHY: Her medication. She didn't take it.

MELANIE: Is she safe up there?

DOROTHY: Well... you know, people with problems like hers – they have their civil rights. Right now she thinks quartz is going to help her.

MELANIE: What do you mean?

DOROTHY: She believes precious stones have power. She's put crystals in each of the corners of the cabin.

MELANIE: There's such a difference between her and her sister!

DOROTHY: No matter what you may think of Victoria's business style, she doesn't rest on her laurels. And you know, she's had her health problems, too.

MELANIE: Yeah, but if she's constantly rubbing people the wrong way people are going to hate her all the same.

DOROTHY: She does what she has to do in a man's world.

MELANIE: I don't want to sound unthankful for being allowed to be up here, but... she's a bitch.

DOROTHY: You think so?

MELANIE: Yeah. whatever...

DOROTHY: All I can say is I did all I could do for her. *(When she says "her" she means "Irene". She sighs.)* Oh, well. She's stayed up in the cabin lots of times before.

MELANIE: Does she have enough supplies?

DOROTHY: Yeah, I think so. *(Pause.)* Um. *(Pause. She is wondering. Almost whispering.)* How did "T" get his name?

MELANIE: Sometimes he works as a guide down at Dinosaur Ridge in Golden. I've been there and I've heard him tell kids "T" is for T-Rex. He's also said that his ex-wife used to say "T" stood for "turkey". Anyway, he says, T-Rex and turkeys... are related – seeing that birds are the dinosaurs' closest relatives.

DOROTHY: *(Pause. Ready to get going.)* Well, I'm heading down. Irene's got her tourmaline and her red jasper. She's set up for the day.

MELANIE: Oh. Well. *(Pause.)* Adios.

DOROTHY: Bye.

DOROTHY *goes over to* MALCOLM *and* "T" *and says goodbye and exits.* MALCOLM *and* "T" *go back over to the pit.*

"T": *(To* MELANIE.*)* The break's still not over yet.
MELANIE: Well, I'm ready to get back to work whenever you are.
"T": Your sister is holding things up.

MALCOLM *gazes at the rock/skeleton in the pit.*

MALCOLM:
Its steps no longer slap in the mud
Yet we see the echoes in the stone.
They speak of our astonishing world.
We're not the only great ones in this universe.
And we're far from being the first ones.

MALCOLM *points out various features of the skeleton.*

MALCOLM:
These bones give the creature a colorful afterlife.
What we do with our minds is flesh out the skeleton,
Explaining how it is that ligaments were in this space
And skin is all around.
In a sense, we bring about a second birth for this
Great ancient lizard.
If we were to leave this creature alone
Science would be silenced.

Pause.

MALCOLM: We don't have a lot of days before the cold sets in.

There is the sound of a soft bird-cry, and an echo of it. They listen to it.

"T": The sounds here tell of eternity. But we don't have all day to wait for that hammer.

"T" *sees something in the distance.*

"T": Well, I guess she's finally getting here. Hallelujah!
MELANIE: Just in time to catch lunch.

ED *enters wearing a straw cowboy hat. He wears a brown and white antelope skin jacket (it is more white than brown). He has a black bandana around his neck. He steps carefully around the site and looks the rock, the rope harness and the block and tackle over.*

ED: Quite a stump you're pulling out of the ground. *(Pause.)* Hello.
MALCOLM: Hello, Ed.
MELANIE: Hi.
"T": Big old oak tree trunk. Had enough of it hogging up the lawn. You going to help us with your brains or your brawn?
ED: You probably got all the help you want.
"T": *(He looks him up and down.)* Maybe not.
MELANIE: *(To* ED.*)* "T" thought you were Marie.
ED: Sorry to disappoint.
"T": I'll get over it. What j'you been up to?
ED: Walking. It's an intensely bright day. You can imagine how they thought about inventing something like a laser.
MELANIE: *(To* ED. *Wanting to make conversation.)* Nice day. But we could use the rain. (ED *does not say anything back to her.)* You know… it's… been dry.

"T": Yep, dry. The deer are on the hillsides kicking up shark teeth – wondering if they can squeeze out another drop of water.

ED: I've found what I thought were shark teeth up here before. Thanks for confirming that.

MELANIE: *(Showing off her recent education with* MALCOLM.*)* This wasn't always mountains. Parts of the land were in the ocean.

ED: Some pretty tough sharks living in Denver now.

"T": You staying long?

ED: No. Just passing by. See you later.

MELANIE: *(She wants to delay* ED *from going. She is in love with him. He has been unresponsive to her.)* What do you think of that Randy Bruce? I mean, winning the primary?

ED: He's one of *them*, isn't he? *(He does not elaborate.)*

MELANIE: But he's not going to be like the Democrats who want only certain qualified people working on excavating dinosaurs.

ED: I'm sure he has his own list of people who are the only ones invited to the party.

SCOTT: *(Offstage.)* I had a school friend, from Genesee Park. That's at eight thousand feet. Like here. He said the first snow would come on the fifteenth of August and the last would be the tenth of June. Those are not the *exact* dates, but...

MS. PAROLE *enters, with her assistant* SCOTT *behind her.* SCOTT *carries a laptop computer.*

MS. PAROLE: *(To* SCOTT.*)* It snows enough in Denver for me.

"T": *(He is not pleased to see two new people up near the site. He looks* MS. PAROLE *up and down.)* Still no Marie.

MS. PAROLE: Who's Marie?

"T": Not you.

MELANIE: *(To* Ms. PAROLE.) Who are you?

Ms. PAROLE: Karen Parole, attorney to Ms. Victoria Van Epps. *(To* SCOTT, *pointing.)* Scott, find yourself a seat somewhere over there. I know you're not a typist, but you're sure faster than me with notes.

"T": Notes?

Ms. PAROLE: For her records.

"T": What in the world...! She knows what's going on here. *We* take the notes. If you'd kindly take yourselves back to Denver we'd be much obliged.

MALCOLM: I'm Doctor Malcolm Lockley. Victoria didn't inform me that she was sending anybody up. What's this about?

Ms. PAROLE: Just what I said.

MELANIE: She'll have access to all the data we collect.

"T": *(To* Ms. PAROLE *and* SCOTT.) What *kind* of notes? *(Pause.)* There seems to be a communication problem here.

SCOTT *and* Ms. PAROLE *make no motions to leave.* SCOTT *types on the laptop. It looks like he is taking down the personal description of those at the site. He stops typing. He looks at* ED. *He inadvertently stares at him.*

ED: I used to have a mole on my arm. But I had it taken off. On account of it looking really threatening. To people who *stared* at it.

ED *leaves.*

MALCOLM: It would be best to let us get on with our work

undistracted.

Everyone is silent as Scott *continues typing.*

"T": Scott, I'll give you one chance to stop that.

Scott *continues typing.* Ms. Parole *is several yards away. She is busy glancing over the site.*

"T": You two have had your one chance. (*He snatches the computer from* Scott's *lap. He throws the computer on the ground, hoping to smash it.*)
Scott: (*Shocked.*) What?
"T": (*Picks up the laptop and throws it down on the ground again. Then:*) Damn, those things are practically indestructible.
Ms. Parole: (*She runs over to where* "T" *is.*) What are you doing? That's private property!
"T": (*Threateningly.*) It's all private property these days, isn't it? (*Pause.*) I said you should get on out of here. (*He picks up the computer once more. He grabs it by its screen and beats the computer against the ground sharply two or three times. He cannot separate the laptop at the hinge.*) These laptops really hold up well in the mountains.
Ms. Parole: You just can't do that!
"T": Then what am I doing, ma'am?

Ms. Parole *cries out in a strange hurt sound, like that of a young hoofed animal getting its leg caught in the teeth of an animal trap.* Scott *picks up the remains of the laptop.* Ms. Parole *cry ends almost as soon as it began.*

"T": I don't have anything against binary numbers. Only

some of the people that use them.
Melanie: It would be best if both of you leave now.
Ms. Parole: This has never happened before.
"T": Then guard against it ever happening again.
Ms. Parole: *(Composed, for the moment.)* How dare you.
"T": We got our own devices in place here. Hazardous stuff. Unshielded pins, exposed ropes. You'll be happier with your microchips in Denver.
Scott: You just can't do things like that. This is completely destroyed.
Ms. Parole: *(To Scott.)* Ms. Van Epps will hear about this. *(She appears to have a brief panic attack – more like a pang of panic. She breathes deeply, twice. Then:)* Expect a bill.
"T": *(To Ms. Parole.)* Sue me if I don't pay.
Ms. Parole: *(To Scott.)* Let's get out of here.

Ms. Parole *huffs out and* Scott *follows.*

Malcolm: *(To "T", once they are gone.)* You went too far, "T".
"T": Sometimes with people like that you have to take the low road. *(Pause.)* Now why were they spying on us? I thought they were happy with what we're doing.
Malcolm: They're impatient. We need to keep the pace up.
"T": What we have here is a place for focus on sustained, significant inquiry. *(Pauses and thinks things over.)* Okay. Well. I apologize. That was a bit too much. I guess I just couldn't find my "off" button.
Malcolm: *(Pause.)* We might as well have lunch now. In the meantime maybe Marie will show up.
Melanie: *Almuerzo.* Lunch.

Scene 3

In Denver, at Victoria's office. Victoria *is leaning on her desk chair.* Randy Bruce *stands on the other side of the desk from her.*

Randy Bruce: These things take time. Meanwhile, you have a thriving chain of supermarkets to run and a lot of property to manage.

Victoria: *(Sarcastically.)* Yeah, so why not just be happy with that, right? *(Answering her own question.)* It's not my fate to accept hand-me-downs and not do anything more. *(Pause.)* Look, I missed the first casino boom. *(Pause.)* You'll get in. You'll modify the existing law.

Randy Bruce: I will. Now, you just relax. You seem to be having a difficult morning.

Victoria: I'm bankrolling you. And my mornings are going to stay difficult until the morning that you are sworn into the state legislature.

Randy Bruce: It is wrong to show any concern for you?

Victoria: Oh, cut it out Randy. You're not the type that really cares.

Randy Bruce: Well, something's obviously irritating you. I'm sorry.

Victoria: *(Opening up a bit.)* One thing that's not happening fast enough is that I have to remove my sister from the deed!

Randy Bruce: What deed?

Victoria: My sister Irene's name is on the deed to the mountain property, you idiot.

Randy Bruce: You always said it was yours.

Victoria: *(Pauses, thinks.)* Well, it's mine, but she's also on the deed. The longer she stays up in the cabin, the faster I can build a case.

Randy Bruce: What case?

VICTORIA: She'll be declared insane. I have to have all the facts, lay them out in the right order. All the details. Find out as much as I can. On the way up to the cabin, for example, she assaulted a woman. *(Pause.)* I'll get permanent guardianship. Or at least she'll be ruled incompetent to manage her own affairs.

RANDY BRUCE: I don't know anything about those kinds of things.

VICTORIA: Yes, because you come from a family as ordinary as boiled potatoes.

RANDY BRUCE: Actually, my mother's family comes from Portuguese stock.

VICTORIA: So, what's that supposed to mean?

RANDY BRUCE: They were the first Westerners to colonize the world.

VICTORIA: That was a long time ago. I suggest you keep campaigning, all right? And re-friend any Indians that you might have had a falling out with five hundred years ago. I would be good to have them on your side.

RANDY BRUCE: Why?

VICTORIA: You didn't grow up here. You're not always "with it", are you? Indians agitate from time to time. They even litigate. Especially when it comes to matters of land being zoned for commercial use.

RANDY BRUCE: I have friends in pretty high places.

VICTORIA: You won't find any Indians there. *(Pause.)* They're a lot harder to deal with than some liberal group.

RANDY BRUCE: I'll pay a visit to the reservation.

VICTORIA: Randy, there *is* no reservation. Maybe that's part of the problem. They live all over the place – among us. But they have their organizations. Some of them want to get into the gambling business, too. I'm not going to have them as partners.

RANDY BRUCE: Then why do I need to know them?

VICTORIA: Randy, I know you were born in Massachusetts, but do you have to be so obvious about it? *(Pause.)* We need to know our enemies, Randy. They hate us and they don't always know at first how to attack us.

RANDY BRUCE: What are the names of some of these Indians? I'll see what I can do.

VICTORIA: Well, it might be advantageous... Sometimes people like you can slow them down by being nice and friendly. You're running for office – talk to them about ... conservation. *(Pause.)* Promise any Indian you come across that you'll see to it that they get a small business loan.

RANDY BRUCE: Is there any particular Indian that I should treat with deference? One's who is maybe a leader of one of their organizations?

VICTORIA: You should be careful of a guy named Ed.

RANDY BRUCE: What's the name of the organization he heads up?

VICTORIA: I don't know. He's young and secretive. But various people seem to know of him.

RANDY BRUCE: Okay.

VICTORIA: Promise any of them that Indian kids can go to college free for the next three hundred years.

RANDY BRUCE: *(He thinks that would be outrageous. Hesitantly:)* Right.

VICTORIA: *(Ominously.)* Though I can now set you up with Boots Brandley – by virtue of your winning the primary – never forget it's the small guys – or who you think are small guys – who can trip you up big time.

RANDY BRUCE: All right.

VICTORIA: I can't wait till the scientist up there has finished! Ms. Parole has gone up there to scope out where my sister assaulted that woman *and* to make sure Malcolm's not dawdling. We've got to get that dinosaur up and out of there! I don't have a whole lifetime for it!

RANDY BRUCE: You sent Jennifer Parole up there?

VICTORIA: No, I sent *Karen* Parole up there. It's her sister, Jennifer, who works as an exotic dancer at Shotgun Willie's. *(She gives him an accusing look.)* Watch your ass, Randy. Be a little more careful where you go out at night now. Make sure your past gets told the way it needs to.

RANDY BRUCE: I've got nothing to hide.

VICTORIA: Yeah, sure. *(Pause.)* So, Karen Parole's up there. With her assistant. They should know the lie of the land if they're drawing up papers for me. *(Pause.)* I'm still tweaking the concept of the whole place. I could be missing something – I've been up there so many times that maybe there's something brilliant that I haven't see because it's always just staring me in the face. *(Pause.)* I need to have an extraordinary plan and phenomenal messaging to attract investors and make sure all the legislation leaves nothing out. It'll be a *multi-purpose* development even though gambling's at the center of it.

RANDY BRUCE: I understand.

Gambling Fever

VICTORIA: You say you do, but it's complicated. *(Pause.)* Just remember this even in your sleep: though Colorado already has two gambling towns, all the casinos in those towns are owned by out-of-staters. That means that except for taxes, Colorado lost. No Coloradoan actually owns a casino! Pine Meadows – our development – will change all that. It will be entirely Colorado-owned and run. And some of Colorado's prized archeology, dug up just nearby, will greet you as you arrive at the largest, most spectacular casino of them all. When you're at Pine Meadows, you'll be humbled to win in such a setting.

RANDY BRUCE: And humbled to lose.

VICTORIA: *(Not hearing him.)* Anyway, the major emphasis in our development will actually be on the *family*. *(Her phone rings. She picks it up, listens for a moment and says into the phone.)* Send her in.

MS. PAROLE *comes in.*

VICTORIA: Hello, Karen. Obviously, it couldn't wait.

MS. PAROLE: We were attacked.

VICTORIA: What? Attacked?

MS. PAROLE: Yes, me and my assistant, Scott.

VICTORIA: Another assault. By my sister?

MS. PAROLE: No.

VICTORIA: Then by whom?

MS. PAROLE: The group in the mountains. In complete disregard of your rights. *(Pause.)* As shaken as we were, Scott and I somehow found our way down to my car. A laptop's been damaged beyond all repair.

VICTORIA: That's very sad.

MS. PAROLE: It was kicked, picked up and thrown!

VICTORIA: Who exactly did it?
Ms. PAROLE: The older guy.
VICTORIA: "T"?
Ms. PAROLE: Yeah.
VICTORIA: It pains me not to have full control up there. That man should not be on my property.
Ms. PAROLE: I couldn't stop hyperventilating.
VICTORIA: The air *is* thin up there.
Ms. PAROLE: What they did was prosecutable in court.
VICTORIA: I wouldn't want to prosecute it anywhere else. Malcolm let this happen?
Ms. PAROLE: He stayed out of it. Like you requested, we were friendly. We were just going to start taking notes when the old guy went nuts.
VICTORIA: You did nothing to provoke him?
Ms. PAROLE: Nothing whatsoever. I don't trust them. They're self-righteous.
VICTORIA: I guess they felt a little invaded. I should have given them some warning. Still, it's my land and I don't have to bow down to them. And certainly "T" is criminal in assaulting a representative of mine. *(Pause.)* Do you or your assistant need to see a doctor?
Ms. PAROLE: No.
VICTORIA: Or a therapist? You never know if there might be some lingering effects. Time does not heal everything. In fact it slowly kills, doesn't it?
Ms. PAROLE: I don't want to see a therapist.

VICTORIA: Glad to hear it. I realize that if either one of you needed to then you'd bill my insurance company for the sessions and that would be the end of cheap premiums with them. *(Pause.)* Oh. Sorry. *(She looks at* RANDY BRUCE *and* MS. PAROLE.*)* Have you two met?

Their silence indicates they have not. VICTORIA *introduces them.*

VICTORIA: Randy Bruce, meet the sister, *Karen* Parole.
RANDY BRUCE: *(Smiling his fake politician's smile. Extends his hand.)* Delighted.
MS. PAROLE: *(Shaking his hand.)* Me, as well. Congratulations on your recent victory.
RANDY BRUCE: Thanks. *(Pause.)* I'm sorry to hear that you were attacked.
MS. PAROLE: Judging from Victoria's tone, it seems that you've run into my sister. I hope it was a mutually beneficial encounter?
RANDY BRUCE: *(Pause.)* Well, it's fine weather we've been having in Denver lately, isn't it? After fifteen years of living out here I still can't get over how many days of sunshine there are in a year! A good state to settle down in and raise a family.
MS. PAROLE: Sun every day helps to keep you productive – that's for sure. *(She looks him up and down.)* Keeps you young, too.

Scene 4

A high meadow in the mountains about a mile away from the excavation site, just after lunchtime. Upstage, something that appears to be made of white and black feathers is in a lump on the ground. Downstage, IRENE *walks. A few moments pass. The sound of the beating of a human heart fades in. The heartbeat will be heard throughout the entire scene.*

IRENE: Oh, that Dorothy. Going on about woman's inequality, the abuse of women, women's lack of power… when I've got a sister and *she* doesn't. *(She walks more and does not say anything for a while.)* Self-generation, cleansed being. *(Pause. She gets closer to the tree.)* My heart's pounding. It's going to jump out of me. *(Pause.)* Black onyx in my pocket. A bracelet of yellow topaz. *(A command to herself.)* Find strength!

First there is a short burst of static, then a radio sounds.

MAN'S VOICE ON RADIO: "There's an altercation at Fourteenth and Steele." *(Another short burst of static.)* "Uh. There's a vicious animal involved."
IRENE: I didn't know the crystals in the cabin could broadcast this far.

There is another short burst of static, followed by:

Man's Voice on Radio: "Undefined kind of animal. Send a backup unit in right away. Over and out."

Irene: Wow. *(Pause. Her mind shifts to an entirely different set of thoughts.)* Dorothy's been in graduate school for like eight years now. Can you actually stay in college for a total of twelve years? *(Pause. She looks around.)* Strength. There's an oak. *(Pause.)* Now, that's strong. *(She walks some more. After a few moments she arrives at the lump on the ground. She notices that this lump is in fact a magpie the size of a man. She screams.)* Ah! *(Pause.)* What huge feathers! *(The big bird gets up. It is* Ed, *wearing a man-sized magpie costume. Fear strikes* Irene. *She does not recognize* Ed.*)* It's alive!

Ed: *(Calmly.)* Irene?

Irene: *(Confused.)* What?

Ed: Irene?

Irene: How do you know my name?

Ed: We've met.

Irene: I don't know you. This is like ah… something out of a …

Ed: Irene. You know me.

Irene: How… how … how do you know me?

Ed: I've been at the dig before. Talking to Malcolm. You've seen me there once.

Irene: You weren't there last night. *(She wonders at the magpie's size. She looks him up and down.)* Were you feeding in uranium country?

Ed: *(Not understanding her.)* What?

Irene: Your size. Look at you! *(Fear seizes her again.)* You're a ghoul… in a tuxedo! (Ed *moves slightly.* Irene *misconstrues the movement.)* Don't come any closer to me.

Ed: Irene, I'll stand still. *(Pause.)* I won't do anything to you. I can help, if you want.

IRENE: You can't fly. Magpies your size don't fly.
ED: What puts it in your head that I'm a magpie? I've got a clan, sure. But it's the Antelope Clan. Though I wouldn't mind being a bird sometimes.
IRENE: She sent you, didn't she?
ED: She? What are you talking about?
IRENE: Victoria. *(Pause.)* Drag your tail out of here! This is my property.
ED: Property? You have a point. In the world of the whites.
IRENE: *(She now understands why he said what said about the pronghorn clan.)* Oh. Antelope Clan? You could be an Indian.
ED: I know you've seen me before. You don't remember who I am? *(Pause.)* It's none of my business, but if you're taking any medication, have you lost it?... or did you forget to take it?
IRENE: *(Retorts.)* That's personal.
ED: Um. Well... you never know, it might relax you if you were to take it. *(Pause, trying to appeal to her "new age" side.)* You'd be doing an Indian a favor if you took it.
IRENE: Indians aren't into Western medicine. They have their own natural remedies.
ED: I'll have to tell that to some of the Indians I know.
IRENE: I still don't know why you're here. *(When she says this, she is thinking of Colorado and the rest of the continent as a place with a long history – with the Indians preceding the Whites:)* I think it's good you're here. What are you going to do?
ED: Oh, the usual.
IRENE: What's that?
ED: What is ... customary.
IRENE: *(Impatiently.)* What would that be? What do you do *up here*?

Ed: I inspect the aftermath of "rainstorms and snowfall". Just like Henry David Thoreau.

Irene *appeared to be becoming calmer but now she lets out a cry of anguish.*

Irene: Oh, no!

Ed: *(In a calming tone.)* Let me be the one who's wild. Who's easily misunderstood as any animal can be. You can never really know what lies under my fur – or feathers, to your eyes. You may see me doing one thing but I'll be doing it to bring on quite the other. *(Still calming.)* Sorry, listen, Irene. *(Pause. Collecting his thoughts.)* I'm human. Do you get that? I'm not maybe exactly what you see now, but I'm … real. *(Pause.)* It was not my intention to cross paths with you and surprise you. I saw you from a distance. I thought you'd seen me. It would have been rude to ignore you. So I came to say hello. That's all. *(Pause.)* I don't want to sound out of line, but I think you should go back to your cabin and do normal things. Like drink water – and take your medicine if you have some. Normal things. Once you're there, sit down. Eat something – you might be hungry. Lie down if you need to. Sleep some – if you feel like it. *(Pause.)* Do you understand?

Irene: *(She stands there and studies* Ed. *Then:)* I understand that you're speaking to me and that I didn't ask for this conversation and it'll probably go on for a while longer and I hope for not too much longer…

The sound of the heartbeat that has been heard throughout the entire scene fades to silence.

Scene 5

It is three-thirty in the afternoon at the excavation site. Malcolm *is in the pit surrounding the dinosaur skeleton. He is sitting at on side of the pit, relaxed, filing down a chisel that has become blunted.* "T", *a few yards from* Malcolm, *works independently. He has a large pair of scissors in his hand and he is trimming the bristles of a brush.* Marie, *Melanie's brawny sister, enters.*

Marie: Oh. My sister's not here?
"T": No, she went down to get you. *(Pause.)* Where's the hammer?
Marie: The what?
"T": The sledgehammer you were supposed bring up – *yesterday.*
Marie: I was supposed to bring up a hammer?
"T": Yeah. I'm sure you remember. *(Pause. There is no answer from* Marie.*)* We're being slowed down, Marie. We need that hammer. I ought not to be trimming a brush right now. And Malcolm's filing a blunt chisel.
Marie: Oh, yeah. The hammer. I had some bad luck. Here's a Spanish word for you: *pavoroso.*
"T": *Pavoroso?*
Marie: Yeah, something scary. *(Pause.)* I was going to the hardware store. A boy came up to me. He was excited. *(Pause.)* I went with him to the end of the row of stores on Main Street. Somebody'd split open a parking meter. And they ran away. Money was falling out the meter.
"T": *Somebody* split open a parking meter? *(Pause.)* You didn't take any of it, did you? It wasn't your money.

MARIE: While we were in the café having pop and our ice cream sundaes, a guy came up to us. He threatened to bust us. For the parking meter. We didn't do it. We didn't see anything.

"T": Who was the guy?

MARIE: A policeman.

"T": Did that boy get you in trouble?

MARIE: *(Taking it to mean that he has asked her if she is pregnant.)* No. I'm just a little overweight.

"T": What happened to the hammer, dammit?

MARIE: I'm getting to that. No, the policeman didn't arrest us.

"T": What'd he do?

MARIE: He said he was going be watching us from now on.

"T": That's his job. What's so scary about...

MARIE: *Pavoroso*.

"T": ... about that?

MARIE: I saw policeman's right hand. It had *six* fingers on it. Talk about *pavoroso!*

"T": No, they're not going to let you be a cop if you've got six fingers on one hand. What are you talking about, girl?

MARIE: *(Making excuses.)* I couldn't carry it the whole way.

"T": It couldn't be that heavy. Not for someone like you.

MARIE: The wind came up and I thought it was going to rain. I didn't want it to get wet.

"T": Where exactly is it? Down near the Rabbit Leg?

MARIE: No.

"T": Where on the trail is it then?

MARIE: There were stacks of rocks.

"T": Get to the point, girl! *(He takes a break from trimming the bristles on the brush.)* Did you get as far as the first cliff?

MARIE: The cliffs of red rocks, you mean?
"T": Jesus! Where's the hammer!?
MARIE: The policeman said leave the café and stay home.
"T": You had an errand to do! *(He thinks the policeman story is a lie.)* And you came up here. You're not at home. *(Pause.)* It's nowhere, isn't it? *(Pause.)* You never picked it from the store. It's down there waiting for us. *(Pause.)* Good help is really hard to find! *(Pause. He rethinks the situation.)* There ain't much choice.

MARIE *walks over to where* MALCOLM *is. He looks at the apparatus and the rock/skeleton below and speaks to* MARIE.

MALCOLM: "T"'s right. It's not going to move as it is. We're going have to split it in two. There's a lot of pressure on the block and tackle. *(Pointing.)* You see that, you can see the stress on the chain, too.
"T": *(He throws his brush and the scissors done on the ground in anger.)* I'll go down the mountain. *(To* MARIE.*)* I'll have to hurry. It's getting late. You watch yourself, girl, and don't go distracting Malcolm! Be back as soon as I can!

"T" *leaves.*

MARIE: *(Going over to* MALCOLM.*)* Sorry I didn't bring the hammer. *(Long pause.)* There's something I need to tell you. You know I'm nineteen and... there's not much to do here. I don't mean you. What you're doing *is* something. I've been thinking of my future. *(Pause.)* I'm going to New Jersey. I can't work for you anymore. Even on a part-time basis.
MALCOLM: Thank you for doing what you could, Marie.

MARIE: I'm strong enough. There's a professional wrestling school. In Millvale, New Jersey. I'll come back, Malcolm. Eventually. I want to. When I'm on tour. To see how things are coming along. *(She flexes her meaty arms.)*

MALCOLM: How do your parents feel about you going into wrestling?

MARIE: They don't mind. Look at me. I'm Marie Gonzales, the girl with the perfect tag-team body. I'm a natural type.

MALCOLM: Hm.

MARIE: You're not mad?

MALCOLM: Try not to get injured.

MARIE: I won't. All that violence you see in the ring – it's faked.

MALCOLM: *(Feigning surprise.)* Really?

MARIE: Yep. It's not like boxing – there you could get killed. *(Pause.)* I'm going to conquer the wrestling world. I'm going to say to them they should play up the Mexican-American aspect with me. They don't have a Chicana in the league now. *(She does a few stretching exercises as she talks.)* You never actually fight. The boss tells you who's going to win. Then you plan out the moves with your partner – the best things you can think of, for the audience. I'll have the Latino audience behind me. But you got to be in good shape.

MALCOLM: I don't doubt that. *(Pause.)* You've thought a lot about this. How come you didn't say anything before?

MARIE: They'll root for me to be on top. For the audience as a general whole, you have to have a gimmick. I'll don't what I'll wear, but it'll be exotic. *(She flexes her muscles.)* I know what everybody says. Wrestlers cheat the audience 'cause it's all a set-up. But the crowd doesn't care if the match is real or not. It's the excitement they want.

MALCOLM: You and your sister are quite different.

MARIE: I'm sorry to have to tell you, but I thought it would be best to tell you in person.

Pause. MALCOLM *puts down the chisel he has been filing and he looks at the block and tackle, as well as the taut chain. While* MARIE *continues to speak,* MALCOLM *moves further into in the pit to get a close up look. He is concerned about the stress being put on the chain.*

MALCOLM: See, Marie, we can't take the chain off because it's keeping the rock in its place. What we do when the hammer comes is …
MARIE: *(Interrupting.)* Okay, you've got a bunch of clashes. Make sure before you end to pull some hair and wap her shins repeatedly. Simulate all the pain. Invite the audience to work out their aggressions through you. Then a heroic ending. *(Pause.)* I'm leaving soon.
MALCOLM: *(He has heard this kind of thing from her before.)* You won't be staying on with us just for a *while longer*?
MARIE: No, I've saved up the money.

MALCOLM *runs his finger carefully over the metal ring or eyelet which gathers parts of the chain together. Suddenly, the block and tackle of the makeshift machine snaps apart. One part of the block and tackle hits him in the face and the gravel and ground underneath him shifts and he falls down. The rock/skeleton moves, gripping* MALCOLM's *legs below the knees in a kind of vice.*

MALCOLM: Marie, uh…
MARIE: Let me see what I can do.

Scared, she steps into the pit and looks for a moment; then she tries to budge the rock/skeleton in order to free him. After a few attempts it is obvious that it cannot be moved.

MALCOLM: Be careful. Don't hurt yourself.
MARIE: I can't move it. *(She feels the ground shifting.)* Oh, no. The gravel's shifting underneath me. Do you feel it?
MALCOLM: Yes.

MARIE *jumps out of the pit. This causes the ground to shift more: it will be even harder for him to get free now.*

MALCOLM: Ow, you jumped out. The gravel didn't like that. It's worse now!
MARIE: I'll try and hook up the pulley.

She retrieves the block and tackle. She cannot get it hooked back up properly.

MALCOLM: You can't. It's broken.
MARIE: You're going to lose circulation in your legs.
MALCOLM: No, more than that.

She tries again to move the rock/skeleton but without success.

MARIE: Tell me how to fix it.
MALCOLM: Let me see the block and tackle.

She shows him the block and tackle.

MALCOLM: *(Looking.)* It's all but shattered.
MARIE: *(Pause. She thinks.)* You can't stay trapped like this.
MALCOLM: Go get "T". He can't be far.
MARIE: What good will that do? He can't move the rock. I won't let you be alone.
MALCOLM: Digging into the eons is no small matter.
MARIE: *(Spotting* ED *in the distance who is hiking.* Wait! Ed. The best luck I've had all day! *(She runs in his direction and shouts to him.)* Ed, come! Come here! Malcolm's in trouble!

ED *enters. He comes towards* MARIE.

MARIE: He's stuck.
ED: *(After he sees that* MALCOLM *is trapped he rushes to him. To* MALCOLM.*)* We'll get you out in a minute.
MALCOLM: I doubt it.

ED *studies the situation and his demeanor changes.*

ED: It does look bad.
MALCOLM: We'll try a new block and tackle. *(Pause.)* Marie, you'll get one.

ED *attempts to budge the rock but knows it is impossible.*

ED: A new block and tackle's not going to work.
MARIE: We'll have a helicopter come up and roll the stone back.
MALCOLM: No, I'll dead by then.
ED: Where's "T"?

MALCOLM: He went down the mountain.
ED: Can we bust some of this rock up?
MALCOLM: We don't have a big enough hammer.

Pause. MARIE *is oblivious to the significance of this remark. She says nothing.*

MALCOLM: Bring a blanket to me, please. Fold it, and put it under my head.

ED *leaves the spot for a moment to get a blanket.*

MARIE: What are we going to do?
MALCOLM: You go ahead, Marie. Catch up with "T". Send him back. You go down the mountain and get help.

MALCOLM *and* MARIE *wait for* ED *to come back. He comes returns with a folded blanket in his hand and puts it under* MALCOLM's *head.*

ED: *(To* MALCOLM.*)* There you are. *(To* MARIE.*)* What we need is the biggest hammer you can find. Go on down and get one up here as fast as you can!
MARIE: All right. *(She hurries off.)*
MALCOLM: "T" will continue the excavation. Besides bringing up the iguanodon, we'll throw my bones into the bargain.
ED: *(Pause.)* You just be quiet.
MALCOLM: Face-to-face with the ages now.
ED: *(Cautioning him to stay positive.)* Now, now. *(Pause.)* We'll hope for the best. We got to go through a whole lot of trouble to get you out of this.

Scene 6

An extensive porch in back of the ranch owned by Boots Brandley in Berthoud, Colorado. BOOTS *and* RANDY BRUCE *are looking out on the back field.*

BOOTS: *(Pointing.)* East. Wide open sky, it's so clear it seems you could almost see to Washington, D.C. Hm. *(Pause.)* In any direction there are any number of enemies. Don't forget that, Randy.

With a firmness that is shallow and fake, but something that he feels is effective, RANDY BRUCE *excitedly thrusts out his hand and shakes* BOOTS's *hand.*

RANDY BRUCE: Mr. Boots Brandley, I can't tell you what a pleasure it is to make your acquaintance.
BOOTS: You won't see this kind of beauty in New York. Or Massachusetts. In the *(Negatively.)* Liberal East, Randy.
RANDY BRUCE: The West is best.
BOOTS: I know, but there's still California and the liberal west coast.
RANDY BRUCE: I don't know what there is about oceans and their coasts.
BOOTS: *(Pause.* BOOTS *has his own train of thought.)* There's something called freedom. There's something called chaos. If order is not constantly shaped then chaos reigns. And we can't let that happen. That's why the Kennedys and Martin Luther King had to be killed.

BOOTS *looks for a reaction from* RANDY BRUCE. RANDY BRUCE *does not know if* BOOTS *is lying or telling the truth about the Kennedys and King.* RANDY BRUCE *stands there with a dumb look on his face. Suddenly,* BOOTS *lets out a big laugh. We do not know what this laugh means. Then* BOOTS'S *mood turns on a dime.*

BOOTS: *(Solemnly, as if in prayer:)* It's a fine day, today. And it's a notable year. Nineteen ninety-two. *(Pause.)* Coasts are necessary, Randy. Five hundred years ago Christopher Columbus brought his ships to the Land of Milk and Honey. And it *is* the Land of Milk and Honey. *(Pause.)* But the world's up in arms, Randy. Common folk know something's not right.

RANDY BRUCE: Something is not right.

BOOTS: But they'll be delivered from that, won't they? *(Pause.)* How?

RANDY BRUCE: People like me will get elected. *(He smiles a fake smile.)*

BOOTS: And that'll change things for them? *(Pause.)* You've whitened your teeth. What a nice smile. But guess that's what everybody has to do now in the days of television. *(Pause.)* Anyway, they have to be convinced that you stand for the solutions.

RANDY BRUCE: Absolutely.

BOOTS: *(Pause.)* What would you say if I were to put my hand on your naked ass?

RANDY BRUCE: What?

BOOTS: You heard what I said.

RANDY BRUCE: Is this some kind of joke? I uh...

BOOTS: *(Chuckles.)* Did I scare you? You shouldn't scare so easily. Naked asses are quite familiar to proctologists, for example. Anything can be all right if it's in the right context, correct?

RANDY BRUCE *is lost.*

BOOTS: You know what I'm talking about, Randy. Your reaching for women's asses has been, and can accelerate to be, even *more* out of context. *(He smiles.)* People are investing in you. They're letting you use the brand. *(Pause.)* There's hope for you, I guess, since you've come to *me*. *(Pause.)* Do you know the law?

RANDY BRUCE: I practice law. Or I *did* practice. Now, it's different, of course.

BOOTS: There are the facts and there are the client's desires. *(Pause.)* So we got this land here... *(He points to the vast landscape before them.)* ... and we got the law.

RANDY BRUCE: Yeah, the law. If things continue like they have been, ... the way laws have been eating away at us ... there'll be no "us" left anymore.

BOOTS: That may sound good on the stump. We do our best for people to believe somebody like you has the solutions. But I hope you're not that simple. *(He means "stupid" by this last word. Pause. He cannot resist chuckling.)* You want to be my friend?

RANDY BRUCE: Yes.

BOOTS: Then be careful how you say "yes" to me.

RANDY BRUCE: *(Realizing his mistake.)* Yes, *Sir*.

A pause.

BOOTS: How do you get somebody to think negatively at the same time you want them to think *positively*?

RANDY BRUCE: *(Being careful.)* I don't know, sir. I don't want anybody to think negatively.

Boots: Well, I'm classifying "the fear of God" into the negative thinking camp. That's the camp you got to get people into.

Randy Bruce: I know you're the expert.

Boots: If I'm an expert I'll tell you this: if you think you're in control or I'm in control I'll only say that *things* are in control. But there's people who *corral* things. Are you ready to compete?

Randy Bruce: I *am* competing, sir.

Boots: I don't know if you have what it takes.

Randy Bruce: I'd appreciate any help you could give me.

Boots: Ah, that's good. You didn't even blink. But I don't imagine you've ever worked in high-pressure sales.

Randy Bruce: No, I went to law school after college.

Boots: But you've represented brands before?

Randy Bruce: Yes, I've had plenty of clients who have brands.

Boots: You're representing the Conservative and Republican brands now. You are in sales now. You will put the pressure on, and we will help you put the pressure on. We think we can win this one. We've created the conditions – the *need* for politicians like you. *(Pause.)* Now. *(Pause.)* How unique are you?

Randy Bruce: I can solve Colorado's problems – like nobody else – and bring prosperity back for all.

Boots: Randy, my home is not a campaign trail stop. It's something much bigger than that. If you're unique, that means you're the only one... that they can't get what is needed from somebody else.

Randy Bruce: I think the primary has helped decide that. I would say, yes... in this election cycle, I'm unique.

Boots: Like a good lawyer, you're qualifying your answer. *(Pause.)* You're sure of yourself, you think you're unique, you have no fear?

Randy Bruce: I have no fear.

Boots: You should have. Your head's in the clouds if you don't. You should be afraid, just as your constituents are afraid. You should be afraid that you're not going to win the election!

Randy Bruce: *(Hesitating.)* Um. *(Struggling for self-respect and authority.)* I fully support all the policies my contributors are asking for.

Boots: Well, that's okay. You're missing something, though. *(Sighing.)* Folks like you – always lacking something like that pack in the Wizard of Oz – you're either missing a brain, a heart or usually... a spine. Then you make a mistake that comes from that lack. Then there's a scandal. *(Pause.)* Well, we have to work with what's out there. If somebody didn't lack something they wouldn't be in politics in the first place! Amen. *(Pause.* Boots *looks* Randy Bruce *up and down.)* Speaking of "Amen": My information may not be complete, so excuse me for asking. You're not a practicing Christian, are you?

Randy Bruce: Not so much.

Boots: That's good. You'll be Reborn then. In your case, if and when the opponent mentions your history of womanizing – it'll probably come out, you'll be able to counter with the fact that you have turned over a new leaf. *(Pause.)* Call my secretary later this afternoon. She'll give the phone number of a pastor I know. You arrange things with him, okay?

Randy Bruce: Yes, sir.

Pause.

Boots: You'll be a rich man, Randy Bruce, if you can apply pressure, if you can sell.
Randy Bruce: I can, sir. I will try my best.
Boots: You won't just *try. (Pause.)* I have people for you to meet. One has very few real chances in this life.
Randy Bruce: I agree with you, sir.
Boots: Now that the primary's over, it's a whole different ballgame.
Randy Bruce: True.
Boots: Will you stop sucking up to me?
Randy Bruce: Yes, sir.

There is a long pause.

Boots: Yep. You're missing a spine.

Scene 7

Victoria's Denver office. A telephone is on her desk. Victoria *exhales a cloud of cigarette smoke and puts out her cigarette in an ashtray. The* Geologist *is an upbeat type of person.*

Geologist: You've got an almost endless supply of good, natural water. That's what you need or you can't do anything up there.
Victoria: I wish it were gold rather than water.
Geologist: If you want gold you're going to have to haul it up there yourself.

VICTORIA: Something like that's going to happen. *(Irritated.)* When are we going to get this off the ground! *(Her desk phone rings one short ring. She picks up the phone and listens.)* I'm still talking with the geologist. *(She puts down the phone.)* I have an urgent meeting with my attorney now. *(There is some turmoil outside her office – voices are heard arguing.)* That's not my lawyer. *(To the* GEOLOGIST.*)* Well, you can go.

Just as the GEOLOGIST *walks out of the office,* MELANIE *bursts in.* MS. PAROLE *trails in behind her.*

MELANIE: You've got to take me up there! In your helicopter. Malcolm's in trouble! The dinosaur skeleton's pinned him down.
VICTORIA: *(To* MS. PAROLE.*)* Who is this girl?
MS. PAROLE: She knows Malcolm.
VICTORIA: I'm in a meeting. Who let you in?
MELANIE: It's a matter of life and death.
VICTORIA: *(Taking* MS. PAROLE *aside so* MELANIE *cannot hear them.)* Could that actually be the case?
MS. PAROLE: She's one of his assistants at the site.

VICTORIA *and* MS. PAROLE *return to* MELANIE.

VICTORIA: *(Without any emotion, fake, as if reading from a press release.)* If there's a problem we'll do anything we can do to help within reason. Are you sure that he's actually pinned under the dinosaur skeleton?
MELANIE: Yes, my sister saw it happen.
VICTORIA: The words of sisters can't always be trusted. Is Malcolm conscious?

MELANIE: Yes.

VICTORIA: What did he say to do?

MELANIE: Bringing up a sledgehammer's not going to do it.

VICTORIA: Is that what he said?

MELANIE: I don't know. I wasn't there. "T" said bring one up, even before, ...and my sister said that Ed said that...

VICTORIA: You must do what Malcolm says. He's an extremely intelligent man. What *exactly* did he say to do?

MELANIE: We've got to save him!

VICTORIA: Just a moment. *(Again takes* MS. PAROLE *aside so* MELANIE *cannot hear.)* I'm very busy right now. *(Pause.)* I have nothing personally against Malcolm.

MS. PAROLE: If anything goes wrong with a rescue attempt you may be liable.

VICTORIA: I could be sued for Malcolm's accident in the first place.

MS. PAROLE: No, actually, you can't. I had him sign a release freeing you from all responsibility for his actions up there.

VICTORIA: Huh. I just saw my opinion of you rise right before my eyes.

VICTORIA: *(Returning to* MELANIE.) I've given Malcolm the power to do as he pleases. If the consensus is that he can be freed with a sledgehammer, who am I to oppose?

MELANIE: We need to get there fast. Take me in your helicopter.

VICTORIA: It's impossible to land anywhere near the site.

MELANIE: You did it before.

VICTORIA: I won't place the life of my pilot in jeopardy. Flying in the mountains is risky. Why don't you call the sheriff's office?

MELANIE: I did. But there's a forest fire somewhere and they're busy. Also they told me what I was describing is a payload that a helicopter is not be able to lift.
VICTORIA: See, common sense. Facts. *(Pause.)* Little girl, what makes you think a helicopter stands ready for me at my beck and call, anyway? *(There is a short telephone ring on her phone. She picks up the phone, listens, and then:)* You might as well send him in.

ED *enters.*

MELANIE: You're here?

ED: *(To* MELANIE.*)* "T"'s back up at the site now. Why are you here?
MELANIE: I'm trying to get help.
ED: Any help you can give is up there.
MELANIE: I thought maybe a helicopter...
ED: It would pull hard on the chains and snap them. Malcolm knows that.
MELANIE: They can bring stronger chains.
ED: Your sister's gone to the hardware store. She's on her way up with the hammer.
MELANIE: I've heard that before. *(Pause. To* VICTORIA.*)* I came here in person to plead with you for help.
VICTORIA: It seems there are better uses of your time.
MELANIE: *(To* ED.*)* Ask her. Ask her for the helicopter.
ED: I said what I said. You should go.
MELANIE: (MELANIE, *hurt, starts crying. To* ED.*)* I've been thinking things about you and I've been *so wrong! (Pause.)* I'll call the hospital, they'll bring in a helicopter.

Ms. Parole: You're looking for an aerial tugboat, my dear, not ambulance.
Melanie: Somebody can send a team in by foot!
Ed: *(Forcefully.)* What are you talking about?!
Melanie: *(To* Ed. *Upset with him.)* You!
Victoria: *(To* Melanie.*)* Leave my office this instant. Do we have to call the police to get you out of here?
Melanie: I can't believe this! *(Pause. To* Ed.*)* You think you're real superior with that hat on of yours! I ought to smash it down on your head. Eat straw, you horse with your dumb ponytail!

Melanie *exits, in tears.*

Victoria: Some people just can't follow instructions.

Pause. The "dust settles".

Ed: I have to talk to you. It's important.
Victoria: That's interesting. Something more important than a life or death story that's unfolding as we speak.
Ed: I need to talk to you about the canyon. I didn't tell you before. We need to talk alone.
Victoria: You object to my attorney being present?
Ed: Actually, I do. *(Pause.)* I'd like to make some progress and... you know what they call lawyers.
Victoria: They call lawyers a lot of things.
Ed: Deal-breakers, for one.
Ms. Parole: *(To* Victoria.*)* I advise you that I should stay.

VICTORIA: *(To* ED:*)* I'm not about to make any deal with you now. *(To* MS. PAROLE.*)*
Parole, leave us a moment, will you?
MS. PAROLE: Don't listen to him.
VICTORIA: *(Carefree, to* MS. PAROLE.*)* It'll only take a minute. So, go. (MS. PAROLE *does not go.)* Karen, please, go!
MS. PAROLE: Don't sign anything. Even a verbal agreement can hold up in court.
VICTORIA: Not if no one else hears it. But I'm not going to say anything.

MS. PAROLE *exits reluctantly.*

VICTORIA: *(To* ED: *)* So. You've had your way. I don't really know you. *(Pause.)* Make it short.
ED: There's me. And my tribe. *(Turning away from him, wincing upon hearing the word "tribe".)* Did you say the word, "bribe"?
ED: Let's not be too smart. Good things happen fast, so don't slow things down.
VICTORIA: So what is it about the canyon that you didn't tell me before?
ED: You don't have to worry about Indian claims on the land you want to develop.
VICTORIA: Then you can go right now. I never did worry about that. And anyway, there's no land being developed.
ED: *(Knowing he is being lied to.)* Right. *(Pause.)* We're not looking for much. We'll work with you.
VICTORIA: I suspect there is no tribe. The only tribes I know of are at the whole other end of the state. Some three hundred miles away.
ED: I said, we'll work with you.

VICTORIA: On what?

ED: Future prosperity, let's say.

VICTORIA: (ED's *phrase, "future prosperity", makes her feel playful.*) Oh, in that case, then, I should have my lawyer present.

ED: Bad idea. *(Pause.)* You see by the way I treated that girl that Malcolm and his people are nothing special to me.

VICTORIA: Malcolm's doing useful work that's important to the area.

ED: So now it's not a development, it's an "area". *(Pause.)* You can count on us to be with you.

VICTORIA: There is no "us". Don't say there is.

ED: There *is* always an "us". And that'll cause you trouble, because *us* doesn't go away like you and your friends want it to. *(Pause.)* There's time for you to come around. I'm on no fixed schedule. I cut and twist wire. I set some stones. The jewelry's done when it's done.

VICTORIA: Get a real job, huh? *(Pause.)* Having time on your hands is not always the best thing. It gives you time to do drugs, like half the Indians I know. *(Pause.)* You're still not being upfront with me. Spell it out and then please get out.

ED: My people want some of what was once theirs.

VICTORIA: From sea to shining sea.

ED: No, it's not like that. *(Pause.)* Now, we both know: you've got a sister. She could get in the way. She could go green on all of us. She could hook up with some conservationists and nothing would be built.

VICTORIA: *(Interrupting.)* Oh, you want a cut of the casino profits!

ED: *(Smiling that she said the word, "casino". She does not notice his smile.)* Let me finish. She has mental problems. She can cause us a lot of problems.

VICTORIA: My sister lacks the dedication and charisma to get anything done.
ED: Are you listening to me carefully?
VICTORIA: Are you talking down to me?
ED: Your sister's part owner of the land. The land's not all yours.
VICTORIA: I'm taking care of that. She's not going to be part of the picture much longer.
ED: What, are you going to kill her?
VICTORIA: I don't like you, man. *(Pause.)* I hope you're ready to prepare for my lawyer what you *think* you might be entitled to – to the finest detail. I've put a lot of time and money into the project I have in mind.
ED: One would not want anything to be tied up in court for, say... ever.
VICTORIA: I need to do a background check on you.
ED: We'll leave you alone. Could we agree on a few basics? You might think they're concessions at first, but... then you'll see that they'll lend a touch of authenticity to the "area". We could even agree on a few basics right now. And then... to mark the occasion... we Indians have a custom. We smoke a little tobacco. It's like shaking on it. A handshake that's stronger than a contract. Because law isn't at stake – honor is.
VICTORIA: That's very cultured of you.
ED: That's right. Indians have culture. You have any tobacco?
VICTORIA: I've quit smoking. *(Pause.)* Listen, there's no way I'm going to agree on a "few basics" with you today or any day in the near future. *(Pause.)* I'm afraid we'll have to end our meeting now. I have to get ready for a doctor's appointment. *(She picks up the phone, presses a button, and speaks.)* Have Ms. Parole come back in, please. *(Pause. To* ED.*)* There's nothing – absolutely nothing – that I trust about you.

Gambling Fever

ED: You don't trust anybody. Me, too. We have more things in common than you think.
VICTORIA: I doubt that. *(Pause.)* You're a loner. You have no tribe. Goodbye.
ED: That's what I like about you: you're sure. Unhesitating as you go down.

VICTORIA: I'm not going down.
ED: You are. I know you are. I can feel it.
VICTORIA: Get out of here. Get out of here right now!
ED: We do have to come to an agreement someday. You realize that.
VICTORIA: *(Yelling.)* Extortion! This is extortion! Parole! Parole, get in here!
ED: You won't go down easily, either.
VICTORIA: Get out of here before I call the cops!

ED *leaves.*

VICTORIA: What did I do to deserve this!? I will never have contact with that young man again in my life. Anyone who works for me is to know that he shall never be allowed near me ever again!

MS. PAROLE *comes in.*

MS. PAROLE: What did you say to him?
VICTORIA: I told him to go fly a kite!

ACT II

Scene 1

The next day at the excavation site. MALCOLM *is still trapped under the rock/skeleton. He is looking at a hawk that flies high in the sky.* "T *is close by.*

MALCOLM:
A hawk soars, tipping its wings
High above an abandoned mine –
That mine, a once promising enterprise.

MALCOLM *breathes in. He exhales, looking backward over his shoulder on his left and then on his right.*

"T": Malcolm, don't scare me.

MALCOLM:
What? Men are small to those on high.
A quick glance, and I could be a field mouse.
"T": But you're not. *(Pause.)* You're scaring me, man! *(Pause.)* Malcolm, you and I have talked about this before: it's man's evolutionary gift to have developed Thought. *(Pause.)* Man squanders this gift when he doesn't think, and I mean think *rationally.*
MALCOLM: I rationally don't think there is anyway out of this.
"T": There's another thing that man has that other animals probably don't have and that's the capacity to hope.
MALCOLM: Hope is fine with me. Except from time to time you have to admit that the cards are stacked against you.

"T": A fine scientist you are, Malcolm. You could have the world at your feet with your discoveries. If only you'd have accepted the more normal ways of excavating a skeleton. *(Pause.)* Well, help is on its way. I don't know if what form, but... this will work out! We have such plans.

MALCOLM: *Los asuntos del mundo y sus designios.* The world and its plans.

"T": A team of mules. That's what would work.

MALCOLM: It's too late.

"T": *(Pause.)* We can't let this happen. *(Pause.)* Melanie. That girl worships you!

MALCOLM: I'm getting tired, "T". When you're tired, you're more familiar with ...death.

"T": You're too young to die, you silly coot. *(Pause.)* One person. One person can make a whole lot of difference in the world. You've got contributions to make. *(Pause.)* I know you don't want a heavy footprint around here. I know there could be other specimens here and we could endanger them. But your life's in danger! *(Pointing to rock/skeleton, the tripod and the chain.)* We can split this and lift with the chain.

MALCOLM: No one should worry if I take root in this ditch and I branch and bud to reach the sky.

"T": *(Pause.)* I said, quit scaring me! *(Pause.)* You want some coffee?

MALCOLM: My friend, I'll just rest now.

MALCOLM *almost nods off.*

"T": *(Worried.)* Now, now, Malcolm, don't you go away, now! I'm here next to you. And I'll be here when Melanie shows up with the necessary means to get you out of this mess.
 MALCOLM: No worries, that's not the way it's going to turn out.

"T" *looks at* MALCOLM *not knowing how to respond to what sounds like a prophecy.* MALCOLM *dies.*

"T": Malcolm, speak to me! Don't pass out on me.

"T" *does not want to accept that Malcolm has died. He nudges his body a few times – like a dog would nudge his master's body. He bends down and places his hand against the side of Malcolm's neck and feels no pulse. There is a pause, then* "T" *stands bolt upright, like a sentinel. There is silence.*

Moments elapse. Night falls. Stars come out in the sky. "T" *takes a few steps and picks up a stick from the ground. He lights one end of the stick with a match that he takes out of his pocket. The stick becomes a burning torch.* "T" *holds it up, he stretches out his arm and waves the torch slowly, back and forth, as one would when trying to signal to aircraft flying in the sky. He looks up to the sky for aid. He walks away from Malcolm's body and goes to the highest point near the excavation site. He waves the torch more. There is no help forthcoming.*

The ABORIGINAL CHORUS *enters and at first looks up to the sky. Light shines on them. Actors of the chorus wear masks so as not to be confused with another character or characters they might portray in the play.*

ABORIGINAL CHORUS:
The stars – oh, what a cold night it is. *(Pause.)*
So mighty and majestic, this planet on which we reside.

ONE CHORUS MEMBER: A man like a seed appears in the rock.

ABORIGINAL CHORUS:
Rock... is old, is the grandfather,
Earth is older, is the grandmother.
Who is the oldest? The sky,
The giver of breath and motion.

(Pause.) We are primates, we are humans,
We occupy every continent on earth
As do the protozoa and the simplest forms of life.
Yet we are not simple.
We make everything complex.

What happened to the humans?
There were those from the west.
Living in what they called their Renaissance.
These pale skinned questors sailed the high seas.

Five hundred years ago they arrived in this world.
Truly, it was an awesome event.
They came here and crushed our ancestors' Neolithic ways.
They brought metal and disease.
They brought us uselessness, redundancy, absurdity, slavery.

ABORIGINAL CHORUS: *(Continued.)*
(Pause.) Let the next five hundred years
Be filled with usefulness, responsibility and justice
Or else the planet will die.

(Pause.) Malcolm has died.
Caught by the Grandfather Rock of time.

The ACTOR WHO PLAYS ED *enters and goes over to* "T". *"T" gently hands the burning torch over to him and* THE ED ACTOR *leaves the stage. The sounds of pre-dawn fill the stage. The dawn light begins and the* ABORIGINAL CHORUS *exits.* "T" *stands straight. He stands as sentinel, watching.*

Music. A silvery morning light fills out. Then, lights come up dramatically on the spot where MALCOLM *was trapped under the rock/skeleton. Where Malcolm's head and upper body were last seen there is instead now a slender pine sapling about three or four feet tall.*

"T": He was my friend. He was clever, a genius at times. He was curious. And he tried to hurt no one. *(Pause.)* But...

"T" *wanders away from the pit area. He looks into the distance.* IRENE *enters. She is not near* "T".

IRENE: What a day. *(Pause.)* Hm.

IRENE *looks up at the sky. She looks all around her in wonder.*

IRENE: Wow. So silvery!

IRENE *sees* "T". *He does not see her. She tells herself to be quiet.*

IRENE: No. Shh, shh, shh.

"T" *still does not see her. She feels a "vibration" within her and she says to herself.*

IRENE: Something's changed here. A lot.

A few moments pass. "T" *has been looking around. He sees* IRENE. *He walks towards her. He takes his time.*

"T": Hello there.
IRENE: You don't like me, do you?

Pause. "T" *looks her up and down before he says anything.*

"T": There's been an accident. Malcolm's gone away.
IRENE: What do you mean?
"T": Stones. *(Pause.)* ...Bones. *(Pause.)* What's gonna happen with the iguanodon?
IRENE: *(Pause. Somehow she perceives what has happened.)* Oh.
"T": We're going to miss him a whole lot.

Scene 2

In an expensive restaurant. VICTORIA *and* SCOTT *sit at a table in the smoking section.* SCOTT *studies the menu while* VICTORIA *smokes a cigarette.*

VICTORIA: I feel bad about what happened to you up on the mountain. You're sure you're all right?
SCOTT: Yeah.
VICTORIA: The least I can do is take you to lunch at the best restaurant I know.
SCOTT: Thank you.
VICTORIA: I don't have much time, I'm sorry. *(Pause.)* You got a new laptop, right?
SCOTT: Yeah. They discontinued what I had. So I have something better, actually, now.
VICTORIA: That's "Time" for you! *(Pause.)* It's shocking. I would have never thought. Malcolm's a peaceful person. *(Pause.)* Try the shrimp scampi. It's to die for.
SCOTT: Oh, okay.
VICTORIA: *(Pause.)* I'm getting tired of the waiting.
SCOTT: It's lunchtime. They're busy.
VICTORIA: No, I mean the process of putting everything together for the project in the mountains. You'd think I was building something on the moon.
SCOTT: It must be frustrating.
VICTORIA: State, county, Indians. Enough to drive anybody crazy.
SCOTT: Well, I hope it comes through.
VICTORIA: *(Flustered, angry.)* What, you question whether or not Pine Meadows is going to be built?

Gambling Fever

Scott: It's complicated, isn't it? *(Pause.)* A lot of investment. *(Pause.)* It's a new business. They're always risky. But I'm not the business type, so I shouldn't say anything.

Victoria: It is only me that thinks that younger people in business today have no concept of an older person's *experience*. They're always rushing to prove that they're your equal. So informal. So ready to give advice.

Scott: I'm sorry. I thought you asked me something.

Victoria: I didn't. *(Pause.)* Tell me. What do your parents do?

Scott: My mom teaches school and my father has a car dealership.

Victoria: Wow. They have a lot in common. What brought you to legal work?

Scott: My parents said, "Before you go to law school why don't you work in a law office first and see if you like it."

Victoria: They're very supportive.

Scott: They always say it's important *not* to follow your dream, but to do what you do best. They say that most people follow their dreams and fall flat on their faces.

Victoria: I bet your father didn't grow up thinking he'd become a used car dealer. *(Pause.)* I didn't grow up thinking I'd be the owner of chain of supermarkets. But then again I didn't grow up imagining that my parents would die in a plane crash in Mexico and I would inherit something that I frankly have no interest in.

Scott: When did that happen?

Victoria: When I was about your age.

Scott: So you didn't want to go into the family business?

Victoria: I didn't build it, so it's not really mine. *(Pause.)* But unfortunately, the world is full of envy. People hate me for what I have. They want what I have even though I don't want it. *(Pause.)* People will do all sorts of things to you to cut you

163

VICTORIA: *(Continued.)* down. That's why we have lawyers in this world. *(Pause.)* There are people, for example, who spread rumors that I'm not good at my job. They say that I inherited a business that I'm running into the ground.

SCOTT: From what I know, nothing could be further from the truth.

VICTORIA: The company's privately owned. How would they know anyway? But you see: that's the way people are. *(Pause.)* I shouldn't let it bother me.

SCOTT: Yeah, well, let people talk all they want.

VICTORIA: And sue for slander if they talk in public, huh? *(Pause.)* But I need my good reputation. You need it when you're making a large proposal to the County. When you're *asking* for something. I hate having to crawl to people to ask. That's what you're reduced to: crawling!

SCOTT: Some day you'll have so much money that that will never happen again.

VICTORIA: I hope.

A FAT WAITER, *who appears to be wearing something like a Grim Reaper costume – and who carries a scythe and also a telephone, enters.* VICTORIA *has been too focused on herself to notice the* FAT WAITER's *appearance.*

VICTORIA: At last you can take our order.

FAT WAITER: I think you'll want to take this phone call first.

He hands her the phone. VICTORIA *puts the phone to her ear and listens. Her reaction is one of surprise.*

VICTORIA: What? Malcolm's dead? On my property?

Gambling Fever

VICTORIA *finally notices the* FAT WAITER'*s appearance.*

VICTORIA: *(To* SCOTT.*)* It's not Halloween yet!?
SCOTT: It's in a few weeks.
FAT WAITER: *(To* VICTORIA.*)* There's something else I you should know. *You'll* be following Malcolm.
VICTORIA: What? *(Pause.)* Are you saying...? *(Pause.)* Is this some kind of joke?
FAT WAITER: If existence is a joke, then, yes, this is a kind of a joke.

There are voices, then the sound of a scuffle.

VICTORIA: What's all the commotion?

MELANIE *and* MARIE *burst in. Somehow the* FAT WAITER *has vanished from the scene.*

MELANIE: *(To* VICTORIA.*)* You let him die like a dog!
VICTORIA: What?
MELANIE: You killed Malcolm.
VICTORIA: You're crazy.
MELANIE: He was pinned down. He died.
VICTORIA: I'm so sorry to hear of his passing. Malcolm was a highly dedicated scientist. I respect him – greatly. That's why he had carte blanche up there. He's an amazing example to us all. He couldn't help but be an inspiration to you. Possibly he lent stability to your erratic life. And also to your friend's, as well. *(She means* MARIE.*)*
MELANIE: My sister and I are holding you responsible.

VICTORIA: Oh, are you now? I also have a sister. She's living up on the property. She's the part-owner who's physically closest to where Malcolm was working. Why don't you confront her?

MELANIE: You're guilty of the most heinous crime. "T" knows that I came to you before. That I asked you for help. That you refused to lift a finger!

VICTORIA: Don't try to malign me. *(Pause.)* You girls should run along now. *(Pause.)* And I wouldn't drag that man "T" into this. His character is easily called into question. *(Pause.)* My research has uncovered the fact that for much of his life, "T" was not sober. He was known in the mountains as "Puddles". Yes, that's what my sources tell me.

MELANIE: All you want to do is bring gambling up there.

VICTORIA: There's already gambling in the mountains.

MELANIE: Yeah, Black Hawk and Cripple Creek. But you want to bring it into Coyote Canyon.

MARIE: You killed one of the greatest men alive.

VICTORIA: Oh, the fat girl speaks! How would she know who's great and who isn't? *(Pause.)* Scott, do I have to put up with this?

SCOTT: You can ask the manager to...

MELANIE: *(Interrupting.)* You killed, all for greed.

SCOTT: Let's go.

SCOTT *gets up from the table. He offers* VICTORIA *his hand. She takes it and rises from the table.*

VICTORIA: *(To* MELANIE *and* MARIE.*)* You're destroyed our lunch. I hope you're happy. *(To* SCOTT.*)* I thought I paid your law office so things like this wouldn't happen!

SCOTT: We're not bodyguards. I'm sorry.

VICTORIA: *(To* MELANIE.*)* You'll never come near me again. I'll swear out a restraining order. *(To* SCOTT, *carefully, so* MELANIE *does not hear.)* We'll go to the Petroleum Club for lunch. On Seventeenth Avenue. The thirty-eighth floor. There's no way the likes of her can get up there.

Scene 3

The master bedroom in Randy Bruce's house. RANDY BRUCE, *in a tux, stands in front of a mirror and adjusts his tie.*

RANDY BRUCE: Keep the momentum going. The election is yours! Just get the money. *(Pause. Sure of himself.)* I *relish* these fundraisers. *(Pause.)* But man, it would be nice to have a line of coke! *(Pause.)* Unfortunately, those days are over. Sacrifices have to be made! *(Looks out the bedroom window.)* My wife. Her garden. What an angel she is. She stays out of the way. The garden is her passion. I don't care what she does as long as she can put on an evening dress once in a while and show up when she's needed. *(Pause.)* Hm, that preacher that Boots sent me to is a real nut! What did he say? "Science is not God speaking. Science is perverted by the left wing. Actually, the Devil created a lot of science. The Devil created evolution to hide God's hand in creation." *(Pause.)* We've got some stupid, ignorant people out there. It's unbelievable that we have to give them the time of day.

A MYSTERIOUS MAN, *played by the* "ED" *actor, enters. He is dressed in street clothes.* RANDY BRUCE *has no idea who the* MYSTERIOUS MAN *is.*

RANDY BRUCE: *(Surprised.)* How did you...? *(Pause.)* What are you doing in here?

MYSTERIOUS MAN: You've attracted my attention.

RANDY BRUCE: How could I do that? I'm in my bedroom. *(Pause.)* Who are you?

MYSTERIOUS MAN: A journalist.

RANDY BRUCE: Oh, really?

MYSTERIOUS MAN: I know all about Victoria's project for the mountains. The money's coming from the richest people in the state.

RANDY BRUCE: *(Smugly.)* If you think that's news that people are interested in, you'd better find another job.

MYSTERIOUS MAN: You're on the wrong side.

RANDY BRUCE: Well, I'm probably not on *your* side.

MYSTERIOUS MAN: Is it true that you used cocaine?

RANDY BRUCE: No.

MYSTERIOUS MAN: We know about your womanizing. *(Gesturing out the window, down to where his wife is.)* You have a perfect wife there. That she's able to put up with you so well...

RANDY BRUCE: Leave my wife out of it.

MYSTERIOUS MAN: If you have to drive somewhere and you're drunk, do you get in the car anyway?

RANDY BRUCE: What kind of a question is that?

MYSTERIOUS MAN: Have you ever killed anyone during one of your nights out?

RANDY BRUCE: Absolutely not! Who sent you? You're not a journalist, are you? Boots Brandley sent you. He's checking up on me before he introduces me to his friends. Listen: I've seen the preacher he recommended. I'm doing as I was told.

MYSTERIOUS MAN: Good.

RANDY BRUCE: Within reason, I've been reaching out to the preacher's audience in some of my speeches.

Mysterious Man: Ah, you say, "within reason"! That'll work for some. (*Pause.*) Listen. There's... uh... information that you don't know ... about Victoria Van Epps.

Randy Bruce: What –

Mysterious Man: Life's better for others, or better elsewhere. That's what she thinks. (*Pause.*) Soon she'll be elsewhere.

Randy Bruce: What's that supposed to mean?

Mysterious Man: Don't worry, she'll support you as long as she's able to.

Randy Bruce: So, *she* sent you. Is she nervous that not enough other people are giving money? They are. I'm not going to use up her fortune. She has things to do with it – I'm in agreement with her on that.

Mysterious Man: She didn't send me.

Randy Bruce: You are *not* a journalist – that much is sure. Get out of my house, man.

Mysterious Man: Victoria's going to be switching sides.

Randy Bruce: She'll never switch sides. She's always been a Republican.

Mysterious Man: I'm not talking about that kind of side. (*Pause.*) When she switches, you'll be happy to go and do things without her.

Randy Bruce: I hope you've had your fun. Now I'm calling the police.

Mysterious Man: I *have* had my fun. (*Pause.*) *I* can leave now. Your problem is, you can't. You're stuck here.

The Mysterious Man *leaves.*

Randy Bruce: You have to deal with all sorts of wackos when you're running for office. (*Pause.*) How did he get past my wife?

Scene 4

On the porch in back of the Boot Brandley's ranch. Boots *and* Victoria *look out on the back field.*

Victoria: You don't have to deal with all the little crap like I have to. How do you do it? What's your secret?
Boots: The secret, huh? *(He laughs.)* People are parts. You keep your eye out for good parts. When you get the right ones you assemble your buggy.
Victoria: Easier said than done.
Boots: I know. And the trick is to make the parts come to you – you never chase after anybody.
Victoria: That would be paradise.
Boots: *(Pause.)* Victoria, look for people with a church background. Mormons, if any are around.
Victoria: Right.
Boots: A lot of people use Mormons. Howard Hughes did.
Victoria: They can't all be good parts. But I'm sure they're all anti-communists.
Boots: Anti-communists?
Victoria: I'm just saying that as an example.
Boots: And example for what?
Victoria: People that are for our way of life.
Boots: There aren't a lot of communists that live in Colorado.
Victoria: But there are a lot of environmentalists. *(Pause.)* And you know, I have a real problem if they don't like what I'm doing. Um… Let me think of Mormons and what they can do for me.
Boots: Well, first of all you have to make sure the environmentalists are painted as unpopular.

VICTORIA: They are – for most people. Because they're out of their minds. They want to shut down businesses.

BOOTS: Make sure that normal folks have an instinctual aversion to them.

VICTORIA: *(Pause.)* I believe they do. *(Pause.)* The planet's not going to die in fifty years! They're *intellectuals!* They *think* they know. But really, they stand in the way of economic growth. We need jobs for people.

BOOTS: There it is, if your environmentalists make a fuss, you mobilize people. Or "good parts", as I have said. Have them say, "We need jobs for *people*."

VICTORIA: But there's not going to be a problem. People are going to recognize that what I'm doing is good for the state. Very good for it. *(Long pause.)* I've wanted to ask you for so long, Boots. How did you get so rich?

BOOTS: *(Chuckles.)* What, am I rich? *(Pause.)* Have you ever noticed the beliefs of the Mormons are never really an issue – people don't care what their religion is about. They have high regard for them because of their morals. *(Pause.)* Mormons rarely disappoint.

VICTORIA: You didn't answer my question.

BOOTS: The flu is a problem.

VICTORIA: What?

BOOTS: The winter flu. It's a *problem* and every year it has to be eradicated. You're on top if you're selling the vaccine.

VICTORIA: *(Does not follow him.)* The flu? A vaccine?

BOOTS: Actually you, Vicky, are selling a vaccine. *(Pause.)* It's *jobs*. It's a vaccine against unemployment. It'll make you rich if you build a good buggy and use that buggy to convey all that you need to. But you have to have good parts.

VICTORIA: Don't I?

BOOTS: Randy Bruce.

VICTORIA: Yeah, so?
BOOTS: Randy Bruce is not a Mormon...
VICTORIA: That is most definitely true.
BOOTS: I wouldn't make light of it. Could taint your vaccine.
VICTORIA: You really think so?
BOOTS: I hope not. We'll know before too long.

VICTORIA *sounds almost crestfallen because she respects* BOOTS *and his opinion so much.*

VICTORIA: I know, I know he's not perfect!
BOOTS: I found out that he's on some escort service's client list. I fixed it. He may win but we don't know how effective he can be.
VICTORIA: Everything is so overwhelming! *(Pause.)* I'm not going to elaborate to you.

One of Boots' assistants, TERRY, *comes in.*

TERRY: Sorry, sir.
BOOTS: What is it, Terry?
TERRY: *(Apologetically.)* We need your set of eyes. For just a moment.
BOOTS: Victoria, will you excuse me, please?

VICTORIA *makes a gesture, meaning, "Go ahead".* BOOTS *leaves. Pause.* VICTORIA *waits. She fidgets.*

VICTORIA: I feel so fatigued!

She looks out into the distance, far upstage. What she sees is incredible. MALCOLM *appears. He is with a living dinosaur, an iguanodon. The young iguanodon is two meters tall; it has a collar around its neck and* MALCOLM *walks it, holding the leash.*

VICTORIA: What's... *that?!* (*Pause.*) Something my sister would see.

MALCOLM *and the iguanodon continue to walk and they exit the stage. Just before he exits he says:*

MALCOLM: Most people don't know that some dinosaurs had stripes, like zebras. Some had spots, like leopards.

A small CHORUS OF TOWNSPEOPLE *numbering three, four or five persons, enters. The actors wear masks so as not to be confused with another character or characters they might portray in the play. The* CHORUS *approaches* VICTORIA.

CHORUS OF TOWNSPEOPLE:
There was that fatality in the mountains.
The one for which you were not liable.

VICTORIA: Correct. (*Long pause.*) Who are you?

CHORUS OF TOWNSPEOPLE:
We're townspeople.
Being that, we're interested in terrible things.
In fact, it could be said that we're *obsessed*
By accidents, diseases,
Crime, and shocking injustices.

ONE OF THE TOWNSPEOPLE: Victoria, you need to call your doctor.

VICTORIA: What?

ANOTHER TOWNSPERSON: There's some important news. The tests weren't in your favor.

CHORUS OF TOWNSPEOPLE: Oh well, it's cancer again. Not necessarily a death sentence –

ONE OF THE TOWNSPEOPLE: But it doesn't look good.

VICTORIA: Nothing's getting in my way! I have important things to do!

CHORUS OF TOWNSPEOPLE: *(Thinking. After a considerable pause.)* Shit happens.

VICTORIA: This is like... coming out of the blue.

CHORUS OF TOWNSPEOPLE: Not so. The doctor said there was a possibility. You wouldn't listen.

VICTORIA: How long do I have to live?

Pause.

CHORUS OF TOWNSPEOPLE:
We are townspeople.
We're obsessed by accidents, diseases,
Crime, and shocking injustices.

The CHORUS OF TOWNSPEOPLE *turn its backs on* VICTORIA.

VICTORIA: *(Flustered, dazed.)* Boots Brandley. You have to have "good parts"? *(Pause.)* I'm worried. I don't *want* to worry. I've got to get out of here!

VICTORIA *rushes off the stage.*

Scene 5

A mountain meadow, with a few trees. A half mile from the excavation site. The day is dark and desolate. The wind blows. MELANIE *wanders, distraught.*

MELANIE: Malcolm. Malcolm. You lifted the world up. Others rip it down. There's such... *(Looks for the right words.)* ... a big hole now. *(Pause.)* Everything's over. You were better than all of us!

There is a voice from behind a tree. It is Irene's. IRENE *loosely chants her words. She lightly "marches" in place as she chants. Each line gets four beats to a 4/4 measure. After each of her lines there is a full four beats of silence before she proceeds to her next line.*

IRENE:
She's walking by the stone sides.
Walking by, walking through.
Walking.
Talking it through.
Under the aspen sky.
Stop.

IRENE *stops.* MELANIE *recognizes* IRENE's *voice but she does not let* IRENE *know that she has heard her.*

MELANIE: *(To herself only.)* Irene.

Though IRENE *is positioned – from* MELANIE's *perspective – behind the tree, it has not been her intention to hide. However, now that* IRENE *discovers that someone else is near, her reflex is to take advantage of her position and stay hidden and not say anything.*

MELANIE: *(To herself.)* Where is she?

It does not take long for IRENE *to be curious about a young female's voice.* IRENE *partially comes out from "behind" the tree.* MELANIE *sees her.*

MELANIE: Irene?

IRENE *says nothing.*

MELANIE: Are you okay?
IRENE: *(Following her own train of thought.)* It's not July. Things aren't so easy. The ants don't show off, carrying huge chunks on their backs. The bees don't fly around like they own the place. It's getting cold. Now the field's ready for topaz.
MELANIE: Have you heard anything from your sister?
IRENE: Why would I hear anything from her? *(Pause.)* I've got food, clothing, shelter, and spirit.
MELANIE: *(Pause.)* Don't let her push you around. She's despicable. I know she's your sister, but I don't care.
IRENE: She does a lot of bad things. She'll probably do some good things – by mistake. *(Pause.)* Anyway, we have to channel our anger into the whole love found in Nature.
MELANIE: Right. Don't talk to me about love.

IRENE *takes out a small crystal.*

IRENE: See this crystal? Lie down, I'll show you.

MELANIE: I don't want to see your crystal.

IRENE: Lie down, I'll show you what it can do.

MELANIE: I don't want to lie down. I don't believe in that stuff. Malcolm's dead. And there's other things that are pretty bad that I don't want to talk about. *(She is referring to her rejection by* ED.*)*

IRENE: This crystal and its corresponding planet are two power points. The crystal is grounded, for you, for us, for the world. There are vibrations between it and the planet. *(She points upwards to the planet.)* The vibrations are calming. They bring you to your center.

MELANIE: I don't want to be in my center. The world is a dump.

IRENE: Anger is a bitter root. *(Pause. Continuing to be supportive.)* You should talk to Malcolm.

MELANIE: I have talked to him.

IRENE: That should make you feel better.

MELANIE: No, I still miss him. (MELANIE *starts crying.*) I'm sad.

IRENE: The dead are more available to talk to us about deeper things than the living are.

MELANIE: He didn't have to die!

IRENE: Lie down.

MELANIE: He was not that old. *(Pause.)* No, Irene. Don't get me madder than I already am. It's all such crap. On a massive scale. Everything's being destroyed. On *our* planet – who cares about some planet up there! There's so much shit going on behind our backs. Lies and more lies!

IRENE: Life has its disappointments.

MELANIE: Life should *work*. People should be able to survive. To thrive. *(Pause.)* Ed, man, he blew it. He could do something to stop Victoria but he's taking her side! *(Pause.)* Malcolm liked him. *(Pause.)* It's so horrible.

MELANIE's *heart has been broken by* ED. *She cries more and falls into* IRENE's *arms.*

MELANIE: I don't want to eat. I can't eat. I don't want to have kids. I don't want to go on. If breathing weren't automatic, I'd stop breathing!
IRENE: *(Trying to comfort* MELANIE, *saying to herself:)* I'll try to be like Dorothy has been to me.
MELANIE: *(Crying.)* The world is hard!

Scene 6

In Victoria's hospital room. VICTORIA *is in bed.* MS. PAROLE *stands.*

VICTORIA: No one's to go up to the canyon. Don't go near Irene.
MS. PAROLE: We'll get a hearing soon. The evidence will make it obvious. She'll be pushed to the sidelines. No, she'll be out of the picture.
VICTORIA: *(Pause.)* Things were better when Malcolm was there. *(Pause.)* We may have an unforeseen problem on our hands.
MS. PAROLE: What?
VICTORIA: Are you a complete idiot? The unforeseen problem is that I'm *here!*

Ms. Parole: Right.

Victoria: I can't sleep. There's always this activity going on. Activity that doesn't have anything to do with me. It's supposed to be quiet here. Library quiet. But if this is a library then the books are on whaling, delirium and doom. *(Pause.)* Down the corridor someone was hacking all night long. After three nights, I realized it was me. *(Pause.)* You don't see me in the morning. Nobody ever sees me when I wake up, coughing for years now.

Ms. Parole: Smoker's cough?

Victoria: Yes, you unperceptive little ambulance chaser. *(Pause. With all the strength she can muster.)* It's my fate to build a casino on my property!

Ms. Parole: I know.

Victoria: *(Shaking her head negatively.)* You don't really know. *(Pause.)* Ever since I was a kid, I knew I had something that set me apart, and that there'd be something that I'd accomplish that would turn out be quite extraordinary. All I needed was time.

Ms. Parole: You've done a lot.

Victoria: That's using the past tense. I'm *doing* a lot.

Ms. Parole: You're making good progress with the development.

Victoria: I almost get to sleep and then I hear groaning, coughing, crying, yelling. Even with a private room you still have that damned echo chamber of horrors called the hospital corridor!

Ms. Parole: Stay calm. You're only here because they're trying to get you to stop smoking.

VICTORIA: *(Thoroughly disagreeing with her.)* Right. *(Pause.)* Think about it: if there are people, like me, gasping for air, maybe, just maybe, we've come a little too late to the party where air is being served. *(Pause.)* If my situation were as grave as it might be or *is*, wouldn't you think that they'd just say, smoke to your heart's content, because... it doesn't matter anymore?
MS. PAROLE: They want you to rest.
VICTORIA: They don't understand what it's like to run a business. Or two or three of them. There are decisions to be made that affect the lives of numerous people!
MS. PAROLE: I can imagine.
VICTORIA: I detect, in the tone of your voice, that you are not taking me seriously.
MS. PAROLE: I am.
VICTORIA: You're lying.

DOROTHY *walks in.*

VICTORIA: Hi, Dorothy. *(Pause.)* How'd you find out I was here?
DOROTHY: I called your office. I was wondering actually if Irene was okay up in the mountains. But then... *(Pause.)* Are you all right?
VICTORIA: There is some question about that. *(Pause.)* Who told you you could find me here?
DOROTHY: Um.

VICTORIA *is not fully "with it" at the moment. She cannot find the strength to grill* DOROTHY.

VICTORIA: This is my attorney, Karen Parole.

Ms. Parole *and* Dorothy *look at each other.*

Dorothy: Hi.

Ms. Parole: *(Not comfortable with the interruption.)* I know who she is.

Dorothy: *(To* Victoria.*)* Is there anything I can do for you?

Victoria: You have a worried look on your face. Wipe it off. I appreciate that you have time, as a grad student, to keep track, when you can, of your cousins. Just don't think you're going to get any monetary reward for it.

Dorothy: No, not at all! That doesn't come into it. I respect you. What you've done... I admire your accomplishments! We need to stick together. *Women* like you prove that...

Victoria: *(Interrupting.)* Woah, right there, Dorothy.

Dorothy: I mean, I marvel at the fact that we're related.

Victoria: I would think that your being a feminist means you believe *all* women are related.

Dorothy: Well, not exactly.

Victoria: I don't want to be pursued because I'm a woman. Either by a man or another woman.

Dorothy: Boy, I'll say this: you have a thick skin.

Victoria: Thick but maybe not tough enough.

Dorothy: Oh, it's tough.

Victoria: Yeah, *you* know. *(Pause.)* Well, enough of your accolades. *(Pause.)* Irene's still in the mountains. It's getting colder every day. She doesn't want to come down to Denver. She can't stand the pollution, she says. She refuses to live in Boulder, where more of her ilk like to live.

Dorothy: Boulder would be a good place for her.

VICTORIA: They all wear the same clothes. I can't tell my sister from the rest of them. *(Pause.)* In Boulder, in the state of California, in the country of Peru. *(Facetiously.)* She'd find the unity and the harmony she's looking for. *(Pause.)* Instead, there's complications. Complications all around.
DOROTHY: Complications?
VICTORIA: In a sense, she should be where I am.
DOROTHY: What do you mean?
VICTORIA: In a hospital. But not this kind.
MS. PAROLE: *(Warning her against saying anymore.)* Be careful.
DOROTHY: She's been in a hospital before. It didn't help. I'm not sure I believe in hospitals for…
VICTORIA: Yeah, well, you're an expert, huh? *(Pause.)* I'm concerned about her safety.
MS. PAROLE: It's not safe up there. The summer is one thing. But when the temperature drops, it's a completely different situation. *(Pause.)* You heard about the accident, right?
DOROTHY: Accident?
MS. PAROLE: The accident with Malcolm, with his clothing being caught, and then he slipped.
DOROTHY: Yes, I know.
MS. PAROLE: Normally it might not have been so dangerous, but when you're piling on the layers just to stay warm, they get bulky and in your way.

Pause.

VICTORIA: Dorothy, there *is* one thing you could do for me.
DOROTHY: What?
VICTORIA: Some of the specifics of what you experienced with Irene – could you tell them to Karen?

DOROTHY: Sure.

VICTORIA: You've tried to help. You've been a *companion* to her when no one else has been allowed to get near.

DOROTHY: Well, I've tried my best.

VICTORIA: You've tried your best and everything's failed. *(Pause.)* It would be nice for the family to have a document that outlines your devotion to her while she's been so troubled and she's found it so hard to manage. *(Pause.)* She cannot, she will not remember what you've done. But this way, she'll be able to thank you for it when she's less... (VICTORIA *shoots a look at* MS. PAROLE, *not caring if what she says is dangerous.*)...insane. *(Pause.)* Who knows what's going to happen to me?

DOROTHY: *(Interrupting.)* Don't talk like that.

RANDY BRUCE *rushes in.*

RANDY BRUCE: Victoria, I just heard. I hope nothing's wrong. What's wrong?

VICTORIA: What have you heard?

RANDY BRUCE: That you're here, in the hospital. *(Pause. Pleased that he has found a room full of women. To the others:)* Hello, everyone. *(Pause.)* You're going to be fine, right?

VICTORIA: Well..., yes. *(Pause.)* Randy. There's something wrong with my leg.

RANDY BRUCE: So that's why you're in here? What happened?

VICTORIA: I don't know. I was just walking and all of a sudden my leg snapped.

RANDY BRUCE: You were just walking, and your leg snapped?

VICTORIA: Yeah, Randy, it snapped right off, right after my wing broke. *(Rolling her eyes.)* People are either too stupid or too delicate, or an offensive combination of the two! *(Pause.)* Actually, I'm in here for some tests. It's just some… female thing I don't want to get into. I need to stay overnight tonight, and last night, and the night before. I guess you've been on the campaign trail. Good. *(Pause.)* Are the campaign contributions still flowing?

RANDY BRUCE: Yeah.

VICTORIA: You're not lying? You're not desperate, right? You didn't show up because you're desperate?

MS. PAROLE: Please, Victoria, not in front of…

RANDY BRUCE: *(Nothing to hide.)* We're all right. *(Pause.)* In twenty minutes I have to be at a rally that's nearby. I called your office to tell you that my last meeting with Boots went extremely well. I met with one of his friends, too. It'll really help *you*, down the road.

VICTORIA: Oh, that's curious. And good.

RANDY BRUCE: When your secretary repeatedly said you weren't in, I forced her to tell me where you were.

VICTORIA: You forced her. How did you do that?

RANDY BRUCE: I told her I had friends in the police department and *(Smiling)* she'd better stop hiding you.

VICTORIA: I should fire her.

RANDY BRUCE: She put up a good fight.

VICTORIA: But you know how to win.

RANDY BRUCE: Yes.

VICTORIA: *(Pause.)* I can't believe it. My cousin gets through the door. You get in. No one's supposed to know I'm here!

RANDY BRUCE: *(Intrigued and maybe sexually interested.)* Oh, she's your cousin!

VICTORIA: She's a feminist so it would be tricky, Randy.
DOROTHY: I've seen you on the news.
VICTORIA: *(To* DOROTHY.*)* I hope you're not playing up to him.
DOROTHY: *(She could be lying.)* I'm not.
VICTORIA: Maybe people are wrong about you, Randy. Maybe there is something to you.
RANDY BRUCE: What? Are you listening to the ads that attack me?
VICTORIA: What else is there to do when you're in a hospital with the television, lousy food, no cigarettes, some kind of medication they're giving you but which you never can remember the name of...? *(Pause.)* No, maybe you do have something, Randy. Maybe you do have appeal. Even *sex* appeal. (Pause.) You know what? I'm tired. *(Pause.)* Visiting hours are over. I'm afraid you'll all have to go now.

VICTORIA *smiles with a fake smile and extends her hand to for everybody to shake it.*

VICTORIA: So nice of you to drop by.

Once everyone has adjusted to the abrupt change of Victoria's mood and her present request, they take their turns at shaking her hand.

Scene 7

In the mountains not far from the former excavation site. The ground is covered with snow. "T" has snowshoes strapped to his feet and is wearing winter gear. There is a toboggan, to the left or right of him, not far away. This toboggan is mounted on a platform that is knee-high or more. "T" never looks directly at the toboggan.

"T": Well, it's the end of February. Some while back Randy Bruce won the election. Victoria lived just long enough to see him do it. *(Pause.)* No time was wasted in getting legislation enacted so a gambling resort could be brought to Coyote Canyon. Strangely, days after Victoria died, Irene did too. *(Pause.)* They say deaths come in threes – that's unscientific and idiotic. But, whew! Malcolm, Victoria and Irene. *(Pause.)* Hah! Existence. *La existencia*, as Melanie's family would say. *(Pause. He looks up at the sky.)* Ah, Malcolm. The horizon shakes whenever I still think of you! *(Pause.)*
MALCOLM: *(Offstage.)* Crusty surface here.

MALCOLM enters. He has snowshoes strapped to his feet and is wearing winter gear. He is relaxed. He greets "T".

MALCOLM: Are you all right?
"T": No, I am not. And Melanie is far worse off than me.
MALCOLM: *Sí, muchos años por delante.*
"T": Now, what does that mean?
MALCOLM: She has time ahead of her.
"T": And you didn't exactly sweeten her next years by your dying.

MALCOLM: I hope she'll continue in paleontology. She has a lot of field experience.

"T": You shouldn't have left her.

MALCOLM: You're right. I should have been less demanding on myself and all of you.

"T": No, it wasn't that. It was the *way* you did things. You didn't want machines. So you exited the primitive way. *(Pause.)* If there's anything I can do not to turn that dinosaur skeleton into a trophy, I'll do it! *(Pause.)* A dinosaur is a testament, not the crown jewels of a resort.

MALCOLM:

All that grows the seeds, the plants and animals known and unknown,
All that buries and erodes the rock, the skeleton, the bone.
– We're either standing on it now, or it's overhead.

I cared less about humans, I know.
I was too into my work to realize what it would do
If I disappeared into the expanse of time and left loved ones behind.
I was too occupied by beings lying in calm creases of strata
To understand that my actions could cause so much pain.

"T": Damn, we had a fine excavation going on up here! *(He looks out to where the great front range valley begins.)* Down there… the city, a city filled with the short-sighted backroom deal makers! A group of people – not the biggest and brightest, but certainly the richest – have pulled together a timetable for constructing Pine Meadows Resort and Casino. *(He turns to* MALCOLM.) I'm concerned about Ed. I think he might be a turncoat. I hate to say that, but what he's up to is strange to me!

MALCOLM:
A magpie visited where my body lay.
It paced around me. Walking the outline of a liver.
That was just before the tree grew.

"T": *(Pause. Not understanding at all.)* Well, whatever you say.

MALCOLM:
Ed has his own.
He knows the antelope way.
He walks, but he may also fly.
(Pause.) He creates. *(He laughs softly.)*
Could it be that *I'm* his creation?

"T": Boy, you've lost me!

"T" *raises his eyebrows, looks at* MALCOLM *sideways.*

"T": Malcolm, you had such gifts. Gifts that barely got used!
MALCOLM: But they were used. *(Looking skyward.)* They were tested for strength under the open sky.

Pause. A dull roar is heard. "T" *takes notice.*

"T": Holy tumbling powder!

"T" *studies an avalanche as it makes it way down the side of a mountain.*

"T": Look at that!

The sound continues and "T" continues to gaze at the avalanche. Pause. VICTORIA, *in ski clothes, enters, goes to the toboggan and stands on it, towards the head of it. She could just as well be "surfing" on a big, long snowboard.* "T" *never looks at the toboggan and* VICTORIA.

"T": Why, there's something peculiar. *(Pause.)* Look there! *(He points straight ahead, towards the audience – not in* VICTORIA's *direction.)* Victoria's riding down the avalanche… standing on a *toboggan!* Or else I've gone snow blind.
VICTORIA: *(Pause.)* Life has betrayed me. I could have been a Henry Ford, an Andrew Carnegie, a John D. Rockefeller. But I've had to deal with things they never had to: government regulations, not to mention envious people always trying to stab me in the back.

IRENE, *in ski clothes, enters and walks over to the toboggan. She steps up on it, and stands in back of* VICTORIA. *She has a gemstone in her hand.*

IRENE: Hold this quartz: chalcedony as white as snow. It'll steady you.

IRENE *holds out her hand, palm up, with the gemstone in it, in front of her. Her hand is stationary.* IRENE *does not move it towards* VICTORIA. VICTORIA *rolls her eyes upon hearing* IRENE's *words, "It'll steady you."* VICTORIA *and* IRENE *then both stand motionless, looking forward into the distance.*

"T": Two relatives on the outs with each other in life. Sisters again in death. *(Pause.)* It was here, in this canyon, eleven years ago. I was looking at the layers of time displayed sideways. I was drunk – I was still drinking in those days. Deer tracks, elk, and dinosaur tracks were all jumbled up in my mind. *(Pause.)* The oddness of this reminds me of what I saw back then eleven years ago: a big horn sheep – you know how they don't approach humans – come up to me. Sniffed me. Baahed at me, then spat at me. *(Pause.)* I looked into the far away red and gray of the Morrison stone and I knew what that sheep was saying to me: stop drinking. *(Pause.)* And so I did. *(Pause.)* Seeing *this* sight, I don't know *what* message there is. Or if there is a message at all. (*He shivers.*) One thing's for sure though: I'm getting cold. And the air is not exactly full of oxygen.

MALCOLM: Cold. *(Pause.)* The cold and the thin air. The brittle surface and what lies beneath.

"T": Well, *I* don't want to lie beneath. Not yet.

MALCOLM *raises one snow-shoed foot up and sets it down.*

MALCOLM: We break the surface.

"T": And you know what happens if it ain't done carefully.

Scene 8

A huge construction site has swallowed up a large area, including the former excavation site. Sounds of backhoes digging, earth-moving vehicles backing up, trap doors of trucks slamming shut. A large building crane is seen in the distance. Workers walk around wearing yellow hardhats. The actors playing the workers wear masks or disguises so as not to be confused with other characters that they might have portrayed in the play.

MIDDLEBURG, OUTERMAN, GRUMBLER, *and* BITTERMARCH, *all in hard hats, sit in a circle on benches or chairs. They are on a break. They play poker. Each looks at his own hand of cards. The "pot" of money is in the center of the circle.* MIDDLEBURG *deals the cards this round.*

MIDDLEBURG: Rumors are just that. Irene Van Epps was an unbalanced person. She took her own life. Nobody pushed her to her death. *(Pause.)* It's steep. It's dangerous. *(He puts a quarter dollar into the pot.)*
OUTERMAN: I guess we'll never know, will we? *(He also puts a quarter into the pot.)*
MIDDLEBURG: By saying that, you're leaving to door open to her having been pushed.
OUTERMAN: You can say whatever you want.
GRUMBLER: *(Putting a quarter in the pot.)* I'm in.
BITTERMARCH: *(Putting two quarters in the pot.)* I'll raise you fifty cents.
MIDDLEBURG: *(Putting two quarters in the pot.)* Okay.
OUTERMAN: *(He studies his hand of cards, then:)* I fold. *(He puts down his cards.)*

MIDDLEBURG: If they succeed in getting people to come they'll make billions.
GRUMBLER: I call. *(He puts two quarters in the pot.)*
BITTERMARCH: You know, one million is a lot in and of itself. Then you think about *two* million. Now, that's not just one million and two dollars, that's one million plus another 'nother whole million.
OUTERMAN: What's your point?
BITTERMARCH: A billion is an astronomical amount. It's obscene. People shouldn't have that kind of money when we get what we do. *(Pause.)* I call. *(He puts two quarters in the pot.)*
MIDDLEBURG: Well, the owners do have to pay a lot of people back.
OUTERMAN: They have to pay themselves back.

MIDDLEBURG *discards three cards,* GRUMBLER *and* BITTERMARCH *each discard two cards.* MIDDLEBURG *deals them each two new cards and three new cards to himself.*

MIDDLEBURG: They pay us, too. Without them...well,... *(Pause.)* We *need* them.

BOOTS *enters and stays to the side of the stage. He gazes over the area around him and listens to the card players as well.*

GRUMBLER: They say Pine Meadows is going to make money for everybody. Whether you're working in construction, or in the hotel or the casino, or even if you're gambling in the casino. *(Sarcastically.)* A win-win situation, ha! *(Pause.)* But somebody's going to have to *lose* money in order for the rest to make it.

BITTERMARCH: Why are places like this always out in the middle of nowhere? It may be convenient for the rich but it's not for me. Working people are always at a poker table whether they want to be or not. They're cajoled into a game where a lot of them are going to have no choice but to *fold*.
MIDDLEBURG: Are you folding?
GRUMBLER: No, I'm in. *(He puts a quarter into the pot.)*
MIDDLEBURG: You either have confidence in the world, or you don't. If you don't, you're never going to go anywhere.
GRUMBLER: You're not addressing the problem. We get sucked into things. There is no alternative.

BITTERMARCH *puts a quarter into the pot.* MIDDLEBURG *puts a quarter in.*

MIDDLEBURG: Life isn't always fair. Better get used to it.
BITTERMARCH: That doesn't mean it has to be brutal.
MIDDLEBURG: Okay, boys, let's see your hands.

MIDDLEBURG, GRUMBLER *and* BITTERMARCH *reveal their hands.* MIDDLEBURG *looks at the cards.*

MIDDLEBURG: The highest hand is Two Pair. *(To* BITTERMARCH.*)* You just squeezed by.
BOOTS: Bittermarch, come over here.

BITTERMARCH *scoops up the money in the pot, puts it in his pocket, and goes over to* BOOTS.

BITTERMARCH: Yes, sir?

Boots: You should reconsider what you said, friend.
Bittermarch: What?
Boots: You say we're out in the middle of nowhere here. This will be *somewhere* soon. Don't you recognize that?
Bittermarch: My family lives down the mountain, sir, where most people live – in town. About an hour and a half away. I miss them. I can't go home every night.
Boots: I'm a family man, so I understand you. But this place has promise. Cities subtract ten years from a person's life because of all the stress. Here we have a pristine environment. People have elbowroom. They *need* that.
Bittermarch: I can't move my family up here 'cause it's too expensive.
Boots: You'll work it out some way I'm sure. It's going to be extraordinary here.
Bittermarch: Well, I'm just ordinary, so...
Boots: Even if you are only here for a short while you will not fail to benefit from it. You're benefitting from it right now.
Bittermarch: That, I am, sir.
Boots: All the luxuries! You can have a Jacuzzi at any temperature you want. A sauna. A gym.
Bittermarch: *(Bitterly.)* You're right.

Ed *enters. He walks over to* Boots *and* Bittermarch. Ed *looks* Bittermarch *up and down.* Ed *hisses like a snake at* Bittermarch *to scare him away.*

Ed: Hssss –

Bittermarch *leaves and rejoins the other poker players. They will continue playing poker silently. It is* Outerman's *turn to deal.*

ED: *(Looking at the vast construction site.)* Well, I've never seen such a big hole in my life.
BOOTS: You don't make underground parking lot for three thousand cars by making a small hole.
ED: I thought you were going to bring customers up here by bus.
BOOTS: We are. But ... there are those who are attached to their automobiles. Eventually there'll be a monorail, directly from Denver.
ED: You're going to be able to make all that happen?
BOOTS: People will come. In droves.
ED: *(Pause.)* It's their destiny.
BOOTS: I couldn't have put it better myself. *(He smiles.)*

MELANIE *enters and stays at the side of the stage.*

MELANIE: Ah, me!

ED *is not pleased to hear her voice.*

ED: What?
MELANIE: *(Pained, enraged.)* No!
BOOTS: *(Pointing in the opposite direction from* MELANIE.*)* The monorail station will be over there.
ED: *(To* MELANIE.*)* Get out of here!
BOOTS: Who is she?
ED: She was an assistant on the dinosaur excavation.
BOOTS: This is private property, young lady.

MELANIE: *(Like a nursery tale, as in, "Once upon a time.")* One day, something went wrong. Was wrong. Became wrong. Not that, *one day* everything was good, had been good, was always good. *(She refers to recent events on the mountain.)* This was bad. It *is* bad. When things look like this, you have a perfect example of "bad". With things like this, you know there are repeat offenders, that things are *staying* bad, they're *not* getting better. *(She approaches* BOOTS.*)* You and your friends are only out for yourselves! When that's happening, the final result's always *bad*. *(Pause.)* Has everybody forgotten about right and wrong? Is there just money now? *(Pause.)* Is it just that... if there's enough *money* in it, it's okay, or not just even okay, but... *great!?* Or maybe even – and this is what sickens me the most — it's *worthy* of our *respect!*

Pause. MIDDLEBURG *puts down his poker cards and walks towards* MELANIE, ED *and* BOOTS.

MELANIE: I don't respect this, or you. *(Pause.)* There are people with a conscience. But they don't have a voice.
MIDDLEBURG: Listen, girl. We're building here. If you don't love this place then leave it.
MELANIE: I love it and that's why I'm *staying*. If I don't stay and fight, then there will be nothing left to fight for. *(Pause.)* Woe to the planet! Woe to you! A dark night falls. Another conspiracy congeals.

Boots: Miss, I appreciate your concern. Now, *some* people – not all – are out for themselves. That's not us. We care about the community. We are the community. You are, too. Don't overreact and reject it. There are no conspiracies. *(He smiles. Pause. He shakes his head negatively.)* Conspiracies – don't happen. They don't happen because there will always be someone with a loud mouth who reveals whatever thing is being planned.

Melanie: I'm not going to be silent. You're not only gaming our society, you're gaming the planet! You're liars and cheaters, and you're *murderers*, too. People, animals, the environment, they're all dying here.

Ed: You need to leave now.

Melanie: *(Angry. To* Ed.*)* You!

Ed: *(Under his breath, to* Melanie.*)* I'm not through with him *(He means* Boots.*)* yet.

No one hears what Ed *has said.*

Melanie: *(Continuing to be angry towards* Ed.*)* You! *(Pause. To everyone.)* Murderers! Malcolm and Irene!

Ed: You know what happened to Malcolm.

Melanie: *(Distressed.)* I don't have any money. Nobody represents me, or people like me. *I* represent me...

Middleburg *whistles to* Outerman. *He and* Outerman *get up and go towards* Melanie.

Melanie: ...and I'm here. Try to get rid of me!

MIDDLEBURG *and* OUTERMAN *get closer to* MELANIE. BOOTS *commands them.*

BOOTS: Take her away from here.

MIDDLEBURG *and* OUTERMAN *put their hands on her.*

MELANIE: *(Loudly.)* All I want to do is stay alive to avenge your crimes. You wait, *one* day, the people will accept that vengeance must be. It must be. Vengeance must be!

MIDDLEBURG *and* OUTERMAN *haul her offstage. Pause.* BOOTS *gazes over the area. There is another pause.*

ED: *(Solemnly.)* She's crazy.

Pause.

BOOTS: No, she's just not experienced enough in the world.

Another pause. The incessant noise from the construction site continues.

NEITHER GOD NOR MASTER

a play with songs

Neither God Nor Master is dominated by the figure of Del. His character is like a fountain of hatred, vile intentions, intolerance, and self-destruction. He is in conflict with his sister, whom he mistreats and threatens, with the Chinese businessman the sister likes, and even with his own body as represented by the character Bloodstream. Because he is so filled with hate and is unable to get the satisfaction of having Sidney Chong murdered or sent to jail on a false charge of rape, he pursues a course of life in which he stays in his room and drinks. Given the atmosphere of Chicago in the twenties, it is clear that if he had the money he could hire Salvatore Clementi (whose radio shop is a front for his murderous activities) to kill Chong. He explains the need to kill Chong to Sal by saying "we've got to hold onto this country." Sal, of course, has suffered from the contempt people express for Italians and answers sarcastically, "Yeah, protect it from wops, chinks, niggers and the rest of the garbage."

Del's intolerance naturally extends to the women who want to improve the circumstance of their lives and who have recently won the right to vote. When his sister tells him of the poor working conditions of her friends in a factory which is causing them to develop arthritis, he doesn't care and doesn't want to hear about it. He wants to force his divorced sister to go back to her former husband and not mix with the likes of Sidney Chong. Del is quite ready to use seductive charm on the weak figure of Reba to make her tell the police she knows that the man had raped Del's sister. The sister and a chorus of women sing a song expressing their need for tolerance and freedom. But society is not willing to grant them these rights. In the figure of Del we see the people who want to enforce the status quo, who want to keep women in their place, send foreigners back to their "flea-infested dumps," and who, like him, are red-blooded Americans. This is Chicago 1923, nearly a hundred years ago, yet we can still hear such views expressed on television, radio, and in newspapers. However, in the play there is hope as the women in the last scene sing *Bold City on the Plain*, concluding with defiant repetition of "no, no, no" to submission of "tyrants" who would lead them "into pain." The women in the play reveal Tait's sympathy for their struggle to be something, to find love which is returned, to have respect and, perhaps more importantly, to have self-respect.

The songs sung throughout the play are some of the many non-realistic elements which give it great dramatic vitality. Two characters especially set the play apart from a realistic, well-made play. The clown acts as narrator, singer, and stage manager. He is not a circus clown, but a figure from the Chinese theatre who is traditionally allowed to speak to the audience. Bloodstream is present when Del is onstage, appropriately dressed in red and wearing red make-up. The music, the sound effects, and the swiftly changing locations without realistic scenery create a world ranging from a dirty bedroom to a street scene with a puppet show being performed. In it, too, there is violence and fighting. With so much anger and hatred poisoning his system, Del causes his own self-destruction and the departure of his Bloodstream from the stage. We agree with Bloodstream who tells him "You had blood, but you didn't have much of a heart."

– Y. S.

Some performers will still have questions about the exact nature of the Clown even after a close re-reading of the play. For one thing, they might wonder what kind of costume he wears. When I played the clown in a staged reading of Neither God Nor Master I was dressed as a rustic person. Under the bluejean bib-overalls, I wore a tan tee shirt. On my head I had a white bandana (with paisley line-design in black). Two points of the folded bandana stuck up in the air after it was fixed on my head. It looked like a crazy crown. It got the right idea across.

– L. T.

NEITHER GOD NOR MASTER

Characters

CLOWN	*male, 20s to 50s.*
DEL	*male, 20s.*
BLOODSTREAM	*male, 20s to 50s.*
LYNETTE	*female, late 20s to early 30s.*
SIDNEY	*male, late 30s to late 40s, Chinese.*
REBA	*female, 20s.*
SAL	*male, 20s to 40s, Italian.*

Minor Characters (to be doubled):

YOUNG WIDOW, PREGNANT WOMAN, ELIZABETH, FIRST POLICEMAN, SECOND POLICEMAN, BEGGAR, FIRST MAN, SECOND MAN, THIRD MAN, OLDER BOY, YOUNGER BOY, *the* BARKER, GIRL, *the voice of the* DOCTOR, *the voice of the* WIFE, *the voice of the* HUSBAND.

The complete cast requirements can be fulfilled by eight men and four women.

Actors playing the minor roles will comprise the CHORUS. *The* CHORUS *will include a* YOUNG WIDOW, *dressed in black, wearing a veil; the* CHORUS *should also include a* PREGNANT WOMAN.

Suggested role combinations for the minor roles are:

FEMALE ROLES #1: YOUNG WIDOW; GIRL
FEMALE ROLES #2: PREGNANT WOMAN; ELIZABETH; *voice of the* WIFE
MALE ROLES #1: FIRST POLICEMAN; FIRST MAN; OLDER BOY; *voice of the* DOCTOR
MALE ROLES #2: BEGGAR; SECOND POLICEMAN; SECOND MAN; *the* BARKER
MALE ROLES #3: THIRD MAN; YOUNGER BOY; *voice of the* HUSBAND

The actors playing SAL, *and* REBA, *can be in the* CHORUS *but they will be disguised so that they are not understood to be* SAL *and* REBA *that moment. Likewise with any other actors who are playing one of the major roles, but who have been "drafted" into the* CHORUS *to increase its size. One important stipulation: the actor who plays* DEL *is never in the* CHORUS.

Place: Chicago; the Bronx.

Time: 1923.

Songs in the play:

#1 Bold City On The Plain, Part I, CHORUS, *Prologue*.
#2 Eric's Products, CHORUS, *Scene 3*.
#3 The Coolie and His Hammer, CLOWN *and* BLOODSTREAM, *Scene 3*.
#4 The Bourgeois State, CLOWN, *Scene 4*.
#5 Don't Wake Me Up Tomorrow Morning, CLOWN *and* CHORUS, *Scene 4*.
#6 A Nice Silhouette, CLOWN *and* CHORUS, *Scene 7*.
#7 I've Always Seen It That Way, CHORUS (FEMALES ONLY), *Scene 8*.
#8 Justice, BEGGAR *and* CHORUS, *Scene 8*.
#9 Bold City On The Plain, Part II, CHORUS, *Scene 11*.
#10 Sadder Things, REBA, *Scene 12*.
#11 Plenty, CLOWN, *Scene 13*.
#12 The Sun Shined at Six P.M., CLOWN *and* CHORUS, *Scene 13*.
#13 I've Always Seen It That Way (Reprise), CHORUS (FEMALES ONLY), *Epilogue*.
#14 Bold City On The Plain, Part III, CHORUS, *Epilogue*.

NEITHER GOD NOR MASTER

Prologue

A cot is to one side of the stage. A jumble of clothes is on the floor near the bed, as well as some empty beer and liquor bottles and some papers. DEL *sits on the cot with his feet on the floor. He is disheveled. His* BLOODSTREAM *stands next to him. The* BLOODSTREAM's *skin color is red (this includes his face.) He is dressed in red. The* CHORUS *is present. The actors who play* LYNETTE, SIDNEY, SAL *and* REBA, *are not in the* CHORUS.

Song #1: Bold City On The Plain, Part I

CHORUS: *(Sings.)*
 Bold city on the plain, we struggle in our
 Hunger for the wonder, but we're encumbered by these chains.
 Bold city on the plain, our days of joy are
 Deferred, we're just a herd led by tyrants into pain.

 For sale at the market by sellers who own us and the land.
 What kind of chance do we really stand?
 We're just numbers they've given us –
 We're slaves, they're the masters, they shit on us.

CHORUS: *(Singing. Continued.)*
> Bold city on the plain, we struggle in our
> Hunger for the wonder, but we're encumbered by these chains.
> Bold city on the plain, our days of joy are
> Deferred, we're just a herd led by tyrants into pain.

The CLOWN walks in. He puts a stop to the song.

CLOWN: *(To the CHORUS and to the audience.)* No. No more of that. You're free people. You're not slaves. *(Pause.)* I've got nothing against singing. Quite the contrary. *(Pause.)* I have an announcement to make. We're going to do something different to start things out.

Pause. The CHORUS looks at him quizzically as he continues.

CLOWN: *(To the CHORUS and to the audience.)* We're living. Breathing. – You know that. *(To the audience only.)* You're living and breathing yourselves. If you're not, then you're a dead audience and I'm in for a tough time. *(Pause.)* All right. In honor of living and breathing, let's bring the rest of the others out here now.

LYNETTE, SIDNEY, *and* SAL *enter.*

CLOWN: Now, get in a group. Form a circle.

LYNETTE, SIDNEY, *and* SAL *join the* CHORUS *and they stand in a loose circle. The* BLOODSTREAM *joins them as well. The* CLOWN *then makes sure that they walk in towards the center to form a tighter circle. All the actors are shoulder-to-shoulder, except* DEL. *The* CLOWN *says to the group:*

CLOWN: Now breathe in.

They all breathe in.

CLOWN: Yeah, expand those lungs. Isn't this better than the dreary way things first got started that song? *(He looks over at the* BLOODSTREAM.*)* Del's bloodstream likes it. He gets his oxygen and he's bright and red and feels as rich as a billionaire. Isn't that right, Bloodstream?
BLOODSTREAM: *(Dizzy, he agrees.)* Whoa. A-huh.
CLOWN: Now, breathe out and step away from the center.

The CLOWN *gestures and the actors move away from each other as they breathe out and occupy roughly the same spots they were in before they tightened the circle.*

CLOWN: That's the way. Now, having pushed out from the center we've established ourselves as Individuals again. Individuals founded this country and our city, Chicago.

DEL *comes forward.*

DEL: I have an announcement to make. *(To the* CLOWN.*)* You're pretentious. *(To the audience.)* What's he talking about!? Control freak!

CLOWN: I have an announcement to make. There will be no farting in this play.

DEL: Yeah, that's real funny.

CLOWN: Del, we're only balancing ourselves before we're thrown off balance... by *you*.

DEL: *(To the audience.)* He's a clown. Don't ever forget it. Don't let him fool you into thinking he's serious.

CLOWN: You, more than I, treat everything like it's one big joke.

LYNETTE: *(To the audience.)* May I have your attention, please? My brother *(She points to* DEL.*)* doesn't want me to have anything to do with *(She points to* SIDNEY.*)* Sidney Chong.

DEL: *(Pause.)* Sis, you're a slut. A slut!

CLOWN: *(To* DEL, *sarcastically.)* You seem hurt.

DEL: Shut up.

LYNETTE: *(To* DEL.*)* Though I love you, you do not have any say over whom I can or cannot see. It's 1923. Women can vote. Finally. (Pause.) We have our leaders. We have those who educate the masses. We are strong in our conviction that anarchism is the answer to exploitation and social inequality.

CLOWN: *(Mocking.)* Social inequality?

LYNETTE: The writings of Emma Goldman and others inspire us to reject despair. Goodman believes, as I do, that anarchism is close to human nature and cannot easily be dismissed by its critics.

DEL: Spare me!

LYNETTE: Indeed, only anarchism will enable humanity to avoid the dead end it's headed for.

BLOODSTREAM: *(Drunk on oxygen.)* Wow, watch her go!

LYNETTE: What is anarchism? It's about sane living. It's about regeneration – through freedom.

DEL: Rah, rah, rah. Let's give her a big hand! *(He claps his hands a few times, then sarcastically:)* And while we're at it, let's give Emma Goldman one, too – wherever she is. *(With relish.)* In jail. *(Pause.)* You know where my sister reads all this crap? In *Mother Earth*. A rag you'd swear was published a hundred years from now. Hah!

The CLOWN *can't resist goading* DEL.

CLOWN: Hey, Del, don't be bashful. Look at Sidney Chong real good. *(Taunting him.)* Your *buddy*. *(Now he refers to* LYNETTE *and* SIDNEY:*)* He and your sister met last year. On the street. He seemed lost and she asked him if he needed directions. Reluctantly, he said yes. *(Taunting* DEL.*)* How many months has it been now?
DEL: *(To the* CLOWN.*)* Shut your face.
SIDNEY: *(Politely, to the audience.)* If you'd excuse me, I'll only take your attention for just a moment. I'm Sidney Chong. I'm a Christian. I mean no one any harm.
DEL: The Chinks, they're taking over our country!
LYNETTE: You're wrong and you're rude. I feel sorry for you.
DEL: *(To* SIDNEY.*)* This is Chicago, not China. You got that, man?
SIDNEY: I understand.
DEL: Don't fob me off with "I understand". You *don't* understand. You still remember the time when you got to this country and someone charged you a dollar for a loaf of bread and you paid it. *Because you don't understand!*
LYNETTE: People of many races try to succeed in Chicago. It's *not* easy. *(To* DEL, *accusingly.)* I wish the situation were better.
CLOWN: Circumstances could always be better.
DEL: In this cesspool of a town?

CLOWN: *(Scolding* DEL.*)* Now, now. I think your assessment might be jaded. Prematurely, since you are so young. It may also be affected by your work. One of your jobs is that you work as a doorman at the Subway Café, correct?
DEL: Yes.
CLOWN: You charge a cover charge.
DEL: Yes.
CLOWN: There is no cover charge to get into the Subway Café. You don't have to pay to get in there. *(Pause.)* This is no doorman.
DEL: Out-of-towners don't know that. *(Whispering to someone close by in the audience.)* You want anything, you tell me. I can get it for you. *(He winks.)* For a price.
CLOWN: *(To everyone except* DEL.*)* Come on. It's time to begin.

All the actors except DEL *and the* BLOODSTREAM *start to walk off the stage but they stop when* DEL *says:*

DEL: Wait a second? What's going on here?
CLOWN: Yes. *(He picks* LYNETTE *out of the crowd and says to them:)* Please come with me.

MEMBERS OF THE CHORUS *and* SAL *leave.*

Scene 1

Del's *room. A quiet soundscape fades up. This soundscape consists of an eerie electronic hum and, from time to time, sounds of short-circuiting electrically charged wires and contacts. This soundscape will be heard again in other scenes of the play.*

Del, Lynette, *the* Clown *and the* Bloodstream *are present.*

Del: Lynette, what have you done? You've rearranged my room. My bed was over there. *(He points to another spot in the room.)*
Lynette: I didn't change a thing.
Clown: She didn't change a thing.

The Clown *exits.*

Del: I won't be able to find anything.
Lynette: You don't have much.
Del: *(Thinking.)* Now, yesterday, Friday, when you came by...
Lynette: Today's Sunday, Del. You need to stop drinking. You're not in control. For example, I'm not actually here. And that's why I'm going, too. I'll see you later.

Lynette *slips away, exiting the stage.*

Del: What's this pile of garbage?

He kicks a pile of clothes and some bottles papers that are on the floor.

Del: I'm counting on Sal.

BLOODSTREAM: Sal, who?
DEL: The guy that runs the "radio repair shop".
BLOODSTREAM: Oh, him. He runs a respectable business.
DEL: A respectable business as a *front*.
BLOODSTREAM: Whatever you say.
DEL: Don't try to play dumb. He'll take care of the Chinaman.
BLOODSTREAM: *(Pause. He thinks, then.)* Radios are dangerous. All that electricity. Gives you cancer.
DEL: Yeah, wireless, the new thing. *(Pause.)* Don't I have a drink around here somewhere?
BLOODSTREAM: Attitudes aren't usually improved by drinking.
DEL: You're right, Miss Sunday School Teacher. I'm going to give up drinking.
BLOODSTREAM: No worries. Your self-discipline will pass.

DEL *approaches the* BLOODSTREAM *and grabs him by the neck and threatens him.*

DEL: Just mind your own business, huh?
BLOODSTREAM: Thank God, I'm not your liver.
DEL: Shut up! Nobody asked you.
BLOODSTREAM: Maybe they should.
DEL: Cut it!

DEL *releases the* BLOODSTREAM. *He kicks some papers on the floor around.*

DEL: Where's a racing form? I need to make a bet.
BLOODSTREAM: You don't have any money to bet on horses.
DEL: No lip!

He punches the Bloodstream *in the gut.*

Del: We've got to stop the Chinaman. They made the Exclusion Act. But still they keep coming. It didn't help.

The Bloodstream, *holds his stomach and aches from being punched.*

Bloodstream: You shouldn't have pursued a friendship with him if you don't like his kind.

Del: I never was his friend. He glommed onto my sister. I was forced to know him. *(Pause.)* It's time to nail Sidney Chong to a big yellow cross. And we'll make that cross with lumber from his own mill…

Bloodstream: Why do you want to crucify him?

Del: Punishment for my sister.

Bloodstream: Lynette has a life of her own. And she's older than you.

Del: I'm still the man. *(Pause.)* Who ever heard of a Chinaman with his own lumber company? But he's building his business empire and the Chinese need wood like anybody else.

Bloodstream: He called you a rooster, didn't he?

Del: What?

Bloodstream: Not to your face. Mr. Chong mentioned it to your sister. Something to do with their form of astrology, I believe.

There is a knock on the door. Del *does not answer it. There is another knock.*

Del: What do you want?

REBA: *(Outside the door.)* It's me, Reba.
DEL: *(Far from overjoyed.)* Oh.
REBA: *(Concerned.)* How are you doing, Del?
DEL: I'm meeting with a panel of experts. They're arguing that a cat has nine lives, and I say nine less, if take off their whiskers.
REBA: Can I come in?
DEL: Well, yeah, sure.

REBA enters. The BLOODSTREAM is invisible to her.

REBA: I've missed ya. It's been real busy at the factory.

There is no response from DEL.

REBA: Some of the girls swear they're getting arthritis because of the machines.

Still no response from DEL.

BLOODSTREAM: *(Pause.)* Del, you could say something. She's such a sweet girl.
DEL: *(To the BLOODSTREAM only.)* She's all yours, you like her so much.
REBA: You're not feeling good, are ya, Del? I could bring you something to eat.
DEL: I'm okay.
REBA: Let's go for a walk along the lake. You up for that?
DEL: No.
REBA: I don't want to go. But I guess I'd better.

DEL *does not respond.*

REBA: I don't want to go and leave you here. You need to get out.
DEL: Button it!
REBA: Please, Del.
DEL: Go where? To the Fireman's Ball? It's not January, is it?
REBA: *(Anxious, hurt and confused.)* No, it's not January.

DEL *toys with her and is sarcastic.*

DEL: But wouldn't you like to go to the Fireman's Ball?
REBA: *(Pained.)* I don't know what you're talking about!
DEL: But you'd like to go, wouldn't you?
REBA: *(Acquiescing.)* Sure, Del.
DEL: *(Mocking.)* Somebody's got to put out the fires and they need our support.
REBA: Oh, Del!

REBA, *upset, almost breaks into tears. She runs out.*

BLOODSTREAM: You have a lovely way with women.
DEL: *(To the* BLOODSTREAM.) Do you do anything useful, like wash shirts?
BLOODSTREAM: I'm afraid if I did, they'd all turn out red.
DEL: Communists are red. You and them are parasites!

The BLOODSTREAM *does not know what to say. The soundscape fades to silence.*

Scene 2

In Sidney Chong's office. Sidney *sits at his desk.* Lynette *sits across from him. The office door is open so that if anyone were to come in, they could see that the two are only talking.*

Sidney: When you grow up not speaking English, you're in a classroom for the rest of your life.
Lynette: We should always keep learning.
Sidney: There's a certain amount of poignancy in learning.
Lynette: There's happiness in it.
Sidney: You discover things. But there's only so much you can do with what you learn.
Lynette: You can do so many things. Almost anything.
Sidney: You're very optimistic. But there are restrictions in life. We are not all-powerful. *(Pause.)* Don't you think it could be dangerous, coming here?
Lynette: I can always say I'm a missionary. *(She chuckles.)*
Sidney: I've already converted.
Lynette: I'm just checking up on you. To make sure you haven't swerved from the path.
Sidney: They can easily find out that you're not a Christian.
Lynette: Christianity always has its last minute converts. I can easily be one anytime it's required. *(Pause.)* It doesn't bother you that I'm not a believer?
Sidney: Oh, you're a believer, just not in the Bible. You have another set of books. There are many faiths in China. We try not to impose on each other.
Lynette: It's nice to be friends. What is remarkable is that you are a man and I am a woman. We are in a country where we are not forced to live separately – I mean, myself with women, and you, with men. *We* can sit here and talk.

SIDNEY: Yes, that is the new world we live in. It does take some getting used to. (*Pause. Not completely comfortable.*) I am not in a country that is mine.

LYNETTE: It *is* yours.

SIDNEY: Many do not accept me.

LYNETTE: Well, they're wrong.

SIDNEY: Certain interactions make me... nervous. Sorry.

LYNETTE: I'm a woman. Certain interactions make me nervous, as well.

SIDNEY: (*Pause.*) You have courage. But you must be careful.

LYNETTE: If I can't live freely, then we don't live in a democracy. We have to enforce our ideals by living them. (*She rises from her chair.*) The meek don't inherit the earth. They remain slaves until the grave. That explains partly why I'm not a Christian. (*Pause.*) I'm not waiting for a reward in heaven. (*Pause.*) Sidney, anarchism liberates us by working against our inhibitions. By working against inertia. On a social level it works to dissolve the barriers that separate man from man. Or man from woman.

SIDNEY: (*Smiling.*) You're such a believer! You're a *preacher*, that's what you are!

LYNETTE: (*Pause. Curious, but playing with his conservatism.*) Would you speak to a Chinese woman the same way you speak to me?

SIDNEY: I didn't know Chinese women who talk like you.

LYNETTE: They exist. Just not in Chicago. There are not many Chinese women here.

SIDNEY: Very few.

LYNETTE: Would you send home for one?

SIDNEY: This is my home now.

LYNETTE: *(Cannot contain her excitement.)* The world is changing – everywhere! And change is necessary. People will try to stop it but they won't be able to.
SIDNEY: You're sure of that? Sometimes things move backwards.
LYNETTE: No, we have momentum. I would be the first to tell you if I sensed the momentum had stalled.
SIDNEY: Women pride themselves in the detection of nuances.
LYNETTE: I'll let you say whatever you want to say about women as long as you agree that we can vote, have jobs and even have the job of president if we want it!

SIDNEY *smiles and chuckles softly. Pause.*

LYNETTE: I shouldn't have asked you to offer Del some work at the lumber company. It hurt his pride. Of course he thinks any Chinese person should be working for *him*.
SIDNEY: *(Agreeing.)* It was well-intended, but...
LYNETTE: He's not in a good state now. Just like he wasn't before. You know he hates everything. It's impossible to talk to him. *(Pause.)* He doesn't realize there's a way out of being exploited. We do not have pure democracy. We need practical applications of libertarian ideals that traditional democracy fails to address. *(Pause.)* Yes, it can be frustrating. It will be frustrating. But frustration is a fact of life.

SIDNEY *looks at* LYNETTE *and can think of nothing to say.*

Scene 3

Salvatore Clementi's Radio Repair Shop. DEL *stands outside. He as tidied himself up ands looks presentable. The* BLOODSTREAM *stands nearby. They look at* SAL *who is in his shop. He is sitting at a table having a meal of fish, spaghetti and wine. He cannot hear them or the* CHORUS. *The* CHORUS *comes in, animated, almost dancing, and sings.*

Song #2 Eric's Products

CHORUS: *(Sings.)*
    Eric's pomade, Eric's shampoo,
    Ask the ladies what they think it does for you.
    They'll say Eric's Products are the only ones –
    Any other brand is for stinky bums.

The CLOWN *enters, joins in the song, and goes over to* DEL *and sings in his face, jeering at him.*

CHORUS *and the* CLOWN: *(Sing.)*
    Eric's pomade, Eric's shampoo,
    Ask the ladies what they think it does for you.

The CHORUS *and the* CLOWN *exit.*

BLOODSTREAM: Hey, do you remember the time you worked for Eric's Men's Products? Selling shampoo and pomade? *(Sarcastically.)* Wasn't that fun?
DEL: I so want to get rid of you.

BLOODSTREAM: *(Pause.)* You're coming to Sal Clementi's radio repair shop and you don't have a radio in your hand.
DEL: Everybody knows what Sal really does.
BLOODSTREAM: Good luck with your meeting. *(Pause.)* Human nature. I don't get it.
Chong's a guy who gave you a job when you needed one. Paid you in good, green Yankee dollars. You turn around and you want him dead.
DEL: He won't stay away from her.
BLOODSTREAM: She won't stay away from him, maybe.
DEL: The whore.
BLOODSTREAM: Where have I heard that before?

DEL *goes into the shop. The* BLOODSTREAM *trails behind him.*

SAL: These bullheads are delectable. You like bullheads?
DEL: I used to fish for them.
SAL: *(He looks at the* BLOODSTREAM.*)* Full of iron. *(He stretches his arms up above his head for a moment. He is a man in good shape. To* DEL.*)* So what's wrong with you these days?
DEL: Nothing.
SAL: You sure?
DEL: Well, I got allergies.
SAL: Allergies? To what?
DEL: Certain people.
SAL: Don't we all? *(He continues to eat.)*
DEL: There's one Chinaman, in particular. *(Pause.)* I've got money, Sal. We've got to hold onto this country.
SAL: Yeah, protect it from wops, chinks, niggers and the rest of the garbage.

DEL: That's not it, Sal. He's not even white. And he's doing it to my sister.
SAL: *(Continuing to eat.)* You been selling lottery tickets outside hotels? That's your racket, isn't it? Or has that changed? You're not going to have enough money to do what you want to do.
DEL: I've got money. I did a little work for somebody who's a real bastard.
SAL: Who?
DEL: I can't say.
SAL: No?

DEL *shakes his head, "no".*

SAL: So many of us are bastards. If you killed all the *bastardi* in the world, you'd wind up with a bunch of swine. *(Pause.)* Listen, neither me nor Johnny nor the Hippo works without being paid half up front.
DEL: I know. It's time to get rid of my allergy. Now.
SAL: So where's the dough?
DEL: I don't have it in my pocket now.
SAL: Then don't bother me, kiddo, I'm trying to eat.
DEL: I'm talking about Chinamen who are like radium infecting our lungs!
SAL: I'm Italian. Marco Polo went to China and they treated him good.
DEL: Is that a joke?
SAL: *(Threatening.)* Are you talking back to me?
DEL: No. Not at all. I know you're eating, sorry.
SAL: *(Pointing to his plate.)* These spaghettis here, Marco Polo brung 'em back from China.

The CLOWN *instantly appears. He has a guitar with him.*

CLOWN: *(Grinning.)* Back again so soon! *(Pause.)* I'll serenade you while you dine.
Song #3: "The Coolie and His Hammer"

CLOWN: *(Sings, accompanying himself.)*
   Popping a rail into the springtime prairie,
   The coolie worked harder than any man.
   The sky was splashing and the steel was hard.
   The coolie shivered...

BLOODSTREAM and CLOWN: *(Sing.)* ...and swung his hammer.

The CLOWN *and the* BLOODSTREAM *continue to sing through to the end of the song.*

CLOWN:
   The boss, he came a-swaggering, he yelled, "That's not straight!
   You have to go back and do it once again."
   The spikes were in tight, they came out with a fight.
   The coolie had a friend...

BLOODSTREAM and CLOWN: ...in his hammer.

CLOWN: *(Singing. Continued.)*
>The boss then cried, "You coolie, you're a slowpoke.
>You brought the spike out and put it in again
>But the way you done it is not to my likin'.
>I dock you one month's pay

BLOODSTREAM and CLOWN: ...you yellow yammerer."

CLOWN:
>The boss then said, "Hey, what'd you just say to me?"

BLOODSTREAM:
>But the coolie hadn't said a single thing.

CLOWN:
>The boss roared, "I won't stand for being talked back to."
>The coolie stood there

BLOODSTREAM and CLOWN: ...and squeezed his hammer.

CLOWN:
>Whiskey – it gave the coolie Dutch courage.
>Whiskey, it made him David 'gainst Goliath.
>He slew the boss and tried to run away
>But the mob caught him

BLOODSTREAM and CLOWN: ...and spared him the slammer.

CLOWN:
   They threw a rope over a limb of an elm tree.
   They put the coolie's head in the noose.
   They let him dangle there for all to see –
   An example of how to properly swing

BLOODSTREAM and CLOWN: ...a railroad hammer.

The song ends. The Clown leaves.

SAL: We all got allergies, kid. Sometimes we just have to live with them. You got a singular reason for wanting what you want and I don't like it. People built this country – people from other places. People wanting to make it on their own, be no slave to nobody. *(Pause.)* Don't come here again unless you got a radio that needs fixing.

SAL *puts his hat on, gets up from the table and leaves.*

DEL: He'd do it if I come up with the money.
BLOODSTREAM: Stop your obsession with the Chinaman. He only gave you work 'cause of your sister. It's your sister you should be obsessed with. *(Smiling.)*
DEL: Wipe that smile off your face.

He punches the BLOODSTREAM *in the face.*

DEL: I'm sick of this is little dance with you.
BLOODSTREAM: You need me. Otherwise you're all hot air, like when you see Sal and you don't have any money in your pockets.

Scene 4

Del's room. The same quiet, humming soundscape heard in Scene 1 is heard again. Sounds of snoring will at times mixed in with it (places where this occurs will be noted). The BLOODSTREAM *is lying on the cot, on his back, sleeping with his mouth open.* DEL *is sitting on a stool nearby. There's a bottle of booze next to him.* LYNETTE *is standing nearby.* DEL *glances through a newspaper.* LYNETTE *stands nearby.*

DEL: The human world is an alcoholic one.

LYNETTE: What does that mean?

DEL: Every year there are more people on the planet – that means more drunks. There's only one direction, it's clear. The direction is down. *(Pause.)* Sis, you deny this. You're a dangerous fool. You think you fight the evils of the world but you're one of the evils, too.

LYNETTE: How so?

DEL: You personally don't spill your blood. You just talk.

LYNETTE: You just talk, too.

DEL: Yeah, but I've never said I'm going to save the world.

LYNETTE: You have, too. You're going to save the world from the Chinese.

DEL: *(Laughing.)* Huh, ha, ha! *(Pause. Stops laughing. Glancing at a newspaper article.)* Ashland and Harrison. A bomb went off. Did your people do it, Lynette?

LYNETTE: My people?

DEL: You and your anarchists.

LYNETTE: Anarchism is nonviolent. It stands against brutality and aggression. Nothing is gained through bloodshed except more bloodshed. Anarchism is peace.

DEL: Yeah, that's your take on it. Your people need violence. It's the only way they're going to change the world.

LYNETTE: No, there's education.
DEL: *(Laughs.)* Yeah, that'll work.
LYNETTE: You seem to be in pretty good health. I'm going.

She turns to go. DEL *moves close to her.*

DEL: Where are you going?
LYNETTE: Excuse me?
DEL: I'm going to take you back to your husband.
LYNETTE: What?
DEL: Your husband. Remember? Walter?
LYNETTE: I'm divorced.
DEL: That doesn't count. You can't be out wandering alone.
LYNETTE: You're out of your mind.
DEL: Chicago's a rough town.
LYNETTE: You're drunk.
DEL: Like the world.

He grabs hold of her.

LYNETTE: Let me go.
DEL: I'll let you go back to Walter.
LYNETTE: He doesn't want me. Our marriage is over.
DEL: You left him. That's not right.
LYNETTE: So it'd be right if it were the other way around?
DEL: If he left you, I would have found him and killed him.
LYNETTE: You talk big.
DEL: You're going back to him. *(Pause.)* You'll stay until he gets here.

LYNETTE: He's coming here?
DEL: I told him to come right away or else.
LYNETTE: Or else what? *(Pause.)* So this is why you asked me to come here? *(Pause.)* This is the craziest idea… He'll take one look at you and take my side.
DEL: At least you'll walk out with him.
LYNETTE: What a waste of time. I'm going.

DEL pulls a gun and makes sure she goes nowhere.

DEL: You've got it wrong, Sis. He still holds a torch for you.
LYNETTE: Nonsense. This is all nonsense.
DEL: People are free to do whatever they want, unless they do something beyond the pale, like you.

He walks around the room, raving.

DEL: There are rules, Lynette. And however wrong they seem sometimes, they're what we got. And we've got a government, too. And sometimes that seems wrong. But it's what we've got.
LYNETTE: *(Sarcastically.)* You're such a staunch supporter of the government, I know.
DEL: I don't want to hear anymore about the anarchy stuff. Woodrow Wilson was right in getting rid of as many of you guys as he could. Humanity will always want property and laws. It will always be petty. *(Pause.)* You're going to stay with me under lock and key until your husband comes and picks you up.
LYNETTE: He's not my husband. *(Pause.)* He's got another woman now. *She* might not let him come.

DEL: Then you'll just stay here till it snows in hell. *(Pause.)* Some people are richer than others. That's just the way it is. No anarchism, socialism, communism, is going to change that. *(Pause.)* "Neither god, nor master," that's your motto, huh? People *want* religion. They *want* masters. They need things kept in line. They can't take the pressure of deciding everything themselves. Never in a million years will people live the way you want them to. Look what your "open living" brings! You, with Yellowman. He's way off-limits, sis.

The BLOODSTREAM *lets out a snore – actually it is heard in the soundscape only. The* CLOWN *comes in with his guitar and goes over to the* BLOODSTREAM.

CLOWN: Did you call me?

Another snore from the BLOODSTREAM *is heard via the soundscape.*

CLOWN: *(To the* BLOODSTREAM.*)* Yes, you did. *(To all.)* You, know, I've been thinking:
the unequal distribution of wealth is shameful. And the extent of corruption is staggering.
DEL: Hey, who has the floor here?
CLOWN: I don't know. Maybe somebody's hearing voices. Maybe somebody's asleep. Maybe they're dreaming. Maybe they're having a nightmare.
DEL: I'm not asleep. *(Insulting him.)* You *clown*. Make yourself useful. *(Pause. He is fraught. He paces for a moment. He stops.)* My sister has a lot of time on her hands. We need to kill some of it. *(Thinks.)* Sing us a song.
CLOWN: I only sing when I feel like it.

DEL: *(Waving his gun.)* Well, feel like it now.
CLOWN: I'm only singing because *I* feel like it. We'll end the nightmare now.

He makes a gesture, similar to what an orchestral conductor might make at the end of a symphonic piece. The soundscape calmly but abruptly ends with his hand motions. The CLOWN *sings, accompanying himself:*

Song #4: The Bourgeois State

CLOWN: *(Sings.)*
    The bourgeois state is a mighty fine state,
    It's armed to the teeth – so you'd better agree
    That freedom's for all – all those who can afford it.
    You label me a jerk.
    – Well, I'm just speakin' my mind,
    But then you silence me.

DEL: *(Singing, echoing the last bit of melody, to the* CLOWN.*)*
You pompous ass!

DEL: *(Waiving his gun at the* CLOWN, *threatening to silence him.)* And that's just what I'm going to do, silence you. *(Pause.)* Or get out of here now!
CLOWN: Thanks for using me and spitting me out, creep.
DEL: No, deep down inside, I know you wanted to sing. Show-off! *(Pause.)* Everybody's trying to horn their way into this country.

The CLOWN *goes.*

LYNETTE: You are distressed. I want you to have a good life.
DEL: Like you do for the Chinaman.
LYNETTE: I demand that you stop talking about Sidney Chong like that.
DEL: You *demand?* It's unbelievable! That's what we get for giving women the vote. The Chinese spread T.B. Of course everybody in your group denies it. Because they're wearing rose colored glasses. But you, you're going to take those glasses off before they get you into more trouble.
LYNETTE: What kind of trouble?
DEL: You know what I mean.
LYNETTE: I don't.
DEL: Don't play innocent with me.
LYNETTE: Why don't you just come out and say what trouble means to you? You're talking about sex, aren't you?
DEL: I'll break your face.
LYNETTE: *(Pause.)* Have you seen Reba lately?
DEL: What?
LYNETTE: You should see Reba.
DEL: Why do you bring her up? I'm not interested in her and her friends getting arthritis.
LYNETTE: That's because they work long hours in a sweatshop.
DEL: Probably run by a Chinaman.
LYNETTE: No, it's not.
DEL: It will be, one day.

LYNETTE *makes motions to leave.*

LYNETTE: I'm going.

The BLOODSTREAM *lets out a snore. This time it is heard coming directly from him.* DEL *threatens* LYNETTE *with his gun.*

DEL: No.
LYNETTE: I'll scream until the neighbors hear me.
DEL: Nobody'll hear. They're at work. Slaving away. In the city of ten-thousand nightmares.

The CHORUS *enters, murmuring:*

CHORUS: Ten-thousand nightmares. Ten-thousand nightmares. Ten-thousand nightmares. Ten-thousand nightmares. Ten-thousand nightmares. *(Etc., ad lib.)*

LYNETTE: *(In the middle of the murmuring, loudly.)* I said, I'll scream!

The BLOODSTREAM *lets out a snore. The* CHORUS' *murmurs crescendo after fifteen seconds and end. The* CLOWN, *with his guitar, walks in.*

CLOWN: We don't want anybody to scream at this juncture. *(To* DEL, *"apologizing" for his intrusion.)* Sorry, just can't get enough. *(Pause.)* Del, you're still sleeping, dreaming and nightmaring. You just can't wake up. You never contacted her ex-husband, Walter. That would we be too much effort for you. *(Pause. Said in the sense of, "and besides...")* And you're drunk. *(Pause.)* If you drank less, you might have sweeter dreams.

231

The Clown *strums his guitar and sings. The* Chorus *joins in, singing sustained background notes during the first two lines of each verse and throughout most of the stanza that begins with* "I don't care".

Song #5: Don't Wake Me Up Tomorrow Morning

Clown *and the* Chorus: *(Sing.)*
Don't wake me up tomorrow morning,
I'd just as soon stay dead asleep.
Sure, I'll miss the birds, singing sweetly in the trees
For all the short life they have left.
Oh, those tasty worms they tear in their clefts!

Don't wake me up tomorrow morning,
I'll avoid the grand mistake –
I don't want to be a fake and say I accept it all.
It's a foul, damned, sick pigsty
In which each of us is forced to lie.

I don't care, I don't care,
I have enough nightmares
While my eyes are closed.
I don't care, I don't care,
You can wake someone else up if you want to get a rise,
Just leave me be, I don't want to get more traumatized.

Don't wake me up tomorrow morning,
I'd just as soon stay dead asleep.
Sure, I'll miss the birds, singing sweetly in the trees
For all the short life they have left.

The Clown *and the* Chorus *just stand there after they finish the song.*

Del: There's some fine things about immigration.

Lynette: Let's not talk about Sidney again. It's not a discussion, it's a monologue.

Del: It's a tragedy. Immigration is fine for the foreigner because he gets out of his flea-infested dump. But he brings fleas here. *(Pause.)* And he and the fleas reproduce. *(Pause.)* You see, an immigrant wants too much. They come here in the first place like that. It's selfish. People have to face the consequences of wanting too much. Of being where they don't fit in, where there's not enough room for them. We don't need them. We can't take them. We can't take Sidney Chong.

Lynette: The United States should be place of refuge and peace...

Del: Look, sometimes you go somewhere and it's not all it's cracked up to be, so then you leave. They should recognize that and move on.

Lynette: Move on to where?

Del: Back home.

Lynette: Tell that to the American Indian.

Del: What's that got to do with anything?

Scene 5

Del's room. DEL *is standing, pacing. He has a gun in his hand.* LYNETTE *sits on a stool. It appears that* DEL *has ordered her to sit there. The* BLOODSTREAM *sits on the cot, his feet are on the floor. He is wide awake and he flexes his arms once or twice. A church bell in the neighborhood rings eight times.*

DEL: Okay. This is for real. I'm wide awake now. *(To the* BLOODSTREAM.*)* Isn't that right?
BLOODSTREAM: Yeah.
LYNETTE: You wouldn't shoot me if I tried to leave.
DEL: I wouldn't test that theory out.

DEL *lets out a loud, big laugh. As he laughs, a church bell in the neighborhood rings out four times.*

DEL: Did you hear them bells? The Catholics keeping time. *(Pause. Raving.)* Do you know where the Philippine Islands are?
LYNETTE: Yes.
DEL: They're in Asia. The islands are home to various unruly peoples. And what happens there? The people are held in line by the Catholic Church. The Church uses the Bible, of course, and supplements that with rattan canes – which they beat the natives with whenever necessary. So much for the Body of Our Lord Our Daily Bread. Nothing works like physical might. You can have all the ideas you want but if you can't back them up with force then you're out of luck. So don't shun force if you want to change the world.
LYNETTE: Are you through?

DEL: No. *(Pause.)* Lynette, you'll never see the Chinaman again.

LYNETTE: Who... do you think you are?

DEL: I'm the World, Lynette. The World is me. The world's a drunk bent on doing what it feels like doing regardless of the circumstances. *(Pause.)* And those that have the power — whether it's the power of the government, or just the power of a gun – a gun like mine — *they* rule. *They* rule, *they* rule, *they* rule.

LYNETTE: You're not the world, you're a dumb, narrow American.

BLOODSTREAM: A red-blooded one...

DEL: ...and I wave the flag with the best of them.

LYNETTE: I want my freedom. You should understand that, as an American.

DEL: *(Pause.)* Remember when we were young? We were in a state of nature. We'd capture and torture anything that crawled.

LYNETTE: You did, maybe. Not me.

DEL: We were young and we were free and we were evil.

LYNETTE: How much longer do I have to stay here and listen to this?

DEL: Home, home. He can go home to China. The world's cruel and race mixing is no answer. See what it's bringing us? The largest stinking cities the world has ever known.

LYNETTE: If you don't like the city, you could go back to Wisconsin.

BLOODSTREAM: Please, offer another pointless suggestion.

DEL: *(Pause.)* Oh, you're doing very well here in Chicago. You fly all over the place like a butterfly, your friends insulating you from reality by all the favors they do you.

There is a knock on the door.

ELIZABETH: Hello, Del? Are you home?
DEL: *(Whispering, threatening. To* LYNETTE.*)* Be quiet.

More knocking on the door. ELIZABETH *talks through the door.*

ELIZABETH: Del? I'm looking for your sister, Lynette.
DEL: Who are you?
ELIZABETH: My name is Elizabeth. Your sister was supposed to be at the settlement house to give a speech. She never showed up.
DEL: *(Quietly, to himself.)* Yeah, I guess so.
ELIZABETH: Del. There's a crippled man on the stoop who told me that he saw Lynette come into the building with you. Can you come to the door, please?

DEL *goes to the door and opens it just a crack so that* ELIZABETH *cannot see into the room.*

DEL: Hello. How are you?
ELIZABETH: I'm looking for your sister, I said.
DEL: She's a free spirit. Um, who knows where she could be!
BLOODSTREAM: *(Pause.)* I don't think you should be in this neighborhood. It can get rough here.
ELIZABETH: I assure you that I'm not comfortable.
DEL: Then leave.
ELIZABETH: She wasn't at her apartment, so the only other place...

DEL: *(He means Sidney's place.)* Oh, there's another place she could be!

ELIZABETH: She's told me about you.

BLOODSTREAM: What has she said?

ELIZABETH: She's here, isn't she?

LYNETTE: Yes, I am.

ELIZABETH: I'd like to see her.

DEL: No. It's a family matter.

LYNETTE: Elizabeth, my brother's not well. He has a gun in his hand.

DEL: *(Pause.)* Ma'am, Miss – whatever you are – suddenly I'm in a sporting mood. *(Pause.)* Let's see. *(Thinking.)* I'll give you three chances which may permit you to see Lynette. Each chance must be met with success. *(Pause.)* Each chance is in the form of a question. First, we'll start easy, answer me this: chop suey, the fortune cookie – name me where they were invented in China.

ELIZABETH: They were invented in the United States.

DEL: *(She is right.)* Great. I told you this would start easy. Now, number two, a riddle: what has strings attached and frees us to laugh?

ELIZABETH *does not reply.*

BLOODSTREAM: I'll give you a clue. It's dead wood, that we imagine is alive.

ELIZABETH: *(Dryly.)* Maybe what you're talking about is a puppet?

DEL: Right-o! You *are* smart. There's some smart women out there. But they've got to know that they need to keep the strings attached or there's trouble. Our stupid imaginations persuade that we're free and then do things we shouldn't do. *(Pause.)* Here's question number three and it's a little harder. Why is there no interest on the principle that a Chinaman should be mixing with a white girl?

ELIZABETH *does not reply.*

DEL: I said, why is there no interest on the principle that a Chinaman should be mixing with a white girl?
BLOODSTREAM: *(Pause.)* Here's a clue: the Chinaman owns a small bank for Chinks and he owns a few other things including a lumber company.
ELIZABETH: I don't understand the question.
DEL: You understand English, even better than Sidney Chong – *Sidney*, that's a fake name if I ever heard one!
BLOODSTREAM: He's just trying to fit in, though.
LYNETTE: Del, stop this now, or I'll have her get the police.
DEL: Listen, I have a gun. That kind of overrules all that.
LYNETTE: Del. You've got to get out of this room. It's a place that won't let you think straight.
DEL: That's an interesting tack to take to plead for all of this to go your way instead of mine.
LYNETTE: I'm serious. If you could only get out of here, go for a walk by the river...
DEL: That sludge pile. Talk to the pigeons...
LYNETTE: You've lost your perspective on a healthy life.
DEL: What, healthy? The poison, Sis, engulfs Chicago.

LYNETTE: Do something simple. Go down to the corner spa and get yourself an ice cream.

DEL *lets out an enormous laugh.*

DEL: That's what I'll do! That'll cure everything. I'll be five years old again and you'll be nine. We'll pick gooseberries and pull off grasshoppers' wings. *(Still laughing.)* Go get out of here. Go before I bust a rib.

LYNETTE *gets up and leaves while she can. She and* ELIZABETH *go out.* DEL, *trying to stop laughing, sits down. Finally, he stops laughing. He is exhausted.*

BLOODSTREAM: Now she's free to go see Sidney.
DEL: He won't be around much longer.

Scene 6

Sidney's home. The CLOWN *plays* SIDNEY's *butler.* SIDNEY *sits, reading a magazine.*

CLOWN: I suppose the Chinese don't embrace anarchy, sir.
SIDNEY: No. It's not a concept that's widely known to them.
CLOWN: A Western concept.
SIDNEY: Yes, I believe so. *(Pause.)* Here's something in this magazine that a friend gave me. *(Pause. Reading aloud.)* "There is a species of assassination which by American standards is infinitely worse than the taking of human life. This is the assassination of civil liberty. It is worse than the taking of

SIDNEY: *(Continued.)* human life because it involves the taking of human life and more." *(Pause.)* What do you think of that?

CLOWN: I don't know. *(Pause.)* Um. I have some exquisite Chinese dragonheads that've been used over the years. I don't need them. I don't know anybody who does. They're rather large. Like the ones used in Chinese New Year's parades. They're very colorful. Made of papier maché and fabric, if I'm not mistaken. Would you or someone else like to acquire them for a small donation?

SIDNEY: A donation?

CLOWN: Yes, sir. A donation to my songwriting career. You know when I'm not working for you, I'm a singer-songwriter.

SIDNEY: Don't I pay you enough?

CLOWN: You do, sir. But my career swallows up money. So I need to augment my income.

SIDNEY: Where'd you get the dragonheads?

CLOWN: I borrowed them.

SIDNEY: You stole them, didn't you?

CLOWN: Yes, sir.

SIDNEY: That's just like you. When will you ever reform?

CLOWN: I'm not sure. But I know you have patience and you will forgive me. That's how Christianity works.

SIDNEY: *(Looking down at the magazine.)* The article continues by saying that the government is limiting free speech. I don't completely understand the connection they are making between free speech and assassination. It ends with: *(Pause.)* "No man of American traditions and spirit can *silently* tolerate a censored press."

CLOWN: Rah, rah! That much is true! We need to be *vocal*. Who gives you these things to read?

SIDNEY: A friend.

CLOWN: That friend wouldn't be Lynette Fisher, would it?

SIDNEY: I have a slight stomachache. I ate some American food last night and it didn't agree with me.

CLOWN: You should be careful. We eat a lot of crap. Would you like some tea?

SIDNEY: Yes, it might calm my stomach. But don't go now. I'll have it in a few minutes.

CLOWN: Is the magazine you're reading by chance called, *Mother Earth*?

SIDNEY: Yes, it's an old issue. Published in 1908.

CLOWN: Why are you reading a fifteen year-old magazine?

SIDNEY: My friend has taken it upon herself to provide me with educational information. It seems that this information has been available to the public for many years.

CLOWN: Hm. *(Pause.)* These Western women can be unceasing with providing such materials. How is it in China?

SIDNEY: The same can be true, sometimes.

CLOWN: *(Pause. Rolling his eyes.)* Women! *(Pause.)* Without them we would not be born. *(Pause.)* They do not want to be submissive to masters visible and invisible. They take offense at social and political repression and feel pangs when hearing reports of injustices grave and slight. They are determined to do something. What do they do? They talk a lot. *(Pause.)* They write. But who reads?

SIDNEY: I'm reading right now.

CLOWN: The time will come when nobody reads anymore. We've already turned that corner. It's called *radio*.

SIDNEY: Radio is quite an innovation.

CLOWN: It signals our doom. It's going to put my singing career out of business. I must be brave in my fight against radio. But I realize it's a losing battle.

SIDNEY: *(He has a thought. Then he sighs.)* Perhaps I'm ready for that tea now.
CLOWN: Yes, sir. Right away, sir. *(Pause.)* Maybe.

Scene 7

Del's room. DEL *and* REBA *sit together on the cot. The* BLOODSTREAM *reads a newspaper, sitting in a corner of the room. The* CHORUS *is present.*

The CLOWN *strolls in. The* CHORUS *will hum their musical notes during the stanzas that begin with the words, "A nice silhouette" and the last stanza.*

Song #6 A Nice Silhouette

CLOWN: *(Sings.)*
   Two lovers seen on a wooden porch.
   They're all warm, sitting close on a wicker settee.
   The sun at their back falls into the clouds.
   Shadows creep up like onions in spring.

   A nice silhouette
   Against the mold'ring sky.
   An artistic silhouette –
   If that sort of thing gets you in the eye.

   How they coo in the open air.
   How they salivate like dogs.

CLOWN: *(Singing. Continued.)*
   This old world might be a mess.
   From their slobbering, you'd never guess.

   A nice silhouette –
   Rub your eyes and plug your ears.
   They shine black now as a silhouette.
   We say that these are their best years.

The CLOWN approaches DEL and sings at him.

CLOWN: *(Sings.)*
   Why care about these numbskulls
   In this proud, destructive world?
   ...The story of an offensive boy
   And his clinging girl.

The CLOWN exits, but not before DEL says to him:

DEL: Now, that's a good one!

The CHORUS exits. DEL then turns to REBA.

REBA: I've never been to Wisconsin. It must be beautiful.
DEL: It's the most boring place in the world. You'll have more fun counting ants in the sidewalk.
REBA: It'd be nice to go there, I think.
DEL: Listen, I need you to do me a favor.
REBA: Okay. As long as it's not going to cause anybody harm.
DEL: Well, it might.

Reba: Why would you want to do that?

Del: Because the person has caused me harm.

Reba: Revenge isn't the answer.

Del: Actually, the person has done something to my sister.

Reba: What?

Del: He's raped her.

Reba: What?!

Del: Yeah. It's horrible.

Reba: Is she okay?

Del: She's hanging in there.

Reba: Has she gone to the police?

Del: Not yet. She's afraid to.

Reba: What do you want me to do?

Del: If you could report it, you'd be doing us both a favor. My sister's embarrassed. She's ashamed. She thinks that you... that if you go to the station, and they can start doing something.

Reba: Is this why you've been feeling sick?

Del: Yes. I've been sickened by the whole thing.

Reba: You don't think *you* should report it?

Del: Don't you like me? *(Pause.)* The police don't.

Reba: Oh. *(Pause.)* What am I going to say? I didn't see it.

Del: Tell them that my sister's been raped by Sidney Chong and she's too afraid to come forward 'cause of what he'll do to her if he finds out she talked. *(Pause.)* I can go to the police after you go. It's just better if you go first and tell them what happened.

Reba: How did it happen?

Del: He lured her over to his place at night and got her drunk. Then he did it.

REBA: Oh, my God!

DEL: It's a capital offence.

REBA: *(Pause.)* I need to go to Lynette. She must be feeling terrible.

DEL: She is. But she doesn't want to see anybody. She feels unclean. Like a leper. She's in bed and won't move.

REBA: A doctor should see her.

DEL: Don't you get it? She's too ashamed!

REBA: If there's going be a case she needs to see a doctor.

DEL: She will, eventually. Um, maybe you can be a witness.

REBA: What do you mean?

DEL: You could say you saw the rape.

The BLOODSTREAM *puts down his newspaper.*

BLOODSTREAM: That's icing on the cake!

DEL: You heard it, her clothes were torn, she was bloody, stains were on her dress... You cleaned her up.

REBA: That's a lot to say.

DEL: You'll be really helping out. It's just a terrible, terrible thing that's happened. *(Pause.)* Don't worry. Haven't you told me you've got a guardian angel watching out for you?

REBA: *(Meekly.)* Yes.

BLOODSTREAM: *(To* DEL, *meaning he's going a bit too far.)* Oh, Del, come on!

DEL: *(To the* BLOODSTREAM. REBA *is not part of that exchange.)* Shut up, you. *(To* REBA.) My sister needs a little guardian angeling. *(Pause.)* If you stick to your story they'll convict him. Justice will be done.

REBA: I don't want to lie.

DEL: She was raped.

REBA: *(She shudders.)* But I didn't see it and I can't talk to her before I go to the police.
DEL: You have to believe me. Don't you believe me? Be an angel to my sister. To me. I've missed you. I'm sorry I've been feeling sick and haven't wanted to see anybody.
REBA: Do you really like me?
DEL: I do, kid.
REBA: You're asking me to do something that's big, Del.

With a disapproving face, the BLOODSTREAM *picks up the newspaper and starts reading it again.*

DEL: I know. You know the situation now. It's delicate. You're a young lady. You're sweet. You're innocent. *(Trying to get on the right side of her.)* You're my little flower. *(Pause.)* They'll listen to you and put the yellowman in jail where he belongs. Then he'll hang for what he's done. Crimes have to be punished. Otherwise we've got chaos. You could be the next victim.
REBA: Yeah.
DEL: My sister will be eternally grateful to you and so will I.
REBA: Oh, Del. Why's there always such serious stuff going on around you?
DEL: Please, help my sister.
REBA: What if they find out I'm lying?
DEL: They won't. *(Threatening.)* Look, if you don't do it, I'll ask Annie Mueller.

REBA *is intensely jealous of Annie Mueller.*

DEL: You don't want me to see her again, do you?
REBA: Don't go near her… I'm not going to say the B-word.

DEL: Well, then...

REBA: All right, I'll do it.

DEL: Okay, then. You'd better go now. Come straight back and tell me everything that they say.

REBA: You're going to be here?

DEL: Yeah. Though I do have a lot to do tonight. I'll wait for you.

REBA: Which police station should I go to?

DEL: My sister lives on Loomis. There's a station on Taylor.

REBA: You're sure you'll be here when I come back?

DEL: Yeah. But I have to take the train somewhere right now. Just a quick errand.

He checks his pockets. He doesn't have the fare for the train.

DEL: Can I get a token off from you?

BLOODSTREAM: *(Disapproving.)* Hah!

REBA: Aren't we walking to the station together? You could get a token there.

DEL: No, I can't go right this minute.

REBA: Why?

DEL: I've got to... find my other pair of shoes.

REBA: If you don't walk to the station with me, I'm not going to go to the police for you.

DEL: Annie Mueller!

REBA: Del! Go to...! *(She prevents herself from uttering the word, "Hell".)* I don't care anymore! Go ahead and see her! You're not nice to me! I'm doing you a favor and you spit in my face! *(She can't stop herself.)* Just... go to Hell, Del.

REBA *bursts into tears.*

DEL: Now calm down, calm down. *(He holds her by the shoulders and gets her to stop crying.)* We're already in Hell, baby. *(Pause.)* Listen, I'll go with you. We'll go out, now. Together.

Scene 8

Sidney's office. The office door is ajar. SIDNEY *sits at his desk. A teapot and two teacups are on his desk.* LYNETTE *and the* FEMALE CHORUS *are present.* LYNETTE *and the* FEMALE CHORUS *sing:*

Song #7: I've Always Seen It That Way

LYNETTE *and the* FEMALE CHORUS *(Sing.)*
　There is a direction and it's to the Free.
　We must head there, or we'll have no dignity.
　 – I've always seen it that way.
　And *you* can feel this inside you, too,
　There's like an inner compass that points the way.

　Though it's not easy getting to the Free,
　That's not an excuse to live unhappily.
　With strong wills and a plan
　We harness our energy, do all we can for woman and man.

　Well, we have our own needs.
　They're akin to others' needs,
　And thus we do join
　Together and fight, so, please:

LYNETTE *and the* FEMALE CHORUS: *(Singing. Continued.)*
  Though each may look different in the noonday light,
  We have like dreams each and ev'ry night.
  We'll not relinquish our care,
  Have courage, contribute, and dare that the world might be fair.

  Well, we have our own needs.
  They're akin to others' needs,
  If we despair we do ourselves in,
  We let the darkness win.

  There is a direction and it's to the Free.
  We must head there, or we'll have no dignity.
   – I've always seen it that way.
  And *you* can feel this inside you, too,
  There's like an inner compass that points the way.

The FEMALE CHORUS *exits. The* CLOWN *enters, carrying an empty tray down by his side.*

CLOWN: Would you like more tea?
SIDNEY: Would you, Lynette?
LYNETTE: No thank you.
SIDNEY: Let me think...

The CLOWN *waits.* LYNETTE *is happy to talk about politics and let the* CLOWN *overhear her.*

LYNETTE: No one knows better than Emma Goldman how arrogant, ruthless and brutal irresponsible authority can become. Obviously she's experienced it herself, personally.
CLOWN: *(Rolling his eyes.)* Obviously.
SIDNEY: *(To the* CLOWN.*)* Yes, I will have some more tea, thank you.

Pause. The CLOWN *leaves.*

SIDNEY: History will show that our era was one of great changes.
LYNETTE: Most people go on with their lives and take it for granted that the authorities speak the truth. Ignorance is our enemy. No matter how busy one thinks they are, if they don't find the time to inform themselves, they're destined to victimization.

There is a knock on the door.

FIRST POLICEMAN: *(Outside.)* Open up. It's the police.
CLOWN: *(Offstage.)* Sir, the police are here and I'm letting them in.

The CLOWN *comes in with the* FIRST POLICEMAN *and the* SECOND POLICEMAN. *The* SECOND POLICEMAN *reads from a warrant.*

SECOND POLICEMAN: Sidney Chang, or Chong?
SIDNEY: Yes.
FIRST POLICEMAN: You have to come with us.
LYNETTE: What?
SECOND POLICEMAN: There's a charge against him.

LYNETTE: What is the charge?

FIRST POLICEMAN: Rape.

LYNETTE: What? Who brought this charge?

FIRST POLICEMAN: We're not allowed to say.

LYNETTE: I am Lynette Fisher. Do the accusations have anything to do with me?

SECOND POLICEMAN: We're not at liberty to say.

LYNETTE: If this man is accused of doing anything against me, the charges are wrong.

FIRST POLICEMAN: That would have to be discussed in court.

SECOND POLICEMAN: We have a warrant, ma'am.

LYNETTE: I just told you. If you consider the situation, you will see that there are no grounds for his arrest. Don't take him to the station. *(To* SIDNEY.*)* They'll take you to the station and you'll be tortured. They'll force you to confess things you've never done.

FIRST POLICEMAN: *(Threatening* LYNETTE.*)* You be quiet.

SIDNEY: Officer, I'll go with you.

LYNETTE: You mustn't.

CLOWN: *(To* LYNETTE.*)* You should just breathe in, hold it, then breathe out.

SECOND POLICEMAN: *(To the* CLOWN.*)* Who are you? *(Pause. He lets that matter drop. Then:)* We're here for Mr. Chang. He can either go peacefully...

LYNETTE: Or you'll beat him to death.

FIRST POLICEMAN: I'm warning you, lady, shut up, or we'll take you, too.

LYNETTE: Then you can have *two* innocent people to brutalize.

SIDNEY: Miss Fisher, just cooperate with them, please.

LYNETTE: You're going to go? Just like that?

SIDNEY: There's no other choice.

Lynette: You might not come back alive.
Second Policeman: All right, that's enough talk!
Lynette: You have a gun. It makes everything so simple. *(Pause.)* This man has rights!
First Policeman: *(Looking her up and down suspiciously.)* You're an anarchist, aren't you? You and your *rights*! *(Pause.)* But then, you don't respect the law.
Clown: Yes, it's very complicated.
Second Policeman: We'll haul you in too, buddy, if you don't shut yours.

Lynette *throws herself against* Sidney.

Lynette: No, you can't take him. *(To* Sidney.*)* They'll kill you.

The two Policemen *take hold of* Lynette. *They pry her from* Sidney.

First Policeman: Let him go, lady.

Lynette *slaps the* First Policeman.

First Policeman: You don't do that to a police officer.
Lynette: I want to read your arrest warrant.
Second Policeman: What good would that do? *(Pause.)* He's Chinese. We don't even need a warrant.
Lynette: Run Sidney! Run as fast as you can!
First Policeman: Stop talking to him. *(To* Sidney.*)* Put your hands behind your back.

Sidney *puts his hands behind his back. Th*e Second Policeman *puts handcuffs on him.*

FIRST POLICEMAN: Okay, let's go.

The TWO POLICEMEN *exit, leading* SIDNEY *out in front of them.*

LYNETTE: I'm going to get a lawyer.
CLOWN: Sure.

LYNETTE *leaves.*

CLOWN: *(To the audience.)* As Del has said, "Justice will be done." *(Announcing.)* Here's a tune that I found on the side of a street. And since I'm not a street person, I can't sing the lead part myself – I just wouldn't do it full justice.

Accordion music starts. A BEGGAR *with an eye patch over one eye enters. Just after he starts singing the* CHORUS *begins to wander in.*

Song #8: Justice

BEGGAR: *(Sings.)*
    He walks along in haste now
    Tryin' to beat the nightfall.
    He's only got one eye –
    It's said the other got lost in a brawl.

    He doesn't want the night to come
    Crashing down before he
    Gets home with his one eye
    And is safe and sound, don't you see? My friend,

BEGGAR, CHORUS, CLOWN : *(Sing.)*
   Justice, justice, you'd better hope you don't require it.
   The flip of a coin is more reliable – best not to test justice.
   Justice, justice – now, don't you get caught in it.
   Don't hold your head high. Vanish into thin air,
   Don't expect to find justice or fairness or reason or truth –
   It ain't anywhere.

BEGGAR: *(Singing alone.)*
   Whatever did this guy do?
   He never asked to be born.
   One day he was just somewhere
   And he ran into a human thorn.

   He was not the right place at right time.
   Fortune's Wheel was not on his side.
   He was "in the way of someone else",
   Or so said the man who made him half-blind.

BEGGAR, CHORUS *and* CLOWN: *(Sing.)*
   Justice, justice, you'd better hope you don't require it.
   The flip of a coin is more reliable – best not to test justice.
   Justice, justice – now, don't you get caught in it.
   Don't hold your head high. Vanish into thin air,
   Don't expect to find justice or fairness or reason or truth –
   It ain't anywhere.

The song and the music end.

CLOWN: *(To the* BEGGAR.*)* Thank you. Thank you very much, sir. Here's a coin for your trouble.

The CLOWN *takes a coin out of his pocket or purse and gives it to the* BEGGAR.

BEGGAR: No trouble.
CLOWN: Some people don't ask for a judge and jury.
BEGGAR: 'Cause there's no point in it.
CLOWN: The world's a crooked place, huh?
BEGGAR: I never said that. I said it was crazy.
CLOWN: Oh.
BEGGAR: But you know, we have music – so it's okay. Just don't talk to me about radio.
CLOWN: *(Disliking radio, too, of course.)* I know.

Scene 9

Del's room. DEL *sleeps on the cot. The* BLOODSTREAM *reads a newspaper. The quiet, humming soundscape fades up. From time to time, sounds of short-circuiting electrically charged wires and contacts are heard.*

BLOODSTREAM: Del, so you got Sidney Chong arrested. *(Pause.)* What if the charge doesn't stick?
DEL: *(Talking in his sleep.)* It'll stick.

Pause. The CLOWN *comes in and talks to the* BLOODSTREAM.

CLOWN: Oh, *that's* the newspaper he reads. *(Sarcastically.)* Top quality: the Chicago Fox-Sentinel News. The rag that prints first and asks questions later – if forced to. *(Looking into the distance.)* You know, looking into the future I can see that Sidney's going to get out. They're roughing him up a bit. He'll get through it. I hope the scratches aren't too bad. *(Looking over at* DEL.) You better move fast or else you're not going to get to his office in time to break in and steal his money.

BLOODSTREAM: He'll get there.

CLOWN: *(Envisioning the office.)* I see the office. On his desk there's a colored photograph of Dongting Lake. *(To the* BLOODSTREAM.) That's in China.

BLOODSTREAM: I assumed that.

CLOWN: *(Continuing to envision the office.)* On a large bookshelf there's a volume which contains a parable about Emperor Shun's overthrow of Yao. Remove that book from the shelf, and the books to the left and the right, and you will find Sidney's locked box. In it, he keeps nine hundred dollars in cash. But Del already knows that. He worked for Sidney. *(Lowering his voice.)* And he rummaged around. *(Pause.)* He wasn't looking to steal paintings. Sidney has several on his walls. *(Pause.)* Chinese paintings are sublime. *(To the* BLOODSTREAM.) It would interest Lynette to know that not only do the paintings of China contain much beauty, they also carry hidden political messages. You see, life in China has also always been unfair.

BLOODSTREAM: You are worse than Lynette. Because you're indirect.

CLOWN: It *is* a fault of mine. *(Pause.)* If the emperor didn't like you, you were exiled to a place called Xiaoxiang. A horrid jungle. Hot and full of mosquitoes. Salamanders there are three feet long. Now, if you painted a painting, and any of those things were in it, it was like saying today, "the authorities are making Chicago unlivable". You get the point?
BLOODSTREAM: No.
CLOWN: Well, I hope Del wakes up soon. This is one time he shouldn't oversleep.
BLOODSTREAM: *(Pause.)* Three-foot salamanders. I like that.

The soundscape fades to silence.

Scene 10

Salvatore Clementi's Radio Repair Shop. DEL *stands outside, with the* BLOODSTREAM. *They look at* SAL *who is sits at a table in his repair shop working on a radio with a screwdriver in his hand.* SAL *cannot hear them.*

DEL: Oh, my aching head.
BLOODSTREAM: *(Angry.)* Yeah, a hangover affects the bloodstream, too, you know.
DEL: I can't believe how fast the Chong's got out of jail.
BLOODSTREAM: Thirty-six hours isn't fast. At least you had enough time to steal the money.
DEL: My sister. Why'd they listen to her?
BLOODSTREAM: She's the one who was supposedly got raped. *(Pause.)* I hope they don't do anything to Reba. You better hope she doesn't tell them about you.
DEL: She won't. She's a good kid. *(Pause.)* Let's go in.

Del goes into the shop. The Bloodstream *trails behind him. When* Sal *sees* Del *he stops his work.*

Del: Hi.
Sal: What's up, Del?
Del: We can go ahead with the job.
Sal: What job? I don't see you carrying a radio.
Del: It's not a repair job.
Sal: That's all we do here. *(Pause.)* I heard you're working for the cops now.
Del: What!?
Sal: Yep. You saw to it that somebody got arrested.
Del: Who?
Sal: A Chinaman.
Del: He raped my sister.
Sal: Why are you going to the police? If your sister got raped, there are others who do a quicker job than the cops.
Del: I needed the police to hold him, so I could do something. I've got the money, Sal. I've got all the money.
Sal: You shouldn't be using the police. It brings you close to them.
Del: Well, I don't need the cops anymore. I've got the money to send the Chinaman away forever.
Sal: If he goes away, the cops will be asking questions. He's been in custody. His arrest was in all the papers. He's not exactly a nobody now.
Bloodstream: *(To* Del*.)* I told you it might not be so simple.
Del: *(To the* Bloodstream*.)* How else could I get nine hundred bucks?

SAL: *(Not hearing that.)* You shouldn't be mixing into the business between a man and a woman.

DEL: The woman is my sister.

SAL: Let me tell you something about me. My father's from Sicily. My mother – she comes from Corsica. I'm not going to bore you with the details of how they met. My mother's family didn't want my father to have her. She had brothers and cousins. They wanted to kill my father. My father took my mother to Sicily. It's only 'cause Sicily has a strong enough "society" as we'll call it, that my father didn't have to look over his back the whole time I was growing up. But you know what? It would have been nice to have two sets of grandparents instead of one. See, that's what happens when families start mixing into the business between a man and a woman. Now don't you tell me that this man–woman business doesn't apply to Sidney Chong and your sister because Sidney Chong isn't a man. That's the kind of thing my Corsican relatives said about my father. We're supposed to leave all the kind of hatred behind in the old world.

DEL *is about to say something.* SAL *stops him.*

SAL: Now don't you say anything. I told you not to come back here without a radio in your hand. Now get. Get before I do something I might not regret.

Scene 11

The gravel pits in a part of town. First, the two men. Then voices of a raging mob.

First Man: There's been a miscarriage of justice! A rapist is walking the streets.
Second Man: How do you know that?
First Man: It was published in the Fox-Sentinel News.
Second Man: Why isn't the man in jail?
First Man: They let him out on bail. But he's dangerous. Too dangerous to be on the streets. We're doing something about it, though. He's been seen and they've chased him over here to the gravel pits on the West Side.
Voices: *(Including those of women and boys, each actor from the* Chorus, *offstage, takes a phrase.):* Corner him! Get the bloody bastard! Foreigner! *(High voice.)* Lynch him! Get him. He's a rapist! *(High voice.)* Lynch him! He'll die for his wickedness! Slanty eyes little yellow son of a bitch! *(High voice.)* Criminal! Lynch him! Get him! He's a rapist! Get the chink. He'll die for it. The bastard!

The Chorus *enters.*

Song #9: Bold City On The Plain, Part II

CHORUS: *(Sings.)*
   Bold city on the plain, we struggle in our
   Hunger for the wonder, but we're encumbered by these chains.
   Bold city on the plain, our days of joy are
   Deferred, we're just a herd led by tyrants into pain.

   Mold for us a corner, give us hope-dope, spangle our cage.
   Convince us with half truths that we're in a Golden Age.
   Yeah, the Indians got the desert and Blacks aren't in the fields,
   So somehow that means that everything's ideal.

   Bold city on the plain, we struggle in our
   Hunger for the wonder, but we're encumbered by these chains.
   Bold city on the plain, our days of joy are
   Deferred, we're just a herd led by tyrants into pain.

The CHORUS splits into two and goes to two sides of the playing area as the action begins. A THIRD MAN runs in.

THIRD MAN: Where is the rapist?
FIRST MAN: He's here.
THIRD MAN: The newspaper said the girl he raped is protecting him because she's mentally ill.
FIRST MAN: She's mentally ill and she's been mixed up with the anarchists.
THIRD MAN: We'll get that Sidney Chong!

SECOND MAN: There. I think he's there. *(He points.)*

SIDNEY, *tired, enters. He has been running.*

FIRST MAN: That's him! He's just like he's been described.

SIDNEY *sees the* MEN *and tries to flee but he can't distance himself from them.*

THIRD MAN: What an ugly animal.
SECOND MAN: Don't let him run.
THIRD MAN: He's tired.
FIRST MAN: He'll pay.
THIRD MAN: Hey, you! We know what you are.
FIRST MAN: Grab him.

The THIRD MAN *grabs* SIDNEY.

THIRD MAN: You scum!
SECOND MAN: *(Grabbing him, too.)* You scum.

The THREE MEN *lead* SIDNEY *around the stage. In fear, the members of the* CHORUS *run out, exiting the stage.*

FIRST MAN: We're going to string you up!
THIRD MAN: Any last words?
FIRST MAN: Why let him talk? He's garbage.
SIDNEY: Please, no.
THIRD MAN: Did you hear that? He said, "Please, no".

The THIRD MAN *laughs and punches* SIDNEY *in the stomach.* SIDNEY *doubles up. The* SECOND MAN *hits* SIDNEY *on the side of the neck.*

SIDNEY: The accusations are wrong!
FIRST MAN: You raped a girl and she wasn't your first.
SIDNEY: I did not rape anyone!
FIRST MAN: It's all in the newspaper.
SECOND MAN: *(Taunting him.)* You read the newspaper? No read English?
SIDNEY: The newspaper is wrong. The police have released me.
FIRST MAN: You worked out a deal with them, not with us.
SIDNEY: Who are you?
FIRST MAN: We are the people.
SIDNEY: I'm a Christian. I have been falsely accused. I love this country.
FIRST MAN: Oh, yeah, sure.
(Sarcastically.) "Give me your tired, your poor,
Your huddled masses yearning to breathe free,
The wretched refuse of your teeming shore.
Send these, the homeless, tempest-tossed, to me..."

FIRST MAN: *(Pause. Continuing.)* A Jewess wrote that. It's sick that they put it on the Statue of Liberty.
THIRD MAN: Enough of this talk.

The THIRD MAN *slugs* SIDNEY.

SIDNEY: *(Low sound from deep within him.)* Oh. *(Dazed.)* I'm innocent.
FIRST MAN: That's what they all say.

THIRD MAN: *(To the* FIRST *and* SECOND MEN.) Let's get it over with.
SIDNEY: I can pay you money.
FIRST MAN: We don't take money. Justice will be done.

SIDNEY *clutches his left arm and falls to the ground and lies there motionless.*

THIRD MAN: He's playing dead.

The FIRST MAN *kicks* SIDNEY. SIDNEY *is limp.*

SECOND MAN: The Chink's doing a good job of it.
FIRST MAN: He ain't moving. We don't know if he's dead for sure.
THIRD MAN: Well then, let's string him up to make sure.
SECOND MAN: I don't want to touch him again. His skin... it's not like yours or mine.
THIRD MAN: Come on, let's get him up.

The FIRST *and the* THIRD MEN *lift up* SIDNEY.

FIRST MAN: So you're not going to help? *(Pause.)* We need a hand.
SECOND MAN: Sorry, I can't.
FIRST MAN: *(To the* SECOND MAN.) Who asked you to come around here, anyway?
SECOND MAN: Who asked you?

The First *and* Third Men *put down* Sidney's *body. A brawl starts with the* First *and* Third Men *siding against the* Second Man. *After a minute,* Lynette *enters. She looks down and sees* Sidney *on the ground.*

Lynette: What have you done to him?

The First Man *sees* Lynette *and looks away and covers his face with his hand to hide his identity.*

First Man: Nothing. Why should you care about a Chinaman?

The Second *and* Third Men *cover their faces like the* First Man *did. The* First, Second *and* Third Men *run out.*

Lynette: Sidney, what have they done to you? *(She bends down and holds* Sidney's *head in her hands.)* Oh, Sidney, you poor man. This is what my brother has done. This is ignorance, this is anger... *(She cries.)* Del, how could you this? You're a monster! Do you have no concept...? *(Pause.)* Sidney, dear. They're burning your lumber company down. It's a good thing you can't see it.

Scene 12

Reba's room. REBA *sits in a chair. On the table next to her is a straight razor.*

REBA: Del, the police called me in. They wanted to be fully prepared. By time they asked for me, the Chinaman was dead. *(Pause.)* I told them that I said Lynette got raped because I was suspicious of Chong. They asked me he raped me. I said no. I said I made up everything. So I took all the blame myself. Even if I'd said you put me up to it, I know they wouldn't go after you. They can't go after you. Everybody knows that you set fire to the lumberyard. That you've left Chicago, you're headed for New York. They won't find you there so easy. It's bigger there than here.

REBA *takes the razor from the table and looks at it.*

REBA: I'm easily misled. *(Pause.)* It was stupid to hope for us. All I know is this world's too hard. I've always been unlucky. *(Pause.)* What I did killed Chong.

She sets the razor down, takes a bracelet off from one of her wrists and sets it on the table.

REBA: Del, you're a different than me. You don't have a conscience and you just go on – go on without one. I can't do that. *(Pause.)* Ah, most of the time the world's too much for me anyway. I don't want to be scared anymore. That's the worst part: being scared.

REBA *picks up the razor again. She slits one of her wrists carefully. She puts the razor down. She sings.*

Song #10: Sadder Things

REBA: *(Sings.)*
I've been thinking 'bout sadder things –
The sorry things that sadness brings 'cause what I've done's so bad.
Now I lay me down, I'm feeling so, so sad.
Once I had somewhere to go, in front of me I saw a rainbow.

But I think only 'bout only sad, sad things, now –
My angel's fallen to the ground, everything's turned 'round.
What more can happen to me?
'Cause of my stupidity,
Things have gone from bad to worst.
Oh, my heart just wants to burst.

Oh, how naïve, how loyal of me.
I went out on a limb all for you.
Now, face to face with my horrid mistake,
There is but one choice to take –
I'll take it.

I've been thinking 'bout sadder things –
Everything is over now – it's the things I can't undo
That bring me to an ending I never thought I'd know.

REBA: *(Singing. Continued.)*
  But that's what happens to the fool who never really wants to know.
  I hear the mice running behind the wall.
  Powder falls, plaster pieces, too.
  This crappy space is just the place
  For a girl like me to let go.

  End this sadness,
  Put this to my wrist.

REBA: *(Speaks.)* You called me your little flower. You were just trying to get me to do what you wanted me to do. I've always been a weed. Growing in places where nobody wants me.

REBA *slits her other wrist and waits, then:*

REBA: It's getting colder. Darker. *(Pause.)* Yep, pull me out by the roots. Maybe I was a flower, just for minute. But now... no.

She makes a deeper cut in one of her wrist. A bell rings three times.

Oh, that's not for me. This is against the law. *(Pause.)* I'm going where the ghosts are.

She weeps and she passes out. She dies.

Scene 13

A street fair in the Bronx. The sounds of that fair. A fair booth is present. So is a large puppet theater. The curtain to the puppet theater's front stage is closed.

A Chorus Member *enters carrying a huge "wanted" poster of Del and places it on a shelf or a ledge of the fair booth. Del has a smirk on his face in the picture on the poster. The poster is as sturdy as a framed painting. The* Chorus Member *exits.*

The Clown *is to one side and strums a guitar. When he starts singing, the street fair sounds fade.*

Midway through the song more lights will shine on the "wanted" poster. The lights will circle or spin around on Del's portrait. The "wanted" poster is like the "star of the show." Though the lyrics of the song may not suggest it, there is a celebratory atmosphere to the proceedings.

Song #11: Plenty

Clown: *(Sings.)*
    Yeah, you're a creep – so what is new?
    Just go to sleep – forever – we've had enough of you.
    You've taken plenty, repayment is overdue.

    Yeah, you've been something – something in *your* eyes.
    Well, you're just a speck of garbage in the belly of a fly.
    Plenty – you've taken so much, you squander'd it all.
    Best to fade on the road, remember my gun always gets a
      reload.

CLOWN: *(Singing. Continued.)*
> Hide out there, keep out of my sights.
>
> It ain't a question of degree, you were born basic'ly vile.
> We'd all be better off without you and your bad seed
> Sprouting and rotting on our planet while you just smile.
>
> Oh, yeah, you're a creep – so what is new?
> Just go to sleep – forever – we've had enough of you.
> Plenty – you've taken so much, you squander'd it all.
> Best to fade on the road, remember my gun always gets a reload.
> Hide out there, keep out of my sights.

(Whispering/singing):
> Always gets a reload.

The extra lights stop shining on Del's portrait. The CLOWN *takes the "wanted" poster from the fair booth and exits as the sounds of the street fair fade up. An* OLDER BOY *enters carrying a canvas sack. A rifle peeks out of the sack. A* YOUNGER BOY *follows him.*

OLDER BOY: Little brother, if you bellyache anymore I ain't going to be your friend.
YOUNGER BOY: I want to shoot rats, too.
OLDER BOY: You're lucky I'm letting you come along. I need somebody to boost up and get over the fence so he can come around and let me onto the railroad tracks.
YOUNGER BOY: I can shoot a rifle.

OLDER BOY: Yeah, but they move real fast when they scoot from under the rails. You're just not *fast* enough.

YOUNGER BOY: Somebody's going to see us.

OLDER BOY: Nobody'll be looking. They're all at the street fair. This is the only time in the whole of the Bronx that you can ever hunt in daylight.

YOUNGER BOY: I can shoot fast.

OLDER BOY: That's not enough. You got to be careful not to shoot a rat that's too close to a rail. Otherwise the bullet ricochets and you could get killed. Now let's get going.

The OLDER BOY *and* YOUNGER BOY *exit. A* BARKER *enters.*

BARKER: *(Yelling.)* The show starts in five minutes! Get your tickets now if you haven't already. We have got a show for you! The grandest, funniest puppets that ever lived! We will take you on a journey to a place – to where, I cannot describe – that would give away the story. Come one, come all!

DEL, *inebriated and half-blind, enters. The* BLOODSTREAM *follows behind him. The* BLOODSTREAM, *who is not is good shape, is using a walking stick to support himself. The* BLOODSTREAM'S *clothes and makeup are not the color of red – they are pink. The* BARKER *approaches* DEL.

BARKER: Our puppet show is economical, sir.

DEL: Not interested.

BARKER: *(Confronting him with his big body, standing in his way.)* The puppeteers are very good, sir. The best in New York.

DEL: I can't see you. *(Trying to force his way by him.)* I have to walk.

Barker: *(Looking him up and down.)* You could use a rest. This is restful entertainment.
Del: Get out of my way. This is my last weekend before I ship out. I'm in the merchant marine. Headed to South America. Far away from radium. Chinese radium.
Barker: A sailor on the high seas! It'll be a while before you have another chance like this!

The Barker leaves. A Girl steps out to ask Del.

Girl: Mister, come see the show. My parents worked very hard to do make it. You'll like it.
Del: I'm going in a different direction.

Del points to some imaginary destination.

Girl: *(Looking at his clothes and looking at him, too.)* Hey, you don't talk like you're from the Bronx. Where are you from?
Del: Out west.
Girl: I hear it's grand there. Did you strike gold?
Del: Yeah, I did.
Girl: Isn't that swell! *(Pause.)* Come to the show. There isn't a fair everyday. This is special, you'll enjoy it.

The curtain to the puppet theater stays shut.

Girl: Oh, it's starting now. See, the curtain's just come up.
Del: Something's turning.
Bloodstream: Yeah, your stomach.

We hear the puppet show but the curtain to the little theater does not open for us. The GIRL, *however, can somehow see the show. As she follows its action her face glows.* DEL *is immobilized by his illness. The* BLOODSTREAM *can hardly move. The following voices are recorded, they should not be "live". They have an electronic reverb to them that makes it sound like they are radio or television voices.*

VOICE OF THE WIFE: Ever since you came back from the war, you only want to get drunk. I want peace in the house.

VOICE OF THE HUSBAND: There cannot be peace where there are grudges.

VOICE OF THE WIFE: I never gave you reason to have grudges, you slob.

VOICE OF THE HUSBAND: You get to live like a princess around here.

VOICE OF THE WIFE: In this pigsty?

VOICE OF THE HUSBAND: It wouldn't be a pigsty if you lifted a finger once in a while.

VOICE OF THE WIFE: How dare you! I'll show you what a broom also does. Take that!

There are sounds of the Wife hitting her Husband.

VOICE OF THE HUSBAND: I'm leaving.

VOICE OF THE WIFE: Yeah, right – go and get something more to drink.

The curtain of the "puppet theater" gradually opens. Instead of puppets on a stage being revealed, what we see is a large, rectangular screen that softly glows. DEL *sees it and feels nauseous.*

Voice of the Husband: I'm a veteran. The very least I expect is some respect from my wife.
Voice of the Wife: You're a veteran of many bars. You're a veteran of a number of strikes, too. Well... I strike *you*.

There are sounds of the Wife walloping her Husband. Laughing voices, exactly those heard on a television laugh track, are heard in response to what the Wife has just said.

Voice of the Husband: Stop.
Voice of the Wife: You lazy man!

Del, *in a daze, slowly and painfully walks toward the puppet theater's rectangular screen. The* Bloodstream *sluggishly follows him. The glowing rectangular screen glows differently, perhaps sending off more light in all directions.*

Voice of the Husband: I've had enough of you.
Voice of the Wife: Don't bite me! Stop biting me. *(Pause.)* Grrrh. You're biting into my neck! *(We hear her struggling against him and hitting him.)* Let me go!

The burst of the television laugh track is heard. The Wife hits the Husband with her broomstick even though he has her by the neck.

Voice of the Wife: How was it that I ever married you? You were a real charmer, you were.
Voice of the Husband: A snake charmer, you snake.

DEL, *followed by the* BLOODSTREAM, *stops approaching the rectangle screen. We now recognize that the rectangle is a giant television screen. Black, gray and white static fill the screen. We hear the Wife beating the Husband.*

VOICE OF THE WIFE: I bet that hurts! *(Pause.)* I've hit you so hard I've knocked your head off! Now I just have to get your head off my neck. *(We hear her tearing his head from her neck.)* There.
VOICE OF THE HUSBAND: Give me back by head!
DEL: *(In a daze.)* Radio. Radio.

DEL *stands stupefied, staring at the large television screen. There is more television laugh track laughter.*

VOICE OF THE WIFE: See, everybody's laughing at you with your head knocked off. *(Pause.)* Now you'll finally have your head examined like I've always said you should. *(Pause.)* Doctor, come here.
VOICE OF THE DOCTOR: Yes. I'm the doctor.
VOICE OF THE WIFE: This man is sick. What's wrong with him?
VOICE OF THE DOCTOR: He doesn't have a head.

A burst of laughter is heard on the television laugh track.

VOICE OF THE WIFE: Thank you, Doctor Einstein.
VOICE OF THE HUSBAND: Nobody appreciates me, doctor.
VOICE OF THE DOCTOR: *(Off in his own world, being the expert.)* Ah, yes, the minute the head is severed, it is severe.
VOICE OF THE WIFE: And we pay you for such expert advice!
VOICE OF THE DOCTOR: It appears that he's keeling over.

A burst of laughter is heard on the television laugh track.

Voice of the Doctor: He's dropped dead.
Voice of the Wife: *(Comically.)* Oh, boo-hoo-hoo.

A burst of laughter is heard on the television laugh track.

Voice of the Doctor: And now a word from our show's sponsor, the New York Fox-Sentinel – who in fact helped write the script for today's show.

Ridiculous incidental music plays.

Del: *(To the* Girl.*)* Turn it off. I've had enough.
Girl: We can't turn it off. Don't worry, it gets funnier.

Del *falls down to his knees and vomits. The* Bloodstream, *a little distance away, crumples to the ground. The ridiculous music fades out as the soundscape consisting of the eerie electronic hum and sounds of short-circuiting electrically charged wires and contacts cross-fades up. The large screen continues to show static.*

Girl: Are you okay?
Del: Go away.
Girl: Alcohol is such a bad thing.

The Girl *leaves.* Sal *enters.*

Sal *goes over to the* Bloodstream.

SAL: So this is the Bronx?

BLOODSTREAM: Yeah. What are you doing here?

SAL: *(Trying to be nonchalant about it.)* Oh, there's radio business here. *(Pause.)* Besides, things got a little to hot for me in Chicago soon after they got hot for Del.

The television screen quivers on and off a few times and then goes black. SAL goes over to DEL and stands over him.

DEL: *(Surprised.)* Sal? *(Pause.)* Is that you?

SAL: Yeah, it's me.

DEL: Everything's spinning in a rotten pool.

SAL: *(Pause.)* Some things don't change. *(Pause.)* I don't like you. Never did. But you can't stay like that. Let me take you over there. *(He points.)* Sit by the railway fence.

SAL bends down, brings DEL to his feet, and leads him over to the spot he is referring to. He has him sit down. The BLOODSTREAM, exhausted and in pain, follows and sits down as well.

SAL: *(To DEL.)* Catch your breath.

DEL: The clown would say that.

SAL: I'm no clown. *(Pause.)* Prop yourself up. Hold yourself straight. You don't want to choke on your own minestrone.

DEL gets situated, with great difficulty, as told. Pause. SAL stands up and looks out over the area. A gunshot is heard. Then DEL cries out.

DEL: Ow!

DEL has been hit by a ricocheted bullet. SAL does not know that and responds to DEL's *cry of pain:*

SAL: Well, you are sick. *(Pause. Sees something moving in the distance.)* Hey, look at those kids. One's got a rifle. What are they doing?
BLOODSTREAM: They're shooting rats. *(He looks listlessly up at the sky.)*
SAL: *(Still looking at the kids.)* Looks like they got one.

DEL *slumps over. He is dead. There is no more movement or sound out of the* BLOODSTREAM, *who stares up at the sky.*

SAL: *(To* DEL.*)* Are you asleep now, boy?

SAL *bends down to* DEL *and looks him over. He puts his hand to the back* DEL's *head.* SAL's *hand is bloody.*

SAL: Blood on the back of your head. What's that all about? *(A long pause.)* You know, Del? Sometimes life can be just a waste of electricity.

SAL *looks around. Nobody has seen him with* DEL. SAL *saunters away, leaving* DEL's *body alone and the motionless* BLOODSTREAM *staring up at the sky. The humming soundscape with noises of short-circuiting fades out. Music starts. The* CLOWN *and the* CHORUS *enter.*

Song #12 The Sun Shined At Six P.M.

Clown and the Chorus (*Sing.*)
The sun shined at six p.m. –
As if it was tryin' to stiff the eve'nin'.
An eve'nin' very ready to muzzle in black
Any upstart color that dared to challenge black.
Cold clouds went east – heavy with their spray.
Now they're o'er the ocean grave.

Sunshine!

Epilogue

A strange lavender light fills the stage. The Clown *walks with the following: the actors who play the* Younger Boy, *the* Pregnant Woman, *the* First Policeman *and the* Second Man.

Clown: We're living. Breathing. – Let's breathe in and out.

A bomb blast is heard. Pause.

Clown: What was that?
Actor Who Plays the Younger Boy: A bomb exploded.
Actor Who Plays the Pregnant Woman: Yeah, that's what it sounded like.
Actor Who Plays theFirst Policeman: The sound of anarchists "playing". They're retaliating. The police killed fourteen of them in a demonstration on Lenox Avenue.

CLOWN: As I was saying... we're living, breathing...
ACTOR WHO PLAYS THE FIRST POLICEMAN: *(Interrupting. Sarcastically.)* The anarchists have all the answers.
ACTOR WHO PLAYS THE SECOND MAN: They're like the Marxists.
CLOWN: No, there's a difference, but... *(Pause.)* So we breathe in.
ACTOR WHO PLAYS THE FIRST POLICEMAN: *(Interrupting.)* No matter what you do, there's always going to be hierarchy, bureaucracy and control.
ACTOR WHO PLAYS THE PREGNANT WOMAN: And women aren't going to be on top.
ACTOR WHO PLAYS THE SECOND MAN: The anarchists are dreamers.
ACTOR WHO PLAYS THE PREGNANT WOMAN: Some of their solutions might work if we gave them the chance.
ACTOR WHO PLAYS THE SECOND MAN: Don't waste my time with them.

DEL *and the* BLOODSTREAM *walk in together. The* BLOODSTREAM *is pink.*

DEL: Well, it looks like I'm rid of you forever.
BLOODSTREAM: And the same for me. *(Pause.)* You had blood. But you didn't have much of a heart.

LYNETTE *comes in.*

DEL: *(To the* BLOODSTREAM.*)* So long, homo. *(He waves the* BLOODSTREAM *out.)*

The BLOODSTREAM *exits. The* ACTORS *who play the* YOUNGER BOY, *the* PREGNANT WOMAN, *the* FIRST POLICEMAN *and the* SECOND MAN *form a small crowd and they listen to* LYNETTE.

LYNETTE: *(Enjoying giving her speech to the crowd.)* Large property owners – they push and push. We can't push back all the time. But we can *sometimes.*

DEL: *(Sarcastically.)* What, you've changed your tune? *(Pause.)* You're for violence now!

LYNETTE: *(To* DEL.*)* Maybe violence is justified *(To the crowd.)* – as long as it's violence to their property and no people are hurt.

DEL: Sounds like the job I did at the lumberyard.

LYNETTE: *(To* DEL.*)* No, that was different. *We're* acting as a group.

DEL: I can act as a group with others. *(Pause.)* Vandalism, huh? I thought with anarchists, you find all the important values: freedom and justice, solidarity and respect for every living being!

LYNETTE: *(To the crowd.)* We have to send them a message: we won't be usurped – citizens run this country, not the rich.

DEL: *(Facetiously.)* Rah, rah, rah.

LYNETTE: *(To the crowd.)* Daily, the rich steal from the poor. They steal the rightful compensation that must be made for a person's time and labor. When they fight against a living wage, what are they thinking? To this exploitation we say, "No!"

DEL: *(Pause.)* Hah! You're sounding more like a communist everyday.

CLOWN: *(Pause. Sarcastically.)* Okay, thank you for all these interruptions. But I'd like to resume. *(Pause.)* Yes, we're free people – to an amazing extent. We're not slaves – to a certain extent. Please, take all this a little less seriously! *(Pause.)*

CLOWN: *(Continued.)* Breathe in. Exhale.
DEL: That's an idea you floated and got away in the beginning. But we're beyond that now.
LYNETTE: I wouldn't say we're beyond it.
DEL: Of course you wouldn't. You never will.
CLOWN: *(To* DEL:*)* You're as incorrigible as she is.
DEL: *(Sarcastically.)* Clown power!
LYNETTE: *(To the crowd.)* We're obligated to, at the very least, fight the good fight.
DEL: Oh, come on. Sis, come with me, huh? *(Pause.)* I'll take you to a perfect world. A little burg. Just like where we grew up. With white picket fences, bird houses high up on poles...
LYNETTE: The perfect place you want to take me to is for the dead. You're dead.
DEL: But you believe in perfect places.
LYNETTE: Don't tell me what I believe. *(She signals to the theater wings.)* Ladies, could you come out here, please?

The FEMALE CHORUS *enters. (Of course, the actor who plays the* PREGNANT WOMAN *is already onstage and she will join them.)*

Song #13: I've Always Seen It That Way (Reprise)

LYNETTE *and the* FEMALE CHORUS: *(Sing.)*
   There is a direction and it's to the Free.
   We must head there, or we'll have no dignity.
    – I've always seen it that way.
   And *you* can feel this inside you, too,
   There's like an inner compass that points the way.

DEL *rolls his eyes upwards.*

DEL: I'm going. *(Snotty.)* To my "perfect world". *(To the* CLOWN, *taunting him.)* Stay with the women, you loser.

DEL *leaves. The* BLOODSTREAM *stays. He will join the full* CHORUS *later.*

LYNETTE *and the* FEMALE CHORUS: *(Continuing to sing.)*
    Well, we have our own needs.
    They're akin to others' needs,
    And thus we do join
    Together and fight, so, please:

    Though each may look different in the noonday light,
    We have like dreams each and ev'ry night.
    We'll not relinquish our care,
    Have courage, contribute, and dare that the world might
      be fair.

The rest of the CHORUS *enters. The* CLOWN *looks around and says:*

CLOWN: I give up. There's only so much inhaling and exhaling people want to do without singing.

Song #14: Bold City On The Plain, Part III

CHORUS *(Sings.)*
    Mold for us a corner, give us hope-dope, spangle our cage.
    Convince us with half truths that we're in a Golden Age.
    Yeah, the Indians got the desert and Blacks aren't in the fields,
    So somehow that means that everything's ideal.

    Resistance is the action, it's the answer.
    We want a better life – not a bitter life.
    Sacrifice is worth it, I'll give my life
    For others to thrive

    In the future. What is the future? Who are the others?
    Our sons and daughters and citizens.
    We won't stagnate. You won't make us
    And the planet die.

CHORUS *and* CLOWN: *(Sing.)*
    Bold city on the plain, we struggle in our
    Hunger for the wonder, but we're encumbered by these chains.
    Bold city on the plain, our days of joy may be
    Deferred, but are we a herd to be led by tyrants into pain?

CHORUS *and* CLOWN: *(Sing. Continued.)*
    No, no, no.
    No, no, no.
    No, no, no.
    No, no.
    No, no, no.
    No, no, no, no, no, no.
    No, no, no, no, no, no, no.
    No, no, no, no.
    No, no!
    No, no!

AFTERWORD

Yvonne Shafer has written about my interest and absorption in Joseph Meeker's *The Comedy of Survival*. I should say a few words about theatrical works that influenced the writing of these plays. The "humors comedy" or the "comedy of humours" devised by Ben Jonson has been a great influence. It is Jonson's practice to have an assortment or a range of characters; each character has an overriding trait or "humour" that dominates their personality, desires and conduct. The character does not change. A character just *is*. Another Jonsonian technique: he, and English writers before and after him, carried on a tradition derived from Greek New Comedy and Latin comedy (and the English plays indebted to those plays) that involved creating a "lowborn" character who would "organize" the action of a play – with the audience not always recognizing this, nor caring if such a thing is underway. With the ancient classic plays, the lowborn character is a slave. This form of character turns up many times as a servant in the English plays. This character form/phenomenon can be seen in Kevin in *Car Door Shave* and Ed in *Gambling Fever* and the Clown in *Neither God Nor Master*.

When discussing character, I like to quote what Susanne Langer wrote in her book, *Feeling and Form*. It might help some performers to understand how better to play their roles in these plays.

> "The personages in the *nataka* (the Sanskrit heroic drama) do not undergo any character development; they are good or evil, as the case may be, in the last act as they were in the first. This is essentially a comedy trait. Because the comic rhythm is that of vital continuity, the

> protagonists do not change in the course of the play, as they normally do in tragedy. In the latter there is development, in the former developments. The comic hero plays against obstacles presented either by nature... or by society; that is, his fight is with obstacles and enemies, which his strength, wisdom, virtue, or other assets let him overcome. It is a fight with the uncongenial world, which he shapes to his own fortunes."

Shakespeare, of course, has also had a profound impact on these plays. What is known as "Shakespearian design" helped structure these works. Moving closer to the present, twentieth century Epic plays by Wedekind, Brecht, von Horváth have also left their mark on my plays. During the years spent on these three plays I also was keenly interested in plays from the Spanish Golden Age (plays by Calderon, Lope, and others) and as well as Kabuki plays, Chinese ("opera") plays and Sanskrit epic plays.

The plays in this book have taken on lives of their own. Their characters have, too. Thus, *Car Door Shave* would like to thank the old Roman comedy, *The Braggart Soldier*, the old English comedy, *Ralph Roister Doister*, Shakespeare's *Measure for Measure*, and Richard Brome's *A Jovial Crew*. (Brome could be said to be a "student" of Ben Jonson). Cappy would like to thank Shakespeare's Falstaff.

Gambling Fever thanks Dr. Martin Lockley who I shadowed for a few years and learned about dinosaur paleontology through him and his colleagues. The action surrounding the dinosaur in the excavation pit owes a debt of gratitude to the image of Sisyphus painted by Camus in his *The Myth of Sisyphus*. The character Ed would like to thank Rosalind from *As You Like It*.

Neither God Nor Master owes a debt of gratitude to the Danish novel, *Hjule* ("The Wheel", findable in the German,

Das Rad), by Johannes Vilhelm Jensen. The novel was also a great influence on Brecht's early play, *Im Dickicht der Städte* which influenced *NGNM*. *Neither God Nor Master* also thanks Jonson's *Bartholomew Fair* and *Punch and Judy* shows as well as poems in German and French (1870-1915) too numerous to mention. The figure of the Clown was influenced by what I have seen and read in Chinese theater. For the character Reba, two short stories by O. Henry were all-important.

Concerning the songs in *Neither God Nor Master*, there is a great deal that could be said but is perhaps better left for another time. Half of the melodies – and even the words – to these songs, were written years ago when I was a teenager and had not yet gone to college.

– L.T.

ACKNOWLEDGEMENTS

With deep gratitude I thank: David Henry Baldwin, Patrick Barrows, Benjamin Boretz, Bruce Boswell, Chris and Laurie Brown, John Calder, Stephanie Campion (artistic director, Moving Parts, Paris), Conall Carr, Conrad Cecil, Pip Chodorov, Denis Conway, Julian Cook, Lucy Cook, Damian Corcoran, Sheila Coren-Tissot, Jill Danger, Fanny Deblock, Charles DeRosa, Carey Downer, Ariane Dubillard, Roland Dubillard, Bill Dunn, Don Elwell, Kai Ephron, Marie Flageul, Gwylene Gallimard, Yves and Sophie Gaudin, Natalia Golimbievskaya, Jim Haynes, Frank and Jean Hoff, Todd Isaacson, Wanda Ivey, David Kulesza, Brian Keane, Julek Kedzierski, Robert Kelly, Michael Kewley, Sungtae Kim, Dita Lang, Hazel Lee, Alan Levine, Scott and Babette Lithgow, Martin Lockley, Joan and Walter Luikart, Leo MacDougall, Maria Machado, Jean-Marie Mauclet, Sally and Dave McFall, Gretchen Minnie, Joseph Meeker, Gladys Meyer, the Motsingers, John Murphy, Robert Orchard, Marjam Oskoui, Pierre Ozoux, Domenico Pietropaolo, Michelle Powell, Robert Rockman, Justus Rosenberg, Paul Scallan, the Segarnicks, Yvonne Shafer, Jim Shutt, Neomal Silva, Darko Suvin, the Taits, John Tallmadge, Ilmar Taska, Walter Teres, Bill Troop, Linda Tyrol, Derek Walcott, Ursula Werner, Norbert Wuertz, Marsea Wynne, Elie Yarden.

I profusely thank the actors who participated in the staged readings at Moving Parts, Paris. A number of these actors are also friends of mine and have been associated with the ongoing process of readying my works for the stage:

Robert Bradford, Heike Brunner, Harlan Chambers, Bill Dunn, Tiffany Hofstetter, Lexie Kendrick, Clara McBride, Jade Nguyen, Mike Powers, Jerry Prillaman, Kim Tilbury. *(Car Door Shave)*

Paul Cavin, Damian Corcoran, Marie-Céline Courilleault, Bill Dunn, N.C. Heikin, Beth Jervis, Elena Luoto, Jerry Prillaman, Darcy Ruscio, Kristina Sherwood, Amanda Stauffer, Thomas Victorio. *(Gambling Fever, second reading)*

Madeleine Barchevska, Juliet Coren-Tissot, Carey Downer, Kim Tilbury, Carla Villacorta, Robert Brazil, Steve Croce, Bill Doherty, Marten Ingle, Jon Allen Russo. *(Gambling Fever, first reading)*

Maurizio Arena, Chris Barry, Robert Brazil, Damian Corcoran, Carey Downer, Bill Dunn, Lexie Kendrick, Claire Naylor, Wilhelm Queyras, Elena Odessa Ray, Jon Allen Russo, Michael Stromme. *(Neither God Nor Master)*

– L.T.

Three Essential Plays

APPENDIX (Songs)

Car Door Shave

Act II Scene 5, Song Fragments

My pil-low's soft but it's stone cold. You could make it warm, I'm nice to hold. Take me in your arms, let's get to bed. Don't be so hard, yeah, I know what I said. My dog might be dead and my lov-er did leave me but I'm still op-en to get-tin' a cat. Salt-wat-er taf-fy and I'm danc-in' with a tun-a!

Bold City On The Plain, Part I

(Sung by the CHORUS. Song #1, *Neither God Nor Master,* Prologue.)

Bold cit-y on the plain, we strug-gle in our hun-ger for the won-der, but we're en-cum-bered by these chains. Bold cit-y on the plain, our days of joy are de-ferred, we're just a herd led by ty-rants in-to pain. For sale at the mar-ket by sel-lers who own us and the land. What kind of chance do we real-ly stand? We're just num-bers they've giv-en us, we're slaves, they're the mas-ters, they shit on us. Bold cit-y on the

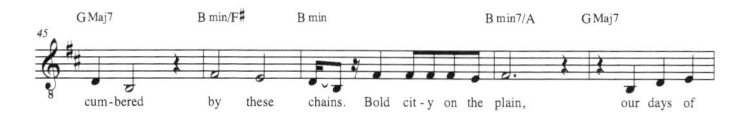

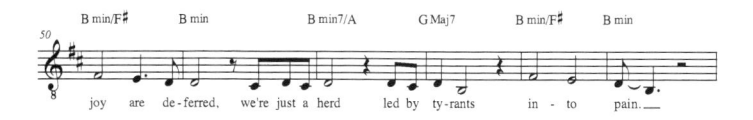

Three Essential Plays

plain, we strug-gle in our hun-ger for the won-der, but we're en-cum-bered by these chains. Bold cit-y on the plain, our days of joy are de-ferred, we're just a herd led by ty-rants in-to pain.

Eric's Products

(Sung by the CHORUS. Song #2, *Neither God Nor Master,* Scene 3)

Eric's Pomade, Eric's Shampoo, ask the ladies what they think it does for you. They'll say Eric's Products are the only ones. Any other brand is for stinky bums. Eric's Pomade, Eric's Shampoo, ask the ladies what they think it does for you.

The Coolie and His Hammer

(Sung by the CLOWN and BLOODSTREAM. Song #3, *Neither God Nor Master*, Scene 3)

Pop-ping a rail in-to the spring-time prair-ie, the cool-ie worked hard-er than an-y man. The sky was splash-ing and the steel was hard. The cool-ie shiv-ered and swung his ham-mer. The boss, he came a-swag-ger-ing, he yelled, "That's not straight! You have to go back and do it once a-gain." The spikes were in tight, they came out with a fight. The cool-ie had a friend in his ham-mer. The boss then cired "You cool-ie, you're a slow-poke. You

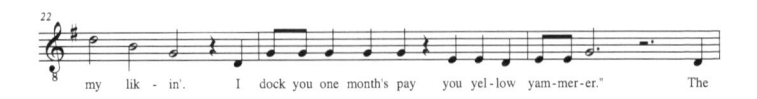

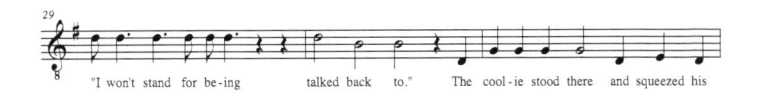

LANCE TAIT

brought the spike out and put it in a-gain but the way you done it is not to my lik-in'. I dock you one month's pay you yel-low yam-mer-er." The boss then said, "Hey, what'd you just say to me?" But the cool-ie had-n't said a sin-gle thing. The boss roared, "I won't stand for be-ing talked back to." The cool-ie stood there and squeezed his ham-mer. Whisk-ey, it gave the cool-ie Dutch cour-age. Whisk-ey, it made him Dav-id 'gainst Go-li-ath. He slew the boss and tried to

Three Essential Plays

run a-way but the mob caught him and spared him the slam-mer. They threw a rope ov-er the limb of an elm tree. They put the cool-ie's head in the noose. They let him dang-le there for all to see, an ex-amp-le of how to prop-er-ly swing a rail-road ham-mer.

The Bourgeois State

(Sung by the CLOWN. Song #4, *Neither God Nor Master,* Scene 4)

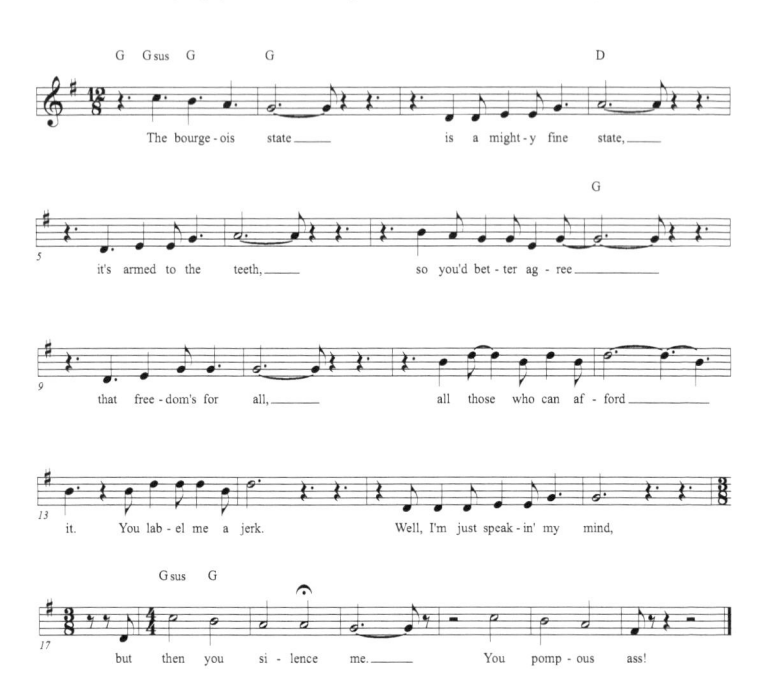

The bourge-ois state is a might-y fine state, it's armed to the teeth, so you'd bet-ter ag-ree that free-dom's for all, all those who can af-ford it. You lab-el me a jerk. Well, I'm just speak-in' my mind, but then you si-lence me. You pomp-ous ass!

Don't Wake Me Up Tomorrow Morning

(Sung by the CLOWN and the CHORUS. Song #5, *Neither God Nor Master,* Scene 4)

Lance Tait

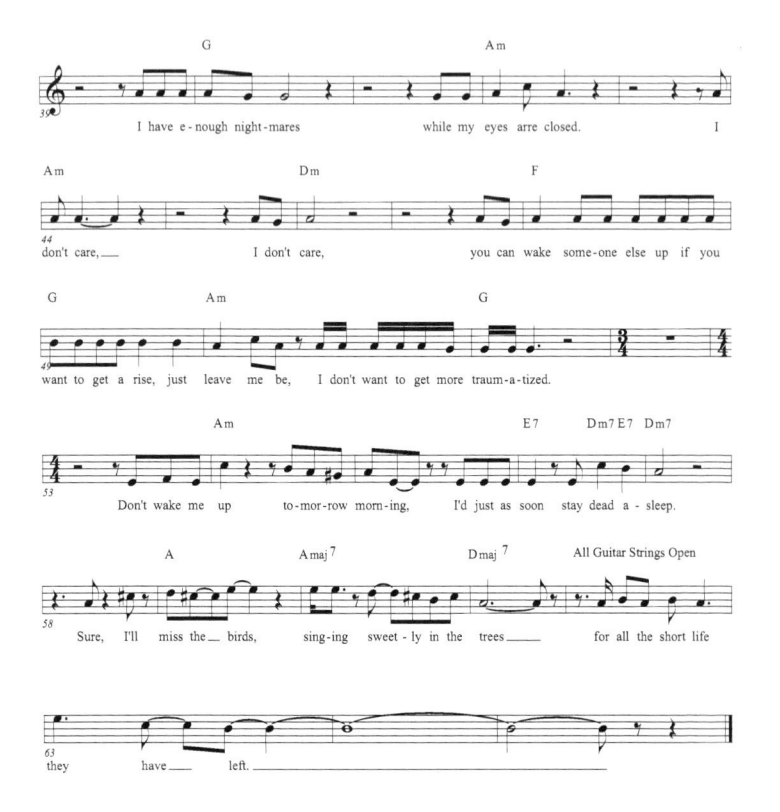

Three Essential Plays

A Nice Silhouette

(Sung by the CLOWN and the CHORUS. Song #6, *Neither God Nor Master,* Scene 7)

Two lov-ers seen on a wood-en porch. They're all warm, sit-ting close on a wick-er set-tte. The sun at their back falls in-to the clouds. Shad-ows creep up like on-ions in spring. A nice sil-hou-ette a-gainst the mold-'ring sky. An ar-tis-tic sil-hou-ette, if that sort of thing gets you in the eye. How they coo in the o-pen air. How they sal-i-vate like dogs. This old world might be a mess. From their slob-ber-ing, you'd nev-er guess. A

301

LANCE TAIT

I've Always Seen It That Way

(Sung by the CHORUS [FEMALES ONLY]. Song #7, *Neither God Nor Master*, Scene 8)

There is a di-rect-tion and it's to the Free. We must head there, or we'll have no dig-ni-ty. I've al-ways seen it that way, And YOU can feel this in-side you, too, there's like an in-ner com-pass that points the way. Though it's not eas-y get-ting to the Free, that's not an ex-cuse to live un-happ-i-ly. With strong wills and a plan we har-ness our en-er-gy, do all we can for wo-man and man. Well, we have our own needs. They're a-kin to o-thers' needs and thus

LANCE TAIT

Three Essential Plays

I've al-ways seen it that way,___ And YOU can feel this in-side you, too, there's like an in-ner com-pass that points the way.___

Justice

(Sung by the BEGGAR and the CHORUS. Song #8, *Neither God Nor Master,* Scene 8)

He walks a-long in haste now tryin' to beat the night-fall. He's on-ly got one eye, it's said the oth-er got lost in a brawl. He does-n't want the night to come crash-ing down be-fore he gets home with his one eye and is safe and sound, don't you see? My friend, jus-tice, jus-tice, you'd bet-ter hope you don't re-qui-re it. The flip of a coin is more re-li-a-ble, best not to test jus-tice. Jus-tice, jus-tice, now, don't you get caught in it.

Three Essential Plays

Don't hold your head high. Vanish into thin air. Don't expect to find justice or fairness or reason or truth, it ain't anywhere. What ever did this guy do? He never asked to be born. One day he was just somewhere, and he ran into a human thorn. He was not in the right place at the right time. Fortune's Wheel was not on his side. He was "in the way of someone else", or so said the man who made him half-blind. Justice, justice, you'd better hope you don't require it. The flip of a coin

LANCE TAIT

is more re-li-a-ble, best not to test jus-tice. Jus-tice, jus-tice, now, don't you get caught in it. Don't hold your head high. Van-ish in-to thin air. Don't ex-pect to find jus-tice or fair-ness or rea-son or truth, it ain't an-y-where.

308

Bold City On The Plain, Part II

(Sung by the CHORUS. Song #9, *Neither God Nor Master*, Scene 11)

Bold cit-y on the plain, we strug-gle in our hun-ger for the won-der, but we're en-cum-bered by these chains. Bold cit-y on the plain, our days of joy are de-ferred, we're just a herd led by ty-rants in-to pain. Mold for us a cor-ner, give us hope-dope, spang-le our cage. Con-vince us with half truths that we're in a Gold-en Age. Yeah, the In-di-ans got the de-sert and Blacks aren't in the fields, so some-how that means that

LANCE TAIT

ev'-ry-thing's i-deal. Bold cit-y on the plain, we strug-gle in our hun-ger for the won-der, but we're en-cum-bered by these chains. Bold cit-y on the plain, our days of joy are de-ferred, we're just a herd led by ty-rants in-to pain.

Sadder Things

(Sung by REBA. Song #10, *Neither God Nor Master*, Scene 12)

I've been think-ing 'bout sad-der things, the sor-ry things that sad-ness brings, 'cause what I've done's so bad. Now I lay me down, I'm feel-ing so, so sad, once I had some-where to go, in front of me I saw a rain-bow. But I think on-ly 'bout sad, sad things, now, my an-gel's fall-en to the ground, ev'-ry thing's turned 'round. What more can hap-pen to me? 'Cause of my stu-pid-i-ty, things have gone from

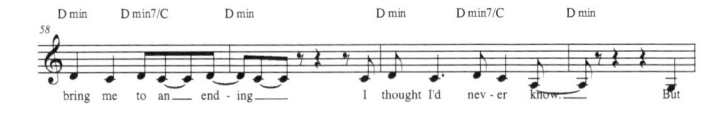

LANCE TAIT

Three Essential Plays

that's what hap-pens to the fool who nev-er real-ly wants to know. I hear the mice run-ning be-hind the wall. Pow - der falls, plast-er piec - es, too. This crap - py space is just the place for a girl like me to let go. End this sad - ness. Put this to my wrist...

313

Plenty

(Sung by the CLOWN. Song #11, *Neither God Nor Master,* Scene 13)

Yeah, you're a creep, so what is new? Just go to sleep, for-ev-er, we've had e-nought of you. You've tak-en plen-ty, re-pay-ment is o-ver-due. Yeah, you've been some-thing, some-thing in your eyes. Well, you're just a speck of gar-bage in the bel-ly of a fly. Plen-ty, you've tak-en so much, you squan-der'd it all. Best to fade on the road, re-mem-ber my gun al-ways gets a re-load. Hide out there, keep out of my sights. It

314

Three Essential Plays

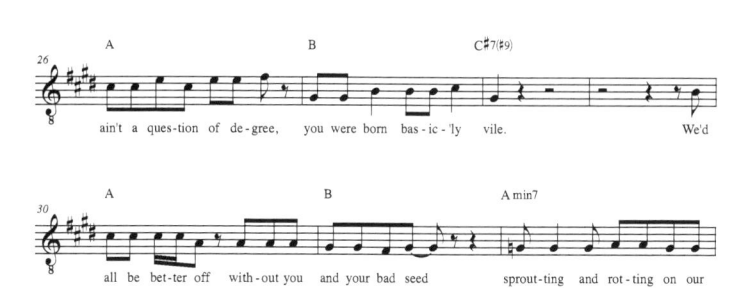

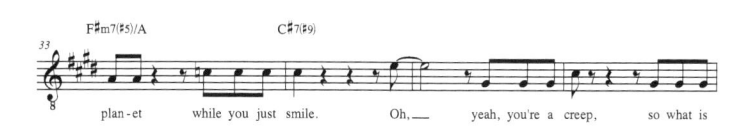

The Sun Shined At Six P.M.

(Sung by the CLOWN and the CHORUS. Song #12, *Neither God Nor Master*, Scene 13)

The sun shined at six p.m., as if it was tryin' to stiff the eve-nin'. An eve-nin' ver-y read-y to muz-zle in black an-y up-start col-or that dared to chal-lenge black. Cold clouds went east, heav-y with their spray. Now their o'er the o-cean grave. Sun-shine!

I've Always Seen It That Way (Reprise)

(Sung by the CHORUS [FEMALES ONLY]. Song #13, *Neither God Nor Master*, Epilogue)

LANCE TAIT

Bold City On The Plain, Part III

(Sung by the CHORUS. Song #14, *Neither God Nor Master*, Epilogue)

Mold for us a cor-ner, give us hope-dope, spang-le our cage. Con-vince us with half truths that we're in a Gold-en Age. Yeah, the In-di-ans got the de-sert, and Blacks aren't in the fields, so some-how that means that ev'-ry-thing's i-deal. Re-sist-ance is the act-ion, it's the ans-wer. We want a bet-ter life, not a bit-ter life. Sac-ri-fice is worth it, I'll give my life for oth-ers to

38
B min7/A G Maj7 B min/F♯ B min B min7/A
thrive in the fu - ture. What is the fu - ture? Who are the
43
G Maj7 B min/F♯ B min B min7/A G Maj7
oth - ers? Our sons and daugh - ters and cit - i - zens.
48
B min/F♯ B min B min7/A G Maj7 B min/F♯
We won't stag - nate, you won't make us and the plan - et die.
53
B min B min7/A G Maj7 B min/F♯ B min
Bold cit - y on the plain, we strug - gle in our hun - ger for the
58
B min7/A G Maj7 B min/F♯ B min B min7/A
won - der, but we're en - cum - bered by these chains. Bold cit - y on the plain,
63
G Maj7 B min/F♯ B min B min7/A G Maj7
our days of joy may be de - ferred, but are we a herd to be led by ty - rants
68
B min/F♯ B min B min7/A G Maj7 B min/F♯ B min B min7/A
in - to pain? No, no, no. No, no,

Three Essential Plays

About the Playwright

Lance Tait's plays have been produced or received staged readings in New York, Los Angeles, Denver, Toronto, Paris, the United Kingdom, and at the American Repertory Theatre. In 2002, in Paris, Tait founded Theatre Metropole. He writes a variety of works for the stage and is also active as a filmmaker. Other theater books by Lance Tait include: *Little Black Book of Comedy Sketches*, *Synesthesia*, *The Black Cat and Other Plays Adapted From Stories by Edgar Allan Poe; The Fall of the House of Usher and Other Plays Inspired by Edgar Allan Poe; Mad Cow Disease in America, Something Special, and Other Plays; Edwin Booth;* and *Miss Julie, David Mamet Fan Club, and Other Plays*. Websites: www.lancetait.com and www.theatremetropole.org.

Made in the USA
Charleston, SC
25 October 2013